D1639676

A Clouded Peace

A Clouded Peace

John Cole

Weidenfeld & Nicolson

LONDON

First published in Great Britain in 2001
by Weidenfeld & Nicolson

© 2001 John Cole

A CIP catalogue record for this book
is available from the British Library.

ISBN 0 297 60721 9

Typeset by Deltatype Limited, Birkenhead, Merseyside

Set in Minion

Printed in Great Britain by
Clays Ltd, St Ives Plc

Weidenfeld & Nicolson
The Orion Publishing Group Ltd
Orion House
5 Upper Saint Martin's Lane
London, WC2H 9EA

For Ion Trewin,
sympathetic midwife
at a long labour,
and for Madge,
who always helps

[1]

Paris, August 2000

They were crossing the Place de la Concorde, dangerously threading their way through the surging, hooting traffic. A man in his seventies and a young girl. I'd have recognised him anywhere: it might have been the Falls in the mid-seventies, rather than Paris in the new Millennium. His hair was gun-metal grey now, in contrast with the auburn tresses of the gawky youngster clinging to his arm.

I rushed to the front of the bus, ignoring the white-on-black warning: '*Par mesure de prudence, ne parlez pas au conducteur!*'

I shouted in the driver's ear. 'S'il vous plaît, Monsieur. Urgence! Me faut descendre tout de suite.'

'Merde!'

He slammed on his brakes, and sullenly opened the automatic doors. Above their hiss, I shouted my thanks, and looked around me. There they were, heading into the cool sanctuary of the Tuileries Gardens. 'Liam! Liam Hughes!' I called. He looked round, so I walked towards him with the old greeting: 'How's about ye?'

'How's about *you*?' came the automatic, if hesitant reply.

Liam didn't recognise me. I'm younger than him, but I've aged more. I thought of Oscar Wilde's epitaph in Père Lachaise Cemetery:

> His mourners shall be outcast men,
> For outcasts always mourn.

I guess I look a bit mournful nowadays, for reasons not unconnected with outcasts, and with Liam. Memory is a scourge, and whatever triggers memory is painful. Yet I was surprised how glad I was to see him, and I'm sure he was glad to see me, once he understood all passion between us was spent.

When last we met, Liam probably classed me as an angry young man. Too right, I *was* angry. Fear – prolonged, debilitating fear – for somebody I loved had stirred up in me a visceral hatred. But a lonely quarter of a century in Paris has left me sure that anger is the most corrosive of human vices, a boil on the surface that conceals the rottenness of the personality within. So I do without losing my temper when I can. Being a serial optimist, I always *think* I can.

At the Tuileries, with the scent of summer flowers caressing us, I could almost see the wheels in Liam's brain turning. So I jogged his memory: 'Alan Houston, 'sieur, 'dame. Late of Belfast, Westminster and other points north of here.' I bowed to the girl, and added with a smile: 'A votre service!' She blushed uncertainly.

Liam, too, was uncertain what to say. Not surprisingly, for this man had ruined my career, wrecked my marriage and my family life, and sent me into exile. And here I was, springing out on him in Paris, during his first visit to France, with what I took to be his granddaughter.

When I say Liam had done all this to me, I mean the IRA had. He was a big shot in the organisation, though whether he took the decision about me, I'll never know. Anyhow, maybe the man I should blame for all that is not Liam, or even some putative Mr O'Big, but Houston, A., the ambitious, obsessive, egotistical non-saint, ex-scholar, general inadequate, and belated convert to humility, who waded into waters that were too deep for him.

Today I live with my memories of a time when I was a medium-sized cog in the politics of my native Ulster, trying to do something called 'bringing peace'. Now I understand that peace grows in the hearts of ordinary people, or not at all. In those far-off days I was more innocent, and much more idealistic.

Since then, the killing has continued, on and off, but mostly on. Even now, the Protestant and Catholic ghettoes are ruled by modern versions of Hitler's Brownshirts, beating and shooting to maintain their perverted law and order.

I'm still working – also on and off, but mostly off – on my book about Ireland. This will never be finished, of course, and nobody would want to read it anyhow.

Why? Because it would be true, unrelentingly true, and gloomy. Whereas what people want to read about Ireland is progress, seismic shifts in attitudes, historic break throughs, the elusive 'Settlement' that has floated, a holy grail, before the lustful gaze of successive political generations.

I'm half-enjoying my half-retirement in a tiny flat on the Left Bank of the Seine, near the Musée d'Orsay, that railway terminal whose astonishing conversion into an Impressionist Palace leaves us British depressed by the lameness of our national imagination. The Greenwich Dome? Need I say more?

What rots my guts is despair that the world still thinks it's just Irish perversity that's to blame for the Troubles. This blithely misses the universal message of thirty bloody years. 'Universal?' Yes, forget the convenient mantra about 'warring tribes', the belief that reciting those words, and perhaps holding up a clove of garlic, or a peace declaration, will preserve everybody else from infection by Irish madness.

It won't, because it was in the Ireland of the seventies that the world lost its post-war innocence. We've kept clear of big wars, thank God, but we still avert our gaze from the brutal lesson of Belfast, Derry and South Armagh: that violence often pays, and certainly holds a veto over democracy.

People don't want to know these truths, because they think they know all there is to be known about the Irish Troubles. Haven't they watched all those boring interviews on telly? What more do they need to know?

But I mustn't succumb to self-pity. Mary always told me that was my besetting sin, that and obsessiveness. Apart from my Hamlet-like tendency to dither. In fact, my wife attributed to me rather too many besetting sins for comfort. I'm sure she was right, and I wish I'd paid more heed.

I liked Edith Piaf, who in my generation didn't? But despite her hauntingly plangent tones, *Je ne regrette rien* is not the final word of wisdom.

Moi, je regrette beaucoup.

When Liam got over his shock and introduced his granddaughter, we stood chatting for about ten minutes. Soon I saw that Deirdre was getting uncomfortable in the hot sun. She looked longingly at the children sailing their boats in the round pond, letting the spray from the fountains cool them. I asked where they were going.

Liam wrinkled his nose.

'A place called the Musée d'Orsay. Deirdre's doing an A-level in History of Art, and Sister Theresa says this is a museum she must visit. Not quite my own cup o' tea!'

I told them I lived close by the d'Orsay, and suggested we should all walk there across the river, by the prettiest of the bridges. I'd introduce Deirdre to one of the staff I knew. Meanwhile I'd take Liam off for his own kind of tea, which I assumed, in the lamentable absence of Guinness, to be a glass of wine. Liam relaxed at the mention of a drink.

'The cardiologist in the Mater Hospital advises red wine for my condition, and that doctor's one man I always obey.'

Deirdre looked doubtful. She had never been out of Ireland before, and was nervous about being separated from her grandfather. But as I assured her that we would be back at the Museum long before she was ready to leave, Liam cut in.

'Don't worry, darlin'. This is a man I would trust with m'life. A man who went all the way for what he believed in. And even though he was wrong, dead wrong, it means he doesn't let you down.'

I was astonished. There were times, years ago, when Liam had given me a different reading of my own character. Still, time heals, I suppose, and I felt quite warm towards him as well, Republican bigot though he was.

As it turned out, we didn't ever get our drink. Later Liam whispered to me that Deirdre was too uncertain of herself to let him out of her sight.

I took them over the Pont des Arts then back along the Left Bank, telling them useful tourists' tricks on the way. We stopped while the girl had a rumble through the boxes of books and pictures on the Quais.

'Granda', can Ah buy this picture for me Mammy? It's smashin'! Daddy gave me some French money before we left.'

She held up an old print of Notre Dame. Liam smiled his assent.

God, she was everything a granddaughter ought to be. Bubbling with enthusiasm and, as she got used to me, ready for every fresh idea about Paris that oozed out of my pride in the city of my exile. She had the creamy complexion of adolescence. Deirdre was gauche, naive, and with those natural good manners that have survived among Belfast youngsters long after they've died out elsewhere. That's why they call my native city backward.

As we walked, she asked how I had come to live in Paris. I caught Liam's alarmed eye, signalling me to be careful. I smiled and said:

'That, Deirdre, is such a long story that the telling would take up too much of your precious time in Paris. Perhaps you'll come here some other time – I hope so.'

'Anyway, Mr Houston, I can only say you're very lucky. Even from what I've seen so far, there's never been a city like this. It's magic.'

Lucky! Well, that was one way of looking at it.

After I parted from them, I pondered how little I had achieved while navigating the shoals of public and private life. How had a man with a satisfying career in broadcasting and journalism, with an intelligent and lovely wife and two fine sons, contrived to lose almost everything? And for motives that, even now, I only half understood? Political ambition? Vanity? Friendship? Duty? Obsessiveness? What fault of character, or chance of fate had made me agonise, and suffer, and lose, both in love and in war?

The inward eye can be either the bliss or the curse of solitude. Across mine that evening drifted the faces of my lost family: Mary, whose mouth had always seemed to smile, before this happened to us; Peter, whose childhood cheerfulness was clouded by anxiety; and Brian, poor, worried Brian, who agonised for all of us.

My mind drifted back to where it all began.

[2]

In 1976 London was a more placid city than it is now. The Athenaeum was different too – more scholars, fewer businessmen.

The porter showed Alan Houston into the Morning Room to wait for his host. He was in his early forties, with blue eyes and fair, curly hair. A suspicion of incipient growth around the waistline? Perhaps.

Alan cut an odd figure in these formal surroundings: his light grey suit might have been slept in and he was carrying an untidy bundle of all ten national newspapers. One of these had already slid to the floor, and the rest looked at imminent risk. Alan's elder son Brian reckoned he never looked at these papers once breakfast was over, but carried them through his working day as a comfort blanket.

The crumpled suit contrasted with a fashionably colourful tie that his wife had bought for his birthday. From time to time Mary tried to take Alan's appearance in hand, but when she saw how his wilful forgetfulness frustrated her efforts, she would roll her eyes and murmur, 'Pierre Cardin lived in vain!'

The clock struck one. Alan sat at one end of a frayed leather couch, glancing at *The Times*. But he was distracted by the stillness of an elderly man with a beard who looked remarkably like Charles Darwin, an early club member whose portrait hung behind him like a shadow. Alan (who always had in mind the interests of his paper's obits editor) wondered if this distinguished-looking old chap was dead. Darwin definitely was; the jury was still out on the Athenaeum's senior member.

But just as Alan edged *The Times* an inch lower to search for any sign of life, the Emeritus Professor of Theology jolted awake, briskly

6

drained his sherry, and went off to lunch, carrying the *University Quarterly*, and humming the signature tune of *The Archers*.

Soon afterwards Alan's host, Charles Corbett, Her Majesty's Secretary of State for Trade, arrived: a handsome man, in that theatrical way other politicians envy – aquiline features and wavy black hair with a natural oil that made it shimmer in the sunlight. In his late forties, Corbett was over six feet in height and retained all the elegance that, ten years earlier, had made him the most eligible bachelor in the upper reaches of the Labour Party. Then he had married a rich Italian – married for love, as his friends discovered when she died from cancer only two years later, sending Charles into a chasm of despair. But to dyspeptic observers – and politics, despite its idealistic pretensions, produces more than a few of those – Charles *must* have married for money. Typical, they said, of upper-middle-class parvenus in the party of Keir Hardie and Ernie Bevin. Oblivious of this animosity, Charles dressed even more immaculately, developed other sybaritic tastes, and aroused further envy among colleagues.

He aroused also the resentment of his party leader, who thought him too clever by half, and too lucky for his own good. That was why, after the election victory, Charles had emerged with only one hip on the cabinet throne, in a run-down Trade Department, two rungs below the chancellorship he coveted.

Alan was surprised by this sudden invitation. It was usually journalists who entertained politicians to lunch, not the other way round.

Charles Corbett came to his point straight away. The secretary of state for Northern Ireland was mortally ill. His resignation would be announced as soon as he'd told his constituency party. Charles was to replace him. Alan emitted a low whistle.

His weakness as a cold-eyed journalist was the modicum of hero-worship he had retained, even in Fleet Street, the home of ulcers and cynicism. He admired Charles, the most radical figure on a dull front bench, and even hoped he might lead the Labour Party one day.

But Alan believed the Northern Ireland portfolio was at best an obstacle course, at worst a graveyard of ambition. Was the Prime Minister just trying to shaft his too brilliant trade secretary? Many of

Tom Sanderson's appointments seemed to be made out of malevolence.

'You look dismayed, Alan. What's wrong?'

'I don't doubt your ability to do the job, Charles. But success in my unfortunate homeland depends on whether the tide happens to be coming in or going out. Just now it's ebbing rapidly. There's too much bloodshed to allow for compromise. You've drawn the shortest of straws.'

Charles grimaced. These Ulstermen were blunt, called a spade a bloody shovel. He said stiffly that he'd already accepted the job. As the only cabinet minister without dependents, he couldn't refuse without looking cowardly. Then he dropped his second bombshell.

'I want you to come to Stormont with me, as political adviser, general dogsbody and a guru who comprehends the Belfast proletarian mind.'

His face lightened into a smile.

'Could be a ladder into politics for you, Alan.'

Alan's stomach turned over. He was still interested in finding a seat at Westminster. But this . . .

Charles, remembering that Alan *did* have dependents, saw a gap in his own logic. 'I suppose there'll be an element of risk for you too. But your family will get all the protection they need. You mustn't be worried about that.'

Alan *was* worried about his family. But he noticed that Charles assumed he would take the job.

The new Northern Ireland secretary had not decided lightly on the recruitment of Alan Houston. Whitehall, hostile to political advisers anyhow, would ask why a suave intellectual like Charles Corbett needed such a craggy *alter ego*. They would scarcely accept that Houston's Belfast working-class chippiness had been noticeably smoothed down by Fleet Street and the BBC.

Corbett foresaw these criticisms, but he himself had the instincts of an outsider. His Jewish parents had escaped from Germany in 1938, so Charles had learned from them how to stand against the world. He believed Alan shared his independence of mind. He had wise political instincts, would never abandon a commonsense solution in favour of whatever fashionable expedient happened to shimmy down the political cat-walk.

Corbett knew that civil servants, especially diplomats, took in pragmatism, not to say amoral expediency, with their mothers' milk. So let political advisers be political, and just occasionally tell you what was right. Above all, in Alan's case, say what might work in Ulster.

[3]

Alan knew nothing of the debate that had gone on inside his host's head. He was simply wondering how Mary – sane, rational, English Mary – would accept exile in Belfast. He also worried for Brian, due to go to Cambridge in the autumn; and for Peter, celebrating his twelfth birthday next week, and just happily settled into a London comprehensive.

Right from the beginning, the risks to his family jangled Alan Houston's nerves, but he suppressed his neurotic nature and talked about his political doubts. Charles, who had few illusions, said he desperately needed Alan's help. The problem since Direct Rule in 1972 was that an inadequate civil service machine had run rings around ignorant and half-interested ministers.

'I'm determined that won't happen to me, Alan. I'll immerse myself in Irish history, culture, poetry, art, drama, whatever it takes to understand. But I'm still scared I might finish up in the same bog of ignorance as my predecessors.'

'I wouldn't argue against the ignorance of your predecessors.'

'Well, I'll finish up the same, unless I have a native guide, preferably equipped with cleft sticks to carry messages, as in Evelyn Waugh.'

Charles talked on persuasively. Alan said he must consult his wife. Charles knew and liked Mary, but she was a strong personality, who might talk him out of accepting. As a successful politician, he liked to get his own way.

Charles played his trump. He had met – in great secrecy, because his colleague's retirement hadn't been announced – the brightest star in the reputedly lacklustre galaxy of the Northern Ireland Office.

'She's called Diana Carstairs – Foreign Office, possibly MI6, I'll find that out soon. A raven-haired, blue-eyed beauty, in a patrician Scottish style – if you care about such things. I'll arrange for you to have a discreet dinner with her tonight. Diana's worked in Belfast for a year, really knows the politics out there. I hope meeting her will remove your doubts.'

Alan did not react to this pre-feminist analysis. His butterfly mind was trapped by the phrase 'out there'. Charles certainly needed a lot of instruction – the natives said 'over there'. However, Alan kept this piece of parochial pedantry to himself; Charles might think he had a chip on his shoulder.

As he walked through St James's Park to the House of Commons, Alan was still thinking about Mary. Ulster was the only subject they ever argued about. Not about its politics, which she found bewildering, more about people's attitudes: he thought her too condescending; she considered that a man who'd spent most of his adult life in London should be less defensive about his native land. She didn't wear her East Anglian heart on her sleeve, did she?

Mary would suspect that he still nursed ambitions to become an MP. Charles's hint at lunch meant that if they made a success in Belfast, he might be able to shoe-horn Alan into a Labour seat. Mary thought that taking an active part in politics was strictly for nutters.

She regarded herself as non-political, a sort of liberal non-voter. She didn't mind Alan's party, so long as they stuck to opposing hanging, making life easier for homosexuals, legalising abortion, that kind of thing. But she got fed up with all their talk about equality, redistribution of wealth, trade unions, higher taxes. Mary always said she couldn't abide class war.

Come to think of it, class was another subject she and Alan argued about. The *Daily Telegraph* meets the *Guardian*.

At last his thoughts reached the chilling area he was trying to avoid. What would Mary think about the danger – the slight element of danger – to her and the boys?

When he reached the Press Gallery he telephoned her from a well-concealed mahogany cabin. He'd be late home, he said, he had to have dinner with somebody. He couldn't talk freely now; it was about a job, but it was quite sensitive, and might come to nothing.

'I'll reveal all when I get home.'

Mary was mystified and irritated, but told herself that, after twenty years of marriage, she ought to be used to Alan's odd ways.

[4]

As Mary Houston thought about Alan's mysterious call, a frown creased her handsome brow. Just two months younger than her husband, she was of medium height with blonde hair and, normally, a serene expression. Ever since university, Alan had thought her the most attractive woman he had ever met. Her deep blue eyes always seemed teetering on the verge of laughter.

Correction. Just recently Alan noticed that Mary had a few lines at the sides of her mouth – of worry perhaps, or irritation? What was the phrase somebody had for marks like that – 'death's first imprint'. Alan shuddered at the thought.

Less effervescent than her husband nowadays, Mary was much calmer and set in her ways. She guessed that, one way or another, Alan was about to disrupt their lives yet again. Mary's youth had not prepared her for being at anybody's beck and call. She came from a prosperous farming family in Norfolk, and had grown up in a rural community that admired her intelligence, beauty and humour. As a teenager Mary had had suitors in abundance. Her father, an ex-soldier, kept a few horses, and Mary and her sister used to ride out with the local pack of foxhounds. Mary had lost her virginity after a Hunt Ball. She kept these memories of her involvement with country sports from Alan's left-wing friends. If political ambition were ever to overcome his good sense, fox-hunting would not look well on a wife's cv for a Labour constituency.

She had met Alan at the Scottish university where he was reading English, she History of Art. Without false modesty, Mary remembered having been a honey-pot for the male undergraduates. Most of those pursuing her, however, were either zealous athletes, who had to be on the river or the track each morning before seven o'clock, and therefore tucked up in bed by 10.30; or else earnest scholars who were hard to detach from their books.

What attracted her to Alan was the contrast with these worthies. He seemed to take both study and games in his stride, and still remain free to devote himself to making her laugh. He wrote his essays in the middle of the night, and claimed that he got enough physical exercise walking the five miles back from the flat she shared with three other women. Sport was for fun, he said, not self-immolation.

She remembered their dates as an unbroken stream of laughter as Alan entertained her with take-offs of anything that breathed – characters from his Belfast youth, his dons and hers, their fellow students, Professor Jimmy Edwards, the comic hero of the period, barmen, waiters, anybody.

Mary guessed that Alan liked being seen with her because she was a slim, bubbly blonde, always ready for a lark, and because most men envied him. She assumed, for all his jeers, that he also liked her posh background, so exotic to a Belfast proletarian. She suspected this old-fashioned class warrior thought that deflowering an English upper-middle-class gel was another blow for Marxism, or whatever crazy doctrine he still half-believed in.

To the surprise of their friends, they parted after graduation, both saying they were too young for commitments. Not *exactly* mutual, though Mary pretended it was. That was her pride, and a sensible understanding that Alan would not be happy unless he put his career before everything else. Still, she could scarcely claim now that she had not understood his priorities, right from the start.

Alan had gone back to Belfast, to learn his journalism on the *Evening Chronicle*. He and Mary exchanged occasional letters, and Christmas and birthday cards, for the couple of years they were apart. She made sure he knew that she was working at the Tate Gallery. One night, he suddenly appeared on her television screen, pontificating about politics. She sent him a note of congratulation to the BBC, he came round to the gallery and they took up where they had left off. They married a year later.

As Mary thought about Alan's enigmatic phone call tonight, she recalled that this would not be the first such disruption in her career. After university she had worked her way quickly up the Tate's staff. She was just about to become Number 2 on Impressionist painting when Alan whimsically decided to abandon television journalism at Westminster, and lead his family off into the wilderness – aka, the North of England.

Why? Oh Lord, something called 'production values' was bugging him. Mary had never bothered to master the arguments, but apparently the teenage technicians Alan had to work with insisted that his words of wisdom must bear some faint relationship to the pictures on the screen. Not unreasonable, Mary thought, but Alan claimed he couldn't say anything sensible about politics in the time the dimwits at home were prepared to devote to understanding the future of the nation. 'Their attention span' the Men in Grey Suits called it. (Mary preferred a smart grey suit to the wardrobe of Alan's bohemian chums.)

He decided to re-educate himself in what he called 'proper journalism', his original newspaper trade. That meant becoming an assistant editor of a provincial paper, as launching-pad for a leap back into Fleet Street.

For Mary, it meant waving a tearful farewell to her Impressionists, and taking on a dogsbody task in a provincial museum, lecturing to visitors about its decent, but wholly indiscriminate collection. On the plus side, she had to bone up on every artist from Giotto to David Hockney, to keep one step ahead of the knowledgeable local punters. Still, it left her, for the first time, feeling very much second-string in their marriage. Mary wasn't a strident feminist, not a strident anything, but she had never been a second-string before.

Only a year after this grand exodus to the North, Alan moved back to London to be political columnist on a national newspaper. Career advancement for him, anti-climax for Mary. She had just begun to settle and make friends, having decided that they weren't all Picts and Scots.

It was good to be back among theatres and galleries, but Alan kept the working hours of the Westminster Village, and there wasn't much social life. So Mary, in self-preservation, had to cultivate her own circle of friends.

Yes, their living standards reflected Alan's much higher earnings, and they moved into a detached house in South London, but their lives became more semi-detached.

That was the point the Houstons were at when Ulster hit them.

[5]

In the eyes of Charles Corbett, Diana Carstairs was the very model of a modern civil servant: decisive, clear-minded, fertile of ideas. What he did not know was how she came to be that way. It was by a painful route.

A privileged child in her Highland family, she had lived in a small and ancient castle, surrounded by miles of grouse moor. Her two elder brothers went to their father's English public school and her parents thought of sending Diana, their last child, to boarding school too, but her mother knew it would not be right.

Diana was a troubled little girl, for no obvious reason. Her home was happy, her brothers, like their parents, adored and petted her. But at the village school she did not make friends, and she abandoned the Brownie pack at the church after three unhappy months. When her mother asked what was wrong, Diana's reply was always the same: 'Nothing.' She did not encourage intimacy, and would never allow her father to cuddle her. Before going to bed she would blow him a kiss, and bestow a secretive smile.

She hated it when her parents annnounced a visit to family friends, but she was also nervous about being left behind with the housekeeper or her nanny. So she went and when she got there usually enjoyed herself, especially if her brothers or the children they were visiting could make her laugh. Everybody assured her anxious mother that she would 'grow out of it'.

Diana Carstairs did grow out of her childhood shyness, in perhaps the only way that shy people know: she became more aggressively determined to have her own way than the average, nice Scottish

Highland girl – much more determined. By the time Alan got to know her, Diana was 'a control freak'.

When he first saw her in the restaurant, he could see why even the cerebral Charles had noticed her sexual allure. Diana was tall, just short of six feet, even though she was wearing low heels. Later in the evening, when the wine had relaxed them, she confessed that she had avoided high heels in case Alan turned out to be 'a short arse'. She explained that she didn't want to set up 'macho resentments' before these became inevitable. The remark made him realise that this lady might make life more combative.

That was all right by Alan. He liked women who knew their own minds, who didn't even contemplate male colleagues trying to walk over them, and he assured himself that it was fine if she stood up to him. However, he did feel strongly about politics.

Diana wore a full-length, multi-coloured skirt – blue, red, black and green stripes, so far as he could remember later. He did notice that her white blouse was stretched tight across her breasts. Her opinions were pronounced ones too.

They had barely tasted their antipasto when she asked whether Charles had told him about the PM's brief.

Alan looked uncertain.

'Yes, in general terms, he did.'

'Then you'd better hear it in the particular terms the PM used to my permanent secretary last week.'

Tom Sanderson wanted the Ulster question settled, one way or another. The political parties out there – that 'out' again, Alan noted wryly, those lesser breeds without the law! – should be given reasonable time to agree on constitutional arrangements. But they must be warned that if they failed London would leave them to their own devices.

Alan found himself echoing her words like a parrot – 'leave them to their own devices'? This was the disaster Ulster politicians often mumbled about, but which wiseacres like himself scoffed at. He told Diana he couldn't believe what he was hearing. She shrugged her shoulders – which disturbed his concentration – and spoke brusquely.

'You must please yourself, of course, but I'll explain Tom's fall-back position, as I understand it.'

After every effort at conciliation had failed, she said, Britain would declare Northern Ireland to be an independent state. Not part of a united Ireland, or anything unenforceable like that – Whitehall would support its membership of the UN, the Common Market, NATO, and anything else it wanted to belong to. Britain would also honour pensions and other benefits people there had paid for throughout their working lives. However, she added, 'What it won't do is to claim any longer a sovereignty it can't enforce. Tom says if Charles doesn't succeed in getting them to agree on something workable, it'll be time to draw stumps.'

It was her jolly sporting metaphor which made Alan explode. Draw stumps indeed!

'Doesn't the Prime Minister know the difference between a game of cricket and an ancient and bloody feud? Doesn't he understand that what the Unionists would see as a threat the Republicans would regard as a promise? Neither side would have any incentive to compromise.'

'Who knows, Alan? But it should make our work exciting, don't you think? We may be in ringside seats for the birth of Ulster's independence. And, I suspect myself, eventual Irish unity.'

Then she put one of her hands lightly on his.

'That's assuming you decide to come. I hope you do.'

When Alan reached home at midnight, he said he must telephone Charles at once. Mary was not pleased – she'd been waiting to know what had happened at both his lunch and this mysterious dinner.

Charles knew quickly that Alan was steamed up. Diana ought not to have been so frank with a man who had not yet accepted the job. Still, perhaps it was all for the best. If he played his cards right, this might be just what made Alan's mind up for him.

'You warned me that going to Ulster's not my smartest career move, Alan. The only reason I've accepted the job is to avert this doomsday nonsense. I don't think any Prime Minister would be so foolish as to carry out the threat. But even a hint that Tom's been playing with such ideas is dangerous.'

Charles then let drop a psychological bombshell, the thought that left Alan no alternative but to accept the job.

'Frankly, I've discovered that the Foreign Office has been peddling such ideas for years. Not my favourite department – they're too fond of splitting the difference between right and wrong. But if the Westminster talking-shop or the Whitehall sausage-machine ever decides that this tosh has any kind of Prime Ministerial backing, it'll cause mischief. Big, big mischief for your native province, Alan.'

[6]

When Mary had heard Alan's key in the lock, she was deep into a biography of Picasso, with some Mozart on the record-player, and a glass of white wine on the coffee table. Who cared if the Lord and Master was out plotting with some dreary politician?

She was surprised to see that it was after midnight. When Alan gave her cheek an absent-minded peck before his telephone call to Charles, she noted a strong whiff of garlic and booze. Apparently his dinner companion had assisted him in a steady evening's carousing.

'These politicians know how to drink,' Mary mused. 'No wonder their waistlines are so expansive, and their wits so dull!'

When Alan came off the phone, he smiled nervously at her. He explained what Charles wanted him to do, his initial doubts about the present unpromising state of politics in Ulster, the disturbing discussion with Diana Carstairs about the PM's crazy ideas, the challenging conversation he'd just had with Charles. Mary asked just one question.

'Who exactly is Diana Carstairs?'

Alan, his mind, as ever, full of politics, looked surprised.

'Oh, didn't I tell you? Sorry! Diana's the civil servant – well, perhaps I should say spook – I've been having dinner with.'

Alan went into some detail about her job, her views, perhaps more than Mary wanted to hear about the brilliance of Diana's mind, and about her appearance. Mary's husband had not been dining with the pot-bellied public servant of her imagining. She detected that he would take the job.

That lowered her spirits. Now that Mary knew the score-line – 'Ulster 10, My Career nil' – she had no desire to sit up half the night to hear his Match of the Day version. But she got it, kick by kick. Diana said this, Diana said that. Charles was being advised to do this, but he might be better to do that. There was some kind of worry, the detail of which Mary didn't bother to follow, about the Prime Minister's attitude. But Alan believed, after the phone call, that Charles and he would be able to sort that out.

The prospect, Mary heard through a poorly disguised yawn, was better than Alan had believed. Sinn Fein, the UDA, the UVF, the SDLP, the UUP and the DUP – all those sets of unmemorable initials! – they were all politically on the move. So there was hope, provided brilliant minds, like those of Charles Corbett, her husband and Ms Carstairs, led the poor lambs through the wilderness of their ignorance. It was an exciting prospect, Mary did not doubt. For him, for all of them.

When Alan said that, of course, she could veto the move, Mary saw he was watching her carefully. This was a dreary family ritual, which he dutifully observed every time he turned their lives upside down. But Alan knew damn well that she would say he must do what he wanted to. Hadn't her Mama told her, more or less on their wedding eve, that it was her duty to put her man's career first, and follow him wherever he had to go?

This had sounded old-fashioned, even in the mid-fifties. But her mother came from an old-fashioned age, and for her this had meant dutifully following a full colonel in the Coldstreams round for as much of the Second World War as the War Office would permit. At least Mama had felt she was part of great events. The Worldwide Fight against Fascism struck Mary as a shade more important than trying to bring peace to warring tribes who were not really at war.

At breakfast the next day, Brian learned about his father's prospective move and was immediately concerned for Alan's safety. Mary noted again the contrast between their two sons: Brian, like his father, was a worrier, whereas Peter was already addicted to the good life, did not bother over-much about schoolwork, enjoyed a laugh and was everybody's favourite birthday guest.

Come to think of it, Peter was rather like Alan as a student. That was before her husband matured into a sober-sides.

Alan sipped his fourth cup of tea, and said there would be little or no danger, either to him or the family. They'd get plenty of advice and, if need be, protection.

It took Mary some time to mention the effect on her own career. Alan – not for the first time – had forgotten about that. He recovered hastily.

'The Ulster Museum'll be ecstatic at the prospect of getting somebody with your experience. I'll soon be meeting people who can help with that.'

An unworthy metropolitan thought struck Mary. How many Impressionists would *they* have on their walls? Second, would there be anything at all from the Renaissance, now she'd added that to her repertoire?

Come to think of it, had Ireland experienced its Renaissance yet?

[7]

'Are you rushing in to work? We need to talk more before I decide about this offer.'

'Nothing to talk about, Alan. You want to take the job, so you take it. I follow on as usual, like an Indian tea-wallah following the troops. End of discussion.'

Mary had taken the day off for an afternoon dentist's check-up, so Alan postponed his departure for Westminster, and they had coffee together.

He was not the insensitive dolt his wife sometimes took him for. Forgetful, yes. When people greeted him outside local shops, he would cheerfully say 'How are you?' when he really meant 'Who are you?' Of course he was self-centred, but only about his work. He certainly worried about Mary's happiness.

Alan resisted a growing sense of unease about his marriage. His own childhood had been clouded by seeing his father and mother grow to dislike each other; he didn't want to repeat that into another generation, as so many of his friends had done.

Not that his parents had great, roaring rows, like some that his schoolmates boasted about – crockery flying around the kitchen, furniture broken, black eyes freely dispensed. The Houstons' was not Belfast working-class marital strife at its most technicolour. More black-and-white irritation, loss of the love that had brought Hilda and Jimmy Houston together in the early thirties.

His sister Pamela, nineteen when Alan was twelve, viewed her parents' troubled marriage with indifference. Pamela, from as early as Alan could remember, was leader of a one-woman Escape Committee. She hated their working-class home, the mean streets, the litter, the

24

dog-shit. She dreamed of a suburban villa. We all have our dreams and Pamela's were petit bourgeois.

She was not much help to Alan, in childhood or later. In his mother's long final illness, it was he who was to come from London to organise the home helps and nursing. Pamela seemed too busy with her social life. She had married happily above herself.

As a child, Alan had a persistent fear that his parents would eventually part. They never did. At least, not until his mother watched her husband's premature coffin lowered into the grave, just after Alan's thirteenth birthday. Jimmy, a heavy smoker, had died of cancer at forty-two. Alan was grief-stricken, Hilda more affected than he expected. Pamela coped well with her grief.

His father's death left Alan with a recurring dream. In this, Jimmy had at last walked out of their home. Alan knew where he lived and where he worked, but he never visited his father, because he thought this might be disloyal. In the way of dreams, this meant disloyal to his widowed mother, of course, because *outside the dream* Hilda was not a separated wife, but a widow, and needed to be cherished.

So his dream made Alan feel guilty about neglecting his father, but somehow unable to do anything about this. As the real years passed, his memory of Jimmy grew fainter, but this made his dreams more painful. If only he had gone to see his father, and told him how much he still loved him!

It was a relief each time he wakened and found that Jimmy was dead. Death was something that absolved Alan from responsibility.

This memory of his parents' marriage was the reason he was determined to make his own better. No, not better. Perfect. Alan Houston was a perfectionist.

He dipped a ginger-snap in his coffee.

'Look, Mary, if you loathe Belfast so much that you can't bear the thought of living there, you must say so now. I'd like to take this job, but I don't have to. It mustn't open some great rift between us.'

Mary bit her lip.

'It's ludicrous to say I loathe Belfast. I just see how parochial it is. Also that it's a foreign, an exotic place, and different from here in ways I don't relish.'

Alan suppressed a yawn. He had survived this seminar before, at many a hard-fought dinner table. Mary said that because her English friends had seen Ulster's quarrels boringly recounted on their television screens for seven years now, they reckoned to know all there was to know about the place.

'Aren't the pillar-boxes red, don't the cars drive on the left, don't people there speak English – more or less, but then look at Glaswegians or Geordies? And isn't Belfast only a couple of hundred miles from Liverpool?'

Mary argued that Ulster people *thought* differently. They laughed a lot in public, more than she found agreeable, but underneath they were so bloody earnest. Earnest about their work, with a grizzly Samuel Smiles addiction to self-improvement, an obsessive interest in money-making. Earnest about their sport, which many of them worshipped. Earnest about their religion, in which they were supposed to worship, but which Mary thought was just a football jersey to signal their prejudices. Above all, earnest about politics.

'What they lack, my dear, is the sense of irony that makes us English an island of sanity in an ocean of enthusiasm.'

Alan had not heard the point about English irony before. He rather agreed with it, though it had often made argument with his most urbane English friends a source of heightened blood pressure.

'I've told you before, Mary, Ulster's not exotic or foreign. These are just people caught in an impossible demographic stew – a minority within a minority within a minority.'

'Oh well, if it's that impossible I wonder how Charles and you, or even this Scottish woman of genius can hope to solve it.'

For once he was silent. This was not an argument he could win.

Alan privately attributed Mary's disillusionment with Belfast to an incident long ago. They had been having breakfast at his mother's, after coming off the overnight ferry. Brian, aged six at the time, went out to explore the suburban street where she lived. No worries in those days, not much traffic, no bombs going off, or paedophiles that anybody knew about. There he was, their curly-haired, blue-eyed innocent, playing happily with a little girl of his own age from next door.

But then he slunk in, red in the face, and chastened. Granny was puzzled. Surely he hadn't quarrelled with Theresa!

'Dad, what *are* we?'

An existential question for so early in the day. With Brian's second question, mind-blowing simplicity broke through.

'But are we *Protestants?* Theresa says she's not allowed to play with Protestants. Her mum fetched her in.'

Whispered explanations from Granny, Mary listening in disbelief.

'Run away, love, and get the toys from the spare bedroom. I think it's going to rain anyway.'

Then, *pas devant l'enfant*: 'Catholic family . . . *he's* very nice, always bids me the time-of-day . . . but *she's* a very bitter Republican. They say her brother's in gaol . . . explosives in his flat . . . I don't really know, mind, it's just what I've heard.'

That had left Alan and Mary disagreeing about visiting Ulster. She had been very good all the time his mother was ill, and then at her death: they went back and forward a lot, and Mary was kind and supportive, to both of them. Afterwards, she even took in Hilda's flight of china birds, to which his sister Pamela wouldn't give houseroom. But they didn't go to Ulster for a family holiday again. Alan remembered guiltily that Peter had never been there.

Mary interrupted his thoughts, in her usual decisive way. 'You don't need to dither, Alan. If Charles's offer interests you, take it. The danger worries me a bit, the boredom even more. But I can cope. Do just make up your mind.'

Alan rose, looking unhappy, and said he'd better go to Westminster. He'd call her later.

As Mary poured herself a second coffee, she thought about her husband. She believed she was still in love, though she hadn't expected the Scholar-Gipsy she frolicked with through university to become so earnest. He was increasingly a Hamlet figure or, to put it less kindly, a ditherer. A ditherer, not a doubter. Most Ulster males, alas, were singularly immune to doubt, which made them insensitive to other people's feelings, especially women's.

She must confess that this was not true of Alan. He still did everything he could to please her, made her smile or laugh more than anybody else. Pity he messed up her career so often and so effortlessly. Yet it still gave her a warm glow to see how besotted he was, quite fervent at times.

Last year, because he complained they hadn't been to Ireland for years, they had taken the car across from Liverpool for a few days. They went on their own – Mary did not want her sons exposed to either danger or bigotry.

It was a daylight sailing, and the captain recognised Alan from their schooldays. After a couple of gins in the master's cabin, he returned to the bridge, and the Houstons went for lunch. A bottle of wine made them both drowsy. Prudently – though with what intent Mary did not care to speculate – Alan had booked a cabin for daytime use. They went there and they slept, eventually.

Alan observed that sex at sea has an irresistible ingredient. Perhaps, he surmised, it was the romantic feeling that came from seeing, through the cabin window, the coasts of four different countries, plus the Isle of Man?

This absurd piece of Celtic romanticism tickled Mary's Anglo-Saxon sense of the ridiculous. She always did see the comic side of sex, so she had recourse to their private simulation of the Deed of Darkness.

'Tum-ti-tum-ti-tum!' she murmured. 'May God bless this ship's designers for putting a foot-board on the berths!'

In the missionary position, Alan needed lift-off.

Mary found him altogether more enthusiastic about bedroom matters than herself. Never mind, *chacun à son goût!* He certainly loved her, and she would bet her last pound on his faithfulness. There had been lots of nubile researchers buzzing around him when he was on the telly, but he showed no sign of taking the bait. In part, this was his Ulster puritanism. Alan really did think marriage vows were meant to be kept.

And Mary? Well, she was not at all religious, half-way between agnosticism and indifference. So she was not a card-carrying monogamist like Alan. True, marriage avoided too many one-parent households, and kept down the cost of the Welfare State, thus reducing her taxes. So she was in favour, sort of.

Occasionally Mary grew bored, even exasperated with Alan. So she couldn't guarantee if Mr Right-plus-One came along, at a moment of extreme ennui, that she wouldn't stray. She did not regard all this as a big deal. She was being honest with herself, right? She didn't *know*.

Just before Mary went to the dentist's, Alan telephoned.

'I've accepted the job, as you suggested.'

Charles Corbett's appointment as secretary of state for Northern Ireland was announced that afternoon, setting off lavish speculation in the press about likely new policies to be produced by this cabinet big-hitter. Alan's appointment as Political Adviser caused even more interest in Fleet Street, for he was one of their own.

What on earth was Alan Houston after? A permanent move into politics? Bloody fool!

[8]

Their first day in Belfast began cheerfully enough. Mary and Alan were on the overnight Liverpool boat, to go househunting before he reported to Stormont Castle the following day. He went on deck to see the sun rise on Belfast Lough. As the ship glided into the docks, he bent his head on its left side to make sure that the Cave Hill, lying above the city's northern outskirts, still looked like a profile of Napoleon. It did, though he noticed for the umpteenth time – with surprise – that the crag they called Napoleon's Nose was really the Emperor's distinctive hat.

As he blinked through the gathering light at the sights of home, his eyes watered. It must be the wind. Belfast was where Alan Houston still felt most alive. His city – spiced with memories, and now flecked with blood – was like most cities, dear to its own people, especially those like himself who'd left it many years before. But Belfast was also despised or derided by English politicians and civil servants, not to mention Nationalist Irishmen.

For dear, dirty Belfast had dared to look out on holy Ireland, *soi-disant* Island of Saints and Scholars, and to plant on its green-rimmed shore an Island of Hammers and Rivets. This less saintly, less scholarly 'Island' was the shipyard sited on Queen's Island, a muddy flat in Belfast harbour. During Alan's childhood, this had been the largest shipyard in the world, the flagship of industrial Ulster, what distinguished the province from the agricultural South. It was the symbol of Ireland's northern iron, too deeply injected ever to be prised out again.

Later, as he and Mary waited to go ashore, Alan listened with pleasure to the lilting tone of the dockers, their sentences lifting to a

30

climax at the end. Despite his years away from Belfast, his own accent hadn't faded much. Evidence, his English friends said, of a provincial chip on his metropolitan shoulder.

Mary nudged him, and pointed to the first soldier she'd seen. He seemed only a boy, but sharp-looking, automatic rifle cradled in his arm, eyes scanning the foot-passengers. Mary noticed that the veins on his neck were standing out with tension. She shuddered.

A newspaper contents bill distracted Alan's attention: '100,000 Orangemen will march today.' Damn! For all his political obsession, he had forgotten that estate agents' offices would be closed for this public holiday.

A woman's voice at his elbow said, 'Oh, God, no – not the Twalfth! Ah'd forgotten the date, Dermot. Shows how long we've bin away. Ah hope to God there won't be rioting.'

Alan felt a chill at his heart. For the first time, he faced the fact that he had been burying in his subconscious: he could be bringing his family into danger.

In his mental telephone exchange, several long-disused lines clicked. What he'd just heard from the woman passenger was a groan of exasperation. That and her husband's name signalled that she was a Catholic. Her worry was about the Twelfth of July – Orangemen's Day, holy festival of banners, bands and kick-the-Pope tunes from the trainer-shod, Brylcreem-burnished Rising Sons of Sandy Row and Glasgow Rangers, who would prance through the centre of Belfast, outshining the more solemn Orangemen.

The marching was a prelude to political speeches at 'The Field', outside the city, delivered to audiences containing a substantial sprinkling of 'the speechless', Belfast's euphemism for those who did not take quite literally their lodges' support for temperance, or even total abstinence. And for the younger, more libidinous Orangemen and bandsmen, the marching was a prelude to fornication behind the hedges that formed the outer boundaries of Loyalism on this, its glorious day.

Alan remembered a visit he'd made to the Durham Miners' Gala. Somebody had told him that if he wanted to understand the British Labour Movement he must attend this colourful event. The Gala was also a festival of bands and banners and oratory and booze and fornication. As he had stood near the ancient Cathedral, nursing his pint pot and treading on a carpet of broken glass, he'd thought how like the Twelfth of July it was.

The difference was that, though the Durham miners were not the darlings of Middle England, their Gala did not tempt anybody into violent reaction. There was no chance that Chelsea or Cheltenham Conservatives would say the march was a provocation, or infringed their civil rights; no risk that somebody would get killed on the fringes of the parade.

[9]

At the breakfast counter in the hotel, a young man with a bundle of newspapers sat down beside them.

'The top of t' mornin' to you, Frances', he said to the pretty waitress.

She giggled. 'Ach, catch yerself on, Mr Corfield, and don't you be sayin' the likes o' that in yer broadcasts, or they'll all be killin' theirselves laughin' at ye. I doubt ye'll nivver pick up the way we talk here. Somewhere in the back o' beyond now, they might say "the top o' the mornin'", but nat in Belfast.'

'What, not even Mickeys like yourself, Frances?'

She blushed and shook her head.

Frances liked her handsome young customer, beautifully dressed, always with a handkerchief in his breast pocket. He had smooth shiny blond hair, so carefully cut she'd love to run her hand up the back of his neck.

She had mentioned the Englishman's bantering style to her younger brother. Michael, aged fourteen, thought the people making him run errands for them after school were the Provies. His father privately doubted that the IRA would devote quite so much time to betting slips.

Michael sternly told his sister that this kind of English imperialist had been patronising Irish people for centuries, and she ought to treat him with contempt. Frances did not mention Corfield at home again. Sure he wouldn't take up with the likes of her anyway.

As she disappeared to cook his breakfast, her customer spoke to the Houstons.

'Good morning to you. I'm Roger Corfield, BBC London, doing a stint out here. You in the news business too? This hotel makes its living off us hacks.'

When Alan told him who he was, Corfield momentarily showed interest in a potential source of information. But soon his own unquenchable desire to communicate, on or off the air, overcame mere journalistic curiosity. He launched into a lecture on the Orange march, repeating the only fact about it that Nationalists found amusing. When the Orangemen's hero, William III – the famous King Billy on a white horse, featured in so much gable art – marched to defeat the Catholic King James II at the Battle of the Boyne, he actually had the support of the Pope.

'All because *Il Papa* had it in for James's ally, Louis XIV, I'm told.'

Over breakfast he gave Mary the benefit of a highly superficial analysis of the Irish Question, larded with improbable comparisons with other theatres of conflict from which he had reported.

Mary smiled politely. Alan wondered why he had left home, when for the price of a bitter in his London local he could hear similar nonsense? It was like taking your holidays in Torremelinos to eat fish and chips *à l'Espagne*.

The Houstons decided to tour areas where they might like to live. This was not a success – security barriers or Orange marchers frequently delayed them. In frustration, they stopped to watch the procession.

The early Lodges were smart, with many members in well-ironed blue suits and bowler hats. Not the London bowler that had been common ten years before, with its curly brim and Brigade of Guards fur. The Orange bowler looked like what foremen in the shipyard wore before safety helmets were introduced – pulled down on the ears, for protection against rivet ends that might be dropped, maliciously or otherwise, from high on the gantries. That was why foremen were derisively called 'Hats'. The tunes they heard at first were military marches from all round the British Isles, mixed with the more rousing hymns. But as the march rolled on sartorial and musical dignity eroded. Bagpipes and flutes replaced silver and brass. 'Men of Harlech' and 'Abide with Me' gave way to the uncompromising lyrics of Orangeism – 'The Sash My Father Wore', 'Derry's Walls', and 'Dolly's

Brae' (over which, so singers in the crowd stridently declaimed, they'd 'kick ten thousand Papishes').

Alan murmured to Mary, 'This is not the language of reconciliation that Charles and I need to hear.'

'I can't take any more of this. It's medieval!'

Alan grinned. 'Later than that – eighteenth century, to be precise, reacting to events in the seventeenth.'

Mary glared at him. Alan decided his history lesson had been a psychological error. He suggested they go to a pub he knew for lunch.

As they came into the University Tavern, a voice greeted them and Alan recognised their breakfast companion from the BBC.

'Hello there,' said Corfield. 'Have a jolly morning dodging the Brethren? How about a Guinness, Mary? *Vin du pays*! On these holy occasions, we all suffer from what I call "the thirst after righteousness".'

While he bought their drinks, Alan found they were standing near several old friends. One by one, they saw and greeted him, and he introduced Mary.

John Atkinson was an economics lecturer at the university. He drank whiskey and chain-smoked cigarettes, was squat and balding, with a sceptical humour. His wife Grizelda, a handsome, tawny woman in black-and-white tweed skirt and red sweater, was a social worker. Soon she was advising Mary about where she might live. Alan quietly wondered how soon his wife would discover that Grizelda's politics were more left wing than hers – or his, or those of almost anybody else he knew. But Grizelda was an understanding woman, so she talked about housing.

A handful of journalists gathered round Alan to see what they could find out about his boss. Conor O'Grady, red-haired, smooth-cheeked, and looking twenty-one, was Northern Correspondent for a Dublin paper. He cut into the polite questioning.

'C'mon, I hear yer man Corbett's a stuffed shirt.'

Alan advised him to wait and see.

The youthful Dubliner believed he knew more than anybody about Ulster politics. Conor's expertise was in 'opinion formers', in the mental gymnastics of Belfast's introverted intelligentsia.

It never occurred to him, or indeed to them, that nowadays the opinions they formed were those of fewer and fewer people. Because of violence, the middle-class culture of people who drank in the University Tavern had no relevance to the working-class ghettoes, Protestant or Catholic. There the feast of reason and the flow of soul had given way to the fist, the baseball bat, and the gun.

Occasionally Conor persuaded a London Sunday newspaper to accept an article, which made him first port of call for newly arrived feature writers from England and overseas. These visiting firemen had to make their minds up quickly. John Atkinson claimed to have heard one well-known American by-liner, waiting to check in at the Europa Hotel, murmur to the loquacious O'Grady: 'OK, OK, Conor, not too much detail, please. Just tell me who are the good guys in the white hats.'

In Belfast white hats are in short supply, but nobody told him that.

As the group ordered their sandwiches, a tall, broad man with a shock of grey hair burst through the swing doors.

'Quick, plug me into m'life-support system, before those ones out yonder stop me oul' heart beating. A double gin-and-tonic, some-body.' As they all stood laughing, he added: 'Youse one have short arms and long pockets.'

Roger Corfield took the none-too-subtle hint. London reporters were expected to buy more than their rounds.

Harry Fergus was a veteran Nationalist MP with a fine line in blarney which charmed and mystified strangers. He concealed a shrewd political brain and a rare empathy with his fellow Belfastmen, of whatever religion or politics, beneath a haze of anecdote, badinage and – irrigated by a few drinks – occasional song. Today he began seriously.

'Have you heard there's a bit of trouble at the bottom of Castle Street? A bunch of our lads jeered the procession, so the RUC shoved them back. Bloody right, too – the Prod crowd was gettin' wild with them. But one of our brave boys, doubtless inspired by the cause of Oul' Ireland and several pints of stout taken on a fastin' stomach, threw a half-brick, and caught a peeler on the cheek – awful bloody mess, he was.'

Harry said the police then drew their batons, more bricks were thrown, and there was the usual running battle, up to the bottom of the Falls Road. He thought the RUC had gone further up than was sensible. Some Provo was bound to get organised with a Kalashnikov to take a potshot at them.

This was the first news of the skirmish to reach the pub. Corfield and O'Grady hurried off to see what was happening, just a mile away. Belfast's battle-field is compact.

[10]

Alan looked anxiously at Mary. Written on her anguished face was the question in her mind: Why are we coming to live in this awful place? The Des. Reses they'd seen advertised in the closed estate agents' windows suddenly seemed even less Des.

Harry Fergus saw that Mary was upset and he jumped in to change the subject.

'Well, son, so I hear you're coming back for a while to this poor oul' city of ours. And your lovely wee wife here. D'ye know, love, I knew yer man here when he hadn't an arse to his trousers, if you'll excuse my Belfast crudity. But he's done well for hisself, hasn't he?'

Mary smiled uncertainly She knew Alan's family had never been that hard up, but Fergus obviously intended to be welcoming.

'This place minds me of a fella suffering from a highly infectious, and probably fatal disease. Ye notice yer friends steerin' clear of ye. You two aren't doin' that, so God bless you both.'

A Falstaffian figure with a rasping Belfast accent came through the door. Sam McCluskey was deputy editor of the *Evening Chronicle*. A new editor had just joined the paper, an Englishman promoted over Sam's head. The managing director, recently sent to Belfast by Group Headquarters, knew only about balance sheets. He judged the liberal line of Sam's editorials might be discouraging business advertisers, who were mostly Unionists. At least, that's what the chaps he met at the golf club told him.

John Atkinson said, 'Give us the low-down on your new editor, Sam. Fred Hargreaves, is it?'

'Well, he read history at Oxford, and his closest friend there was our distinguished permanent secretary, Sir Richard Heston.'

Harry Fergus choked on his second gin.

'Holy God, a friend of Dick Heston's! Don't tell me he'll be under the influence of that arrogant bastard. That man's got about as much affection for this place, Prods or Micks, as my Granny had for snipe-shooting.'

Alan pricked up his ears. So far he'd only spoken to his permanent secretary on the telephone, but Sir Richard was sure to be a significant figure in his new life.

'What exactly do you find wrong with Heston, Harry?'

'Listen, Alan, there's him and there's the retiring secretary of state himself, and I'd be hard put to it to tell you which of them's the more cantankerous. I will say this for Dick: he's quite without pomposity – "shows no side", as he'd put it himself. That other wee blirt is so full of his own importance that he can hardly walk for the swagger. Good riddance to him, God forgive me, though I know he's dying.'

He lit another cigarette, blew a smoke ring, and posed a rhetorical question.

'Why is it, whenever I meet a five-fut-four-inch, pooter-chested little twit, he turns out to be either a staff captain in the Provies or Her Majesty's secretary of state for Northern Ireland?'

Others piled into the debate about the retiring minister and his permanent secretary – disagreeing, filling out their characters with irreverent, not to say irrelevant stories, and shouting 'Ach, catch yerself on!' – until many were talking simultaneously at the tops of their voices. Mary found it hard to follow the arguments: this was her first experience of an Irish pub just before the Holy Hour, when reasoned conversation is not the norm.

Harry Fergus swerved into anecdote.

'Listen, listen! Have ye all heard the one about the paramilitaries economising on aerosols? Y'know them graffitis about the Pope and Queen? Now they just write FTP or FTQ.'

John Atkinson said in West Belfast you'd always had to mind your Ps and Qs.

The landlord was minding his closing time at three o'clock.

'Finish up your drinks, ladies and gents, please.'

As he collected glasses, Conor O'Grady burst in, his face ashen. He asked urgently for a whiskey, and drank it neat.

'They've shot a peeler,' he gasped. 'I was only ten yards away from him when he fell.'

Harry Fergus asked, 'Is he bad?'

'He's dead. Half his fuckin' head blown away. A Provo sniper. The bastards! One of his mates told me he was a Catholic with four children. Roger's broadcasting the news now.'

He turned green, and hurried towards the Gents, his handkerchief over his mouth.

The colour drained from Mary's face. When Alan asked if she was all right, she nodded her head, but didn't speak. She could still hear the last echoes of the Orange bands. They sounded to her like a dirge.

Alan, too, was horrified by the murder. Down the years, paragraphs in London newspapers about the latest Ulster atrocity produced in him a tut-tutting anger, no different from his English friends. But to hear such news from a reporter who had seen a man's head blown apart just a few minutes earlier brought him nearer the heart of horror.

John Atkinson, whose steady whiskey drinking had left him redder in the face than the others, suddenly said he wanted to recite a poem before they dispersed. His wife, Grizelda, looked at the floor, her face a pale mask.

'It's about the Orangemen,' Atkinson said, 'and about those who hate them. Louis MacNeice was wise enough to desert this bloody city for the BBC in London. He died five or six years before these Troubles, but he must have sensed they were coming.'

A sudden soberness left Atkinson's previously slurred voice sounding out clearly.

> Why should I want to go back
> To you, Ireland, my Ireland?
> The blots on the page are so black
> That they cannot be covered with shamrock.
> I hate your grandiose airs,
> Your sob-stuff, your laughter and your swagger,

Your assumption that everyone cares
Who is king of your castle.
Castles are out of date,
The tide flows round the children's sandy fancy;
Put up what flag you like, it is too late
To save your soul with bunting.

As they filed out of the pub, Mary was weeping quietly.

Fear comes in many forms. Ever since Alan had accepted the job in Belfast Mary had suffered a gnawing anxiety, but this was partly plain irritation that her own career was being disrupted yet again. It was not the genuine, gut-wrenching fear she felt now as she came to terms with the death of a man only a mile from where they had been having one of those interminable political discussions she hated.

From that moment Mary perceived emotionally that these Troubles were not about boring Ulster politics at all. They were about brutality, fear, loss of human feeling, bitterness, bigotry. What folly had brought her here to face, on her first day in Belfast, the death of a policeman with four children, and to listen to a poem of disillusionment?

Mary shuddered. She would still be shuddering several months later, when she followed their furniture van to Belfast.

[11]

Estate agents were closed the next day too, so Mary went home to London. The policeman's murder had blunted her appetite for house-hunting. Alan telephoned Charles from the hotel. This first death of his stewardship had left the secretary of state angry and sad.

'We *must* get a truce, Alan. There's too much suffering here. I went to see Rory Campbell's widow. The three daughters were weeping, the little boy of eight trying to look brave. It brought home to me that this isn't just a political crisis. It's a continuous drip of family tragedies. In my whole political life I've never felt so inadequate as in that little house.'

He said Mary Campbell wondered if her neighbours had set Rory up to be murdered.

'The police don't think they could have, not so near the city centre. But I understand why she's suspicions – the Campbells've had a lousy time since he joined. The IRA regard Catholic RUC men as Quislings, and even more legitimate targets than their Protestant colleagues. Then, ye gods, they complain it's a sectarian police force!'

Charles explained that his private secretary, Bill Simpson, had arranged the visit to Rory Campbell's home.

'I learned another useful, though distressing fact. One of the police escorts blurted out what Bill hadn't told me. Bill's own father, a police sergeant, was murdered by the IRA last year. When I asked him about it his eyes filled with tears, but at least I've got a source who knows more about police attitudes and the difficulties of recruiting Catholics than Dick or Diana.'

Later that day Alan found his new boss in an office furnished to resemble the drawing-room of a stately home. This was what

Stormont Castle had once been. It had housed prime ministers of Northern Ireland, from the first one, Lord Craigavon, a veteran of resistance to Home Rule before the Great War, right up to Brian Faulkner, who had been in charge until Ted Heath declared Direct Rule. Charles and his team were to live and work there.

As Alan entered, Charles rose from a sofa.

'Welcome aboard! Maybe I should say *Morituri te salutamus.* God, they're a gloomy bunch, my advisers. Dick Heston has a good mind, though he's disturbingly arrogant, a professional "blunt Northerner". He makes local politics sound like a chess game that always ends in stalemate.'

'You're making me feel gloomy, Charles.'

The secretary of state grinned mischievously. 'Whitehall has been so seared by the narrow-mindedness of Protestant politicians that it tends to confuse the leader *pro tempore* of the Ulster Unionist Party with the Fallen Angel, Satan. Understandable perhaps, but not conducive to the politics of compromise.'

Alan knew why Unionist politicians made such a bad impression. Compared with the Nationalists, he said, they were stiff-necked, charmless, always appearing to have an eye out for the main chance. The Nationalists were far more agreeable to meet, wanted to explain their case, often to the point of tedium. Unionists were so arrogant they couldn't be bothered, so they just hired yet another useless London public relations agency.

Having delivered himself of this first, sweeping piece of political advice, the political adviser wanted to know more about Dick.

'What does he think about the Nationalists, people like Harry Fergus? I had a drink with Harry yesterday – sensible man, once you've penetrated the blarney.'

Charles said that his permanent secretary didn't rate the constitutional Nationalists either. He seemed to regard the IRA as the only 'real people' on the Catholic side. His own feeling, after Constable Campbell's death, was that they were all too real. Whatever political moves he decided on, something had to be done about combating terrorism.

'Murder's a bit subversive of democratic politics. That's one truth we're missing, all of us at Westminster. This province of yours, Alan, is robbing us of our political innocence.'

'How do you mean?'

'Once violence enters our calculations, where do we stop? What other terrorist outfits round the world are scheming to second-guess the ballot box? Your Republicans out here, Alan, could be international pace-setters.'

Alan chewed his lip reflectively. Irish Republicans thought of themselves not as pace-setters, but victims. He decided this was a piece of political advice his chief should be spared for now. It might depress him further.

Charles said they would have the first dinner of his kitchen cabinet that evening. These were the people he was going to rely on for advice on everything.

'By the way, I ought to warn you: you've met Diana Carstairs – great personality, marvellous mind, pleasant appearance – but that woman is seriously addicted to power.'

'I noticed, all four things.'

'Something else may help you understand Diana. Her first job after university was in the Prague Embassy. She had a brief affair with a Czech politician. It blighted her career a bit.'

'I thought diplomats were encouraged to get close to local politicians.'

'Not that close. MI6 said he was in Czech intelligence. Diana maintains that's nonsense and anyhow they didn't discuss anything secret, but she failed to convince her interrogators back in London. The foreign secretary of the day didn't fancy the scandal of a sacking, but it scuppered her chances in the FO. That's why she finds herself in a backwater.'

Alan ignored that 'backwater' and Charles returned to Dick and Diana's attitudes.

'These are a tough pair of Whitehall warriors. Dick can be forceful to the point of rudeness. Only four of us in my *cabinet*, but from a preliminary recce of positions, there's little risk that viable options won't get mentioned – and demolished.'

He began to fidget with his papers. Alan smiled. Some things never changed. When he used to meet ministers as a journalist, a private secretary would enter after half an hour or so, holding a slip of paper. This was probably blank, but it enabled the Great Man to murmur, 'Awfully sorry, something has come up,' and terminate the meeting.

Advisers were apparently treated the same. Charles said he must read through his papers for the cabinet's Economic Committee, and dictate a minute before dinner.

'I can already see this new job is going to tear me down the middle. My life at Westminster versus my life at Stormont.'

When Alan had showered, he took a short walk in the castle grounds. The building was uninspired, but mellow – mock Scottish Baronial, somebody had called it. The grounds were well tended – masses of rhododendrons, tall oaks, conifers and elms. Dutch elm disease has never spread to Ireland. Prevailing wind, apparently.

Stormont's rooks were making a raucous tumult in their evening roustabout. That apart, Alan felt himself embalmed in deep tranquillity. After a few weeks at Stormont, he would find the atmosphere enervating.

A policeman suddenly fell into step thirty yards behind him, a Sten gun looped on his shoulder. Alan was puzzled that he had an armed guard even within the fortified castle grounds.

'Hello, constable. What's the score?'

'Nil all, so far,' replied the ruddy-cheeked policeman. 'We haven't let the bastards get one of yiz yit, so we haven't.'

Until that cheerfully chilling remark, Alan hadn't taken the danger to himself seriously. It was just a theoretical factor in discussions with Mary. Now fear seemed to spread from the region of his testicles and set off a tremor in his heart.

Alan Houston had often wondered whether he was a coward. He certainly hadn't enjoyed it much at school when the gym teacher, an ex-sergeant major in the Grenadier Guards, had put him in the ring with two other boys. It was all right when Alan was in the majority, but he didn't like two boys thumping him.

Being killed was worse. To pick up Charles's phrase, it was 'subversive of democratic politics'. Also painful, he assumed.

[12]

The man who greeted Alan as he entered the dining-room did not look at all like a permanent secretary. He had expected Sir Richard Heston to be tall, slim, silver-haired – in fact, favouring the disguise dished out to apprentice mandarins at Sunningdale Civil Service College. Dick, however, was below medium height and beginning to develop a pot-belly, and his dark hair was thinning at the temples. Aged about fifty, he had an air of twitchy discontent that hinted at a quarrelsome nature. His suit was expensively tailored, but of an unusual cloth, black with a thin silver stripe. When Diana got to know Alan better, she remarked that it was strange that their permanent secretary spent so much money in order to be badly dressed.

Dick, already half-way down his first whiskey, began to question Alan about his family.

'Our elder son's going to Cambridge in October. That's Brian. Peter's twelve, and he's just started at secondary school in London. I suppose he'll go to a local grammar school, though I'd have preferred a comprehensive.'

Dick grunted. 'You'd do well to think less about your educational prejudices and more about his safety. Most of our people here – English officials, that is – leave their families at home, or even if the wife comes, send their children to boarding-schools. I'd better get one of my security people to talk to you.'

Alan felt again the chill of fear. He had pushed to the back of his mind the thought that Mary or the boys would be in any danger. Dick's remark fed his doubt and guilt.

Diana entered, and began to talk about Charles's visit to the dead

46

policeman's home. She shuddered. 'Oh, God, that poor family just symbolises the futility of what we're doing here.'

Dick moved impatiently from foot to foot.

'I've lived through so many murders of soldiers and policemen now that I've learned to suppress my emotions. This may offend you, Mr Houston, but I notice that English soldiers' deaths attract worse headlines back home than Irish policemen's.'

Alan felt sick. Diana looked pained. Neither said anything. After an awkward pause Dick changed tack. Speaking with ostentatious formality, he said:

'The secretary of state has instructed me that you must be given all relevant information.'

He bounced on the balls of his feet. Alan was to learn later that Dick always did this when he was about to become aggressive.

'First time I or my predecessors have let any locals into the loop. Can't pretend I approve.'

Alan struggled to suppress an angry response and Diana looked out of the window. Dick had something more to add to Alan's bizarre introduction to civil service life.

'Before the S of S joins us, I'd better tell you something about my own past life, otherwise you might hear it from one of your more bigoted compatriots.'

It turned out that Dick had been a youthful candidate for the Catholic priesthood, but had lost his faith before ordination. He added pawkishly that the civil service, unlike his first choice of career, involved a *minimum* of commitment.

'I trust you'll keep your trap shut about this, Mr Houston. You can imagine the reaction in the Orange Lodges if they knew the permanent secretary was as near-as-dammit to being a Papish priest. Or, indeed, what the other lot up the Falls would say if they knew that I was – as they uncharitably say out here – "a *failed* priest".'

Charles burst cheerfully into the dining-room.

'Have I spent long enough on my red boxes to deserve a drink?'

'Try the whiskey, Secretary of State,' Dick answered. 'Black Bush, they call it. Perhaps the principal compensation for your service in this vale of tears.'

Charles had one whiskey before dinner, and a glass of red wine with his roast beef. Dick was thirstier. As soon as the main course was cleared away, the steward left the whiskey bottle at his elbow.

He gradually became both garrulous and aggressive. Diana, who was drinking tonic water, frowned nervously each time Dick refilled his glass. Alan guessed that these two were allies against any political boss, and that she didn't want him to make a fool of himself. So even somebody close to Dick didn't know what he might come out with next! As the level of the whiskey bottle lowered, Diana looked as if she were perched on the lip of a volcano.

Charles said he would prefer at this first gathering of his kitchen cabinet for him and Alan to pick Dick's and Diana's minds, rather than attempt anything more formal. He had skimmed through the mountain of paper they had provided.

Dick and Diana exchanged glances. They preferred the system they had used with their previous boss who, to put it charitably, had not been proactive. They had given him 'option papers' which left him little real option. As Diana once said skittishly to Dick, 'Permanent officials rule, OK?'

Alan pretended not to notice that Dick was getting drunk.

'Do you think the IRA might consider a ceasefire?'

'Put that right out of your mind, Mr Houston. When I heard you came from Belfast, I feared we'd be in for some cheerful "return of the native" stuff.'

Charles looked pained. 'Dick, may I suggest we use first names? Including myself. Makes it seem friendlier.'

Dick nodded irritably, and took another sip from his glass. He was now well into a monologue, and nobody was going to stop him. His inebriation set off a stammer – not that of a nervous man, but denoting an inner rage. Yet he remained surprisingly articulate. Dick was clearly an experienced drinker.

'T-t-take it from me, laddie – er, *Alan* isn't it? – your Provie compatriots will n-n-never call it off. Once they stopped, they'd never be able to crank the V-v-volunteers – if you'll pardon the eupesism . . . euphemism – never be able to crank the so-called Volunteers up again.'

Alan knew permanent civil servants often displayed territorial jealousy, but he hadn't expected hostility like this. Charles was just surprised by Dick's openness. *In vino veritas*, he supposed. Well, Dick's state might teach him things he needed to know about his Permanent Secretary. Charles sat back to enjoy the tingle of excitement he always felt when he couldn't guess what might be coming next.

It wasn't only Dick who had a Them-and-Us attitude. Diana, too, adopted an amused, even disdainful tone about Irish people. Neo-imperialist, Alan's left-wing friends might have called it, if they hadn't been singing from a different song-sheet on Ireland.

At a lull in the conversation, he tried to explain to this unreceptive audience what he thought made Ulster politics different. After all, that's what he'd been hired for.

'Even the most thuggish, the least educated people here take politics in with their mother's milk. That's because of demography. The Catholics are a minority within a minority. They're vociferous in their victimhood.'

Diana was disappointed in Alan, who seemed to her like an apologist for his native land. But she didn't interrupt.

'In most other places, certainly in Europe, it's only the intelligentsia that thinks politically. For the average Joe, politics is about mundane things, like taxes, prices, jobs, how many immigrants the Government lets in. I wish it was like that over here, but it's not.'

Charles looked thoughtful, Diana doubtful. Dick's brain was switched to 'transmit, not receive'. By 11.15 he was ready to give his conclusions on the Irish Question.

'After long experience of this unholy bog, it's my considered opinion that the bastards should be left to stew in their own juice.'

When Dick added that the Prime Minister was right to think the unthinkable, Alan pricked up his ears.

'That's what the British public wants. What's happened out here in the last few years is brutalising public life – courts, police, army, even the civil service. On the mainland as well. In the end, it'll erode liberal values.'

Charles judged that an interruption might still be worthwhile.

'Perhaps liberal values that abandon people in pain aren't worth as much as we thought.'

A more sober civil servant might have paused at this, but Dick scarcely noticed. Oblivious of the impression he was making on his new boss, he chuntered on. Nobody interrupted. His diction grew less secure.

Some aggressive drunks need to concentrate on a single butt. Dick's target for that evening was Alan.

'Let me tell you my credo of how Britain is governed, Alan. First of all, unlike you politicos, I don't have too high expectations of what governments can achieve. My own public service commitment is to recognise that life is a pool of excrement, and that my task is to guide the citizenry towards the shallow end.'

He chuckled at his own joke, filled his whiskey glass, and re-launched the diatribe.

'Trouble about your native patch, brother, is that I'm not at all sure a shallow end exists in this particular shit-heap.'

Charles decided to talk to the PM about how much longer his permanent secretary should remain at Stormont. Diana tried to switch the conversation to likely public reaction to the murder of a Catholic policeman on Orangemen's Day. But Dick Heston could no longer see that she was trying to rescue him.

'Most Prods'll be incadnescent . . . inca . . . anyway, furious; the Micks'll be over the moon. And the Brits'll just be glad it's not one of theirs.'

Charles spoke quietly. 'Rory Campbell was a policeman for whom I bear responsibility. What I want to know is how I'm going to prevent murders like that.'

It was as if Dick had not heard him.

'Where was I? Ah, yes, my professorial lecture on the art of government. Well, Alan, you can forget all that Labour Manifesto nonsense, on which you were doubtless weaned, bowing down to the party's working-class gods, what's left of them.' He thought for a moment, smiling to himself. 'I don't think many of this present lot would want to sing that Keir Hardie knew their father. They'd be more at home with Ramsay Mac's Duchesses.

'And you can also forget the competing Conservative fantasy, that all key decisions are taken at country-house weekends by people who've been together at Eton and Cambridge, or in the Guards.'

He studied his whiskey glass. 'Hotbed of spies and traitors Cambridge was, in my days at the Other Place. Nowadays England – I mean Britain, don't I, though who gives a bugger about the woad-covered Picts and Scots . . . ?'

He caught Diana's eye, and murmured: 'Saving your presence, m'dear – I never think of you as a true Scot, not like Billy Connolly.'

He hiccoughed several times before continuing.

'Anyway, I'll tell you who rules Britannia, Comrade Houston. It's ruled by the civil service, by clever young scholarship boys like Yours Truly. Our network's stronger than either Eton's or the trade union brothers'. And we don't give a damn for any of them.'

Charles rose to his feet, and said firmly: 'Time for bed, I think. I've still a lot of work to do on my boxes.'

The rest rose too, but as Dick staggered towards the door, he delivered a parting salvo.

'We're going to sort out your benighted island, Alan, and if you care to call that a mandarins' plot, be my guest! And the cabinet secretary's guest too, come to think about it.'

Dick emitted another loud hiccough and left. Diana hurried down the corridor after him.

The secretary of state suspected all mandarins thought like that, though he was surprised to hear Dick include the cabinet secretary, Sir Philip Radley, among his plotters. Charles had always regarded the austere Radley as above political intrigue. You learned a little every day, he mused.

When they were alone, he smiled at Alan.

'Don't take it personally, my boy. Civil servants, when sober, conceal their arrogance, and leave us poor elected blokes to dream on in our delusions of democratic power. Dick has just made an error in tactics, as he'll realise when he wakes tomorrow morning.'

He thought for a moment, then added, 'Assuming, that is, that he's able to remember what he said. Not remembering what you've said or

51

done is always the worst part of a hangover. I've suffered it myself, when I was younger and even more foolish than I am now.'

[13]

It was too late for Alan to telephone Mary that night. He began his call the next morning with what he intended to be a fervent cry of love. 'The sooner we get you over here, my darling, the happier I'll be.'

'Why this excessive uxoriousness, O lord and master?'

Alan poured out the story of his new permanent secretary's drunken diatribe and the political anxieties it aroused in him. Mary had no charity to spare for Alan's office troubles. She was still raw from her visit to Belfast, from the worries about making her family's home there.

Alan said he was not looking forward to the weeks when he would be living as well as working in the same building as Dick Heston. 'I can see already there's a considerable downside to this job,' he said.

'You can say that again.'

Mary was thinking not about manoeuvrings at Stormont, but of the dangers to her sons and herself. Also the dangers to her husband, which he seemed incapable of imagining. Alan's self-absorption this morning set her teeth on edge. Mary did not like being valued merely as an antidote to Sir Richard Heston.

For many years the Houstons had spoken on the telephone every evening they were apart – loving, laughing conversations that made up for separation. But this call was less happy. Alone in South London, Mary found herself, for the first time, bored with Alan's voice.

She had always been aware of his faults, of course, but his obsessiveness about work – broadcasting, newspapers, now politics – was becoming a disease. Hadn't she a career too, for God's sake?

Mary Houston was a practical woman. She was able to tell Alan she had sold their house in London for more than the asking price. (He had only half-absorbed what this price was.) The solicitors thought the sale could go through by Peter's autumn half-term, assuming they would be ready to move by then.

She paused, accepting his absent-minded congratulations.

'Yes, my dear, but have you made any progress in finding somewhere for us to live in Ulster?'

It took Alan some time to say he had at least cleared his mind about the district they should live in. Ye gods, Mary silently intoned, addressing the Yellow Pages, which lay open on her desk. Originally, he had wanted a house in North Belfast, where he had been brought up. This had an enduring place in the geography of his imagination, he said sententiously. Just to walk there lifted his spirits.

Alan had long nursed an idyll of living in a Belfast house with views of the sea, the shipyard, the city, and the hills. Mary knew almost by heart his 'Athens of the North' view of Belfast. This did not save her from a fresh recital. She leafed through the phone book, noting the numbers of furniture removers. When she got to the end of her list, Alan was still talking.

'Sadly, the RUC tell me there have been more murders on the Antrim Road than anywhere else. So North Belfast is out.'

'Murder *is* a consideration.'

Mary hoped they might live near the university in South Belfast. Grizelda Atkinson, with whom she'd talked several times since their meeting in the pub, told her it was the place in Ulster with most life about it. It was where the Atkinsons lived.

Mary had now discovered that Grizelda's experiences as a social worker in the Belfast slums had left her more left-wing than anybody else she was to meet in Ulster. But Mary, unlike Alan, did not think a person's politics mattered as much as their general good sense. So she accepted Grizelda's opinion that this was a place where she would have more congenial company, and be near to theatres, restaurants and galleries. It would also be convenient if she found work at the museum.

Mary had no difficulty in deducing that Alan did not want to live in South Belfast. Under her questioning he admitted the security authorities had no objection to the university area.

'Does the geography of your imagination not stretch south of the City Hall?' she asked. 'I understand you don't need a visa.'

'Look, Mary, don't you realise that South Belfast is *inland*? What's the point of being in a port city and out of sight of the sea?'

What Alan did not mention was that South Belfast was also on the wrong side of the river from Stormont, with all this meant in hold-up on the bridges, security checks, the general Buggeration Factor in his life. North Down was a touch bland, but Mary would have a car. And at least Alan could cheer himself by looking across the Lough to the blue hills of Antrim.

He jerked himself back to practicalities.

'I think you're going to have to leave this to me, Mary. What with you being over there, and the security people breathing down my neck, it's the only practical way. If I can find something half-decent in North Down we'll all be safe as houses.'

Safe, Mary thought, but bored out of my mind, and knowing that people are being shot or blown up a few miles away, that the conversation will be about little else, and that there's precious little any of us will be able to do about it.

She said nothing, which was perhaps a mistake. Mary was not an extrovert, never had been. She left that to Alan. In their marriage, this contrast had always worked out well.

Alan cheerfully concluded the call by revealing that he had discussed their house-search with Diana.

'Diana says North Down – the Gold Coast, as she calls it – is where all the Brits live.'

'I thought you didn't like to hear civil servants and army people called "Brits". Aren't your lot over there all Brits too?'

He could tell she was trying to rile him, but didn't guess that his reference to Diana might be the cause. Alan Houston was a perceptive man only when he was thinking about politics.

[14]

Mary and Peter moved to North Down at the end of October. She had not, after all, left the search for a house to Alan. Instead she asked estate agents to send her lists. Grizelda gave her a bed for the few days it took them to select a house.

Alan found time – 'in the midst of his busy schedule', as those sycophantic supplementary questions to the Prime Minister always say – to look at the house she had found for him, in the district where he said they had to live. Mary could see his mind was no longer geared to domestic matters. This was presumably because it was engaged with 'the Great Game', as her oldest schoolfriend, who was married to an ambassador, insisted on calling diplomacy. Could Ulster be as fascinating to Alan as the Schleswig-Holstein question was to others?

Their new home was fine. She and Peter – and Alan, if you counted the hours between 10 p.m. and 8.30 a.m. – were snugly settled into their modernised Edwardian villa, with a well-stocked garden. This was more comfortable, even luxurious, than anything they'd lived in before. If she were just a hausfrau with no pretensions, it would seem ideal.

But, sadly, she had no job, and found herself surrounded by overly sociable neighbours, whose interests seemed limited to family, schools, holidays, horses, dogs, golf and bridge, with a little sideline in flirtations and affairs among people she'd never heard of. Oh, for the buzz and energy of the frantic professions – politics, broadcasting and journalism – that she had grown used to among Alan's friends!

Life couldn't be a perpetual coffee morning, however worthy the causes. In a middle-class area like this scarcely anybody *knew* a family directly affected by the Troubles. They hadn't shared the pain. Neither had Mary, of course, but she did suffer the gloomiest premonitions about her family and herself. They had not caught anybody for the policeman's murder. Apparently when it came to helping the RUC, the Nationalist community closed ranks. Even to convict the murderer of a Catholic policeman! She would never understand this place.

What hit Mary most personally was the effect 'the Situation' was having on her marriage. She blamed the Troubles for converting her once lovable, funny, caring partner and friend into such a failure as husband and father. If he would only take the time to raise his head from work occasionally, wouldn't he see how miserable she was?

If Mary was worrying about her marriage, Alan had other anxieties he kept from her. In an attempt to understand attitudes among the paramilitaries, he had a drink most evenings in Republican or Loyalist ghettoes. He had built up his list of pubs before Mary arrived in Ulster, and even when she complained about his coming home late, Alan did not mention these expeditions because he knew she'd be frightened.

At first he'd taken a police minder in plain clothes. Charlie Ponsonby was good company, and the gun concealed in his shoulder holster gave Alan some hope of escaping if hard men decided to beat him up, or worse. But nobody could call Charlie inconspicuous. He was 6 ft. 2 in. tall, and his feet, though clad in suede shoes for these outings, were size 12.

Once, in the Irish Volunteer up the Falls, Alan saw a man at the bar looking fixedly at the policeman's feet. He hurried away, and talked animatedly into the phone, keeping his gaze on them.

'Charlie, let's get out of here quick. I think we've been twigged.'

As the car sped away, Alan decided he'd better do his ghetto drinking alone. He told his escort that, much as he enjoyed his company, and the secure feeling it gave him, he couldn't hope to get under the skin of the paramilitaries if they suspected the man with him was a cop.

Ponsonby shrugged his shoulders.

'Up to you, Mr Houston, but my bosses won't be happy about you going to that sort of place on your own. In the Republican pubs, if they found out your identity they'd take you into the hills and put a bullet in your head, without thinking twice. The Loyalists are liable to get you into a brawl, with fists and boots. These are vicious people, sir. You don't want to be fooled by their cheerful manner over a drink.'

'I've got no illusions, Charlie. But I've got a job to do.'

He found himself wondering whether he was cut out for the job. After he had dispensed with Charlie's services there was a frightening episode in a Loyalist pub, uncannily like what his minder had predicted. Alan was having an almost rational conversation with two heavily built men in the black leather jackets that seemed to be uniform hereabouts. A drunk pushed into their group, and addressed the bigger of the two.

'You in the Orange, big fella, eh? Which Lodge, eh?'

Alan's companion murmured: 'As well as bein' full as the Boyne, this guy's several slates short of a load.'

Then he turned to the intruder. 'If it's any of your business, arsehole, I'm in LOL Number 274, Ballyrichmond Temperance Defenders. Now, piss off.'

The man was too simple-minded to take offence. He drew his sleeve across his nose, and addressed Alan.

'Hiya, thin fella, which lodge you in, eh? Y'on the Square as well, eh?'

Alan tried to ignore him. He didn't know the terminology of either the Orange or Masonic Orders well enough to tell a convincing lie.

'Like he says, piss off,' was the best he could manage.

His two drinking companions looked at him, suddenly alert. This language seemed out of character. They'd been wondering what this stranger in a suit was doing in their pub. Conversation suddenly dried up. Alan spoke urgently.

'I need a pee.'

He went towards the lavatories, doubting whether they'd assume prostate problems in one so young. Even outside the Gents the smell of urine was overpowering, and somebody had been sick in the vestibule. Alan shuddered, fear gripping his heart.

'What a miserable place to die!' he thought.

Suddenly he saw there was a side exit from the pub. He stumbled through it and ran to his car. His hand shook as he fumbled with the ignition key. After what seemed an age, the engine coughed into life. The tyres protested as he turned on to the road. Through the corner of his eye he saw the two men he had been drinking with gesticulating. Alan did not think they were kindly signalling that he'd left something behind. They were inviting him to return to have his neck broken.

As the sweat broke on his brow, Alan pondered – not for the first time – whether he was a physical coward. How would he have reacted as a soldier? Or was this brand of politics more frightening than battle?

He hurried home to Mary, but didn't tell her about his experience. She was already anxious about security.

Once he had tactlessly advised Mary to count her blessings. Sometimes she did. At least Peter was happily settled in the local school, ten minutes from home by car. She drove him there, and picked him up most days, though there was a bus. He was pleased when he was selected for the school football team, and soon scored his first hat-trick. Mary gave Grizelda a bitterly amused account of how miffed Peter was at Alan's lack of interest in this.

'It just shows how steeped in his work Alan is. He's normally a doting father, as well as something of a football nut.'

She said it reminded her of a story she'd heard about a man whose wife decided to leave him, and thought a car journey would be a suitably unemotional *mise en scène* for the confession.

'But the husband was busy finding the wavelength for the football results, so she had to repeat her whole performance when they reached home.'

Grizelda laughed, and Mary said she thought if Alan and she were ever to reach that stage, it wouldn't be football that diverted his attention. 'He would come into the house so busy thinking about the existential relationship between Sinn Fein and the IRA that he wouldn't even see my note on the mantelpiece saying, "Flying to Rio with Lionel – your dinner's in the oven."'

Grizelda raised her eyebrows, and Mary assured her she was just a little fed up that evening. Her friend wondered about the Houstons' marriage. Later, Mary wondered too, especially about who might be cast as 'Lionel'.

Alan treated marriage like his politics, pragmatic to a fault, whereas Mary had a philosophy of marriage. She believed in a union of equality, sharing everything from joy and sorrow to bank accounts. Alan wasn't interested in money and didn't know what to spend it on, so he had fallen in with her practical ideas and was happy for her to manage their savings, such as they were.

Mary also believed that marriage meant sharing interests, as well as just living together. In the past, Alan had always taken an interest in her career, though he was occasionally forgetful about it until she gave a sharp jerk on the reins. Since they had come to Ulster, she felt shut out of his working life. Admittedly she was not fascinated by the minutiae of Northern Irish politics, but this change had made their marriage less intimate, as did her lack of a job. They had nothing much to talk about in the evenings.

Mary could not decide whether Alan was simply too preoccupied, or whether he had found a more congenial ear for his evening gossip about work. Diana, perhaps?

[15]

Brian came over from Cambridge for Christmas. Telephone calls with his mother had left him uneasy. Mary and Brian had always shared mocking jokes about Alan's idiosyncracies, but on the telephone she gave a less light-hearted character analysis.

'Your father has always been trapped between his proletarian and moralistic upbringing in Ulster and the odd trades of journalism and broadcasting. They're both bourgeois and amoral, and now he's trying to graft on a new requirement – to be a serious public servant working in an impossible cause.'

'Impossible? Do you really believe that, Mum?'

'Ulster politics are hopeless, Brian, and dangerous to dabble in.'

What she did not tell Brian was that the Houstons' marriage felt less happy than before. He did notice himself that his parents seemed more distant from each other. Some days Alan appeared so preoccupied with his own thoughts that he spoke much less than usual. Where was his old, garrulous Dad?

The one part of Christmas Brian enjoyed was seeing Peter again. Although six years separated them, they had always been friends. Walking along the Lough shore, Brian asked his brother how he liked Ulster. Peter said the house was great, there was plenty of room for his model railway.

And school? Peter wrinkled his nose.

'Fine, really, if I had a taste for working as hard as you do. Friendly blokes, good fun. And I'm doing OK at football.'

At first the boys had guyed Peter's accent, which was South London cockney. One aggressive character had called him 'a glipe'. Brian looked puzzled.

'I know,' said Peter, rolling his eyes. 'That's what I asked the guy at the next desk. He said it meant I was an "eejit".'

Brian asked casually if their mother was taking the move to Ulster calmly.

Peter frowned. 'Dunno, Brian, but she's less fun than she used to be, that's for sure. A bit ratty most of the time. Not so much with me, more with Dad.'

Peter kicked a pebble from the path on to the beach, and suddenly shouted, 'Race you back to the house, ye great eejit, ye glipe.' Before Brian could answer, he was disappearing round a bend in the road.

The family row on Boxing Day blew up suddenly. Peter had gone to play with his railway. Alan asked Brian if he had met the Master of his college yet – he was a former head of the Civil Service.

'Oh, yes, Sir Anthony ... Didn't I tell you about his little talk?

At last, Brian thought, he had an anecdote that would make both his parents laugh. Peter was right – there hadn't been many laughs over Christmas, except on the box.

When Brian had received an invitation in his first week to a drink with the Master, he'd assumed it would be a general get-together for freshers. Instead, he was on his own. Sir Anthony didn't waste time on small talk. No sooner had he put a minuscule glass of extremely dry sherry before Brian – who thought he'd asked for sweet – than he plunged in.

Just before term began he'd had a visit from an old acquaintance in the public service – 'security, that kind of thing'. This man knew what Brian's father was doing in Ireland. His advice was to be careful about personal security.

Brian had a gift for mimicry. He continued his account in the supposed tones of Oxford in the thirties.

'"Nobody wants to put the wind up ye, m'dear chap. Indeed, it's an outside chance that the boneheads in the IRA'll ever have heard of ye."'

Brian resumed his normal voice: 'At least that was good to hear.'

Sir Anthony had said the security people just wanted Brian to know they were available on the phone, day or night. If he ever saw anything untoward – shady characters hanging around the college, watching him in a pub . . .

'At this point Sir Anthony gives me a wintry smile, and smirks.

'"That's assuming ye ever intend to rest from yer academic labours long enough to visit a public house . . ." That was his idea of a joke and I laughed, dutifully.'

The Master had then handed him a series of telephone numbers printed in small, meticulous script, and indicated that the meeting was over.

To Brian's disappointment Mary treated the incident as anything but a joke. She turned to Alan, and spoke icily.

'Have the security people not warned you about any precautions Brian or the rest of us ought to take?'

Her tone confirmed for Brian the new and edgy relationship between his parents. Alan reddened, and murmured:

'I've had more than enough security advice that Dick Heston wished on me.'

'What's that supposed to mean?'

Alan stumbled into saying more than was wise.

'Nobody's mentioned Brian, but I did have a visit from a low-level character from MI5, who talked absolute gibberish about sending Peter to a boarding school in England.'

Mary's face drained of colour. Then she exploded.

'And you didn't think of telling me anything about this? Don't I have any say in Peter's safety?'

Alan, looking uncomfortable, said wearily: 'I decided not to worry you, Mary, just because it was such a load of conspiratorial nonsense. I'd already suggested you pick Peter up from school as often as you can. That's what I call a sensible precaution.'

Brian had never seen Mary so angry.

'It may not have occurred to you, but it's the boys' and my lives you're playing Russian roulette with.'

She suddenly fell silent, and nobody else spoke. Alan guessed she was about to explode. Mary had a slow fuse, but when she reached its end he had always made sure to stand well clear.

'I ought never to have come to this godawful country, ruining my own career, losing touch with my friends, and suffering the ennuis of the most boring set of suburban dead-brains I've ever encountered. If I'd stayed in London, you could have lived politics twenty-four hours a day with your brilliant chums at Stormont.'

Alan looked stunned. He had not begun to realise how fed up Mary was.

'Charles and Sir Richard would have kept your argumentative faculty fully exercised, and doubtless that Mensa-plus Foreign Office lady, Diana Carstairs, who crops up so often in your conversation, would have provided all the intellectual and other stimulus you need.'

This was the first Brian had heard about Diana. What was his mother on about? He couldn't imagine his serious, middle-aged father as a likely target for diplomat-temptresses. Alan spoke at last.

'We can discuss security properly, Mary, when you're in a calmer mood.'

She glared at him, and said she was going to bed.

'Sorry about that little spat, Brian. Your mother's a bit on edge. Nothing to worry about. The security man was a grotesque playing at le Carré.'

Brian asked precisely what the man had said. Alan gave a comic version of the encounter.

'He was a cadaverous man, dressed in a British warm overcoat, had a black toothbrush moustache flecked with grey and a bald pate. Didn't smile much, and he certainly set out to put the wind up me about the family. His branch were keeping an eye on you at Cambridge, he said – and now I know the truth of that nonsense, I'm sure Sir Anthony's sensible assessment of the risk is dead right. Then he got on to Peter.'

Alan said the man droned out that his branch had prep schools all over the country they could recommend, and the civil service offered generous financial help. He had replied that boarding schools were not within the tradition of his family. The reaction was a growl.

'He said he'd forgotten I was a Labour chap, rather than a normal official. Made me sound like some kind of pervert! Then he scratched his baldness, and speculated that there must be *State* boarding schools, if I felt strongly about that.'

Alan said he'd explained huffily that his objection to boarding schools wasn't political. He believed family bonding went on for as long as you could keep your offspring in the nest. Several autobiographies by people whose emotional lives were stunted at their prep schools had confirmed him in this view.

The MI5 man said such books were usually written by very odd characters indeed. Boarding school from the age of seven hadn't done him any harm. Alan said he'd let this pass, implying phenomenal self-restraint.

Brian began to depart for bed. At the door he turned.

'All the same, Dad, you ought to consider if Peter wouldn't be safer at a school in England.'

The Saturday was cold and crisp, and Alan suggested they should go for a walk. Mary, who had a heavy cold, said she would stay at home.

'But don't you need to take your tame RUC man with you?'

'There'll be no danger where we're going.'

'Do be careful,' she said, stifling a sneeze.

He drove with Brian and Peter to a favourite haunt of his youth, the Cave Hill, which looked down over Belfast's northern outskirts to the Lough, glinting in the sunshine. As they walked up the hill, Alan addressed his sceptical sons on the beauties of Belfast.

'This must be one of the handsomest city and seascapes I've seen in half a lifetime's travel. D'you know, the one press distortion I find hardest to stomach is the myth that the whole of Belfast is ugly.'

Brian grinned. 'Well, Dad, the reporters seem fairly unanimous about that one.'

Alan snorted, and said most visiting firemen didn't emerge from the Europa Hotel and Stormont often enough, except to investigate riots or murders.

'These rarely happen – surprise, surprise! – in Areas of Outstanding Natural Beauty. Most victims of these Troubles die, as they live, among dereliction and squalor. Not that they often have time to worry about their surroundings before a bullet or a car-bomb blows them away.'

Alan began a sub-Marxian lecture on how the bourgeoisie, including London journalists, were insulated from the Troubles, because these affected only Catholic and Protestant working-class ghettoes. But his sons were deprived of this treat as the slope grew steeper, and his breathing louder. The boys were finding the climb easier than their father.

As they approached the summit the weather was closing in. Up at Napoleon's Nose, the crag that dominated the hill and the city below, the mists were swirling, now obscuring the rock, now revealing it in a shaft of sunlight.

Alan remembered from his schoolboy cricket, played on a ground just below the hill, that this was how you foresaw when rain would stop play. The skipper, crouched at silly mid-off, would look up at the crag and murmur: 'It's coming in five minutes, boys. Keep their score down now, and we'll run through them like a dose of salts when the wicket's wetted.'

Belfast's weather, like its people, was volatile. The early morning sun disappeared, and threatening clouds were cascading down towards them. Suddenly, through the gloom, Alan saw two men approaching, two fierce-looking Alsatians bounding along in front. As the men saw Alan and his sons, they spoke urgently to each other.

Alan bade them good morning. The shorter one grunted a reply, and shaped to pass on. He wore a tweed sports jacket over a tartan shirt and corduroy trousers, and walked with Belfast's rolling gait, just a hint of swagger. He had fair hair, beginning to grey, and deep blue eyes. A handsome man, and Alan guessed he knew it.

His companion was turning bald and carried too much weight, like a boxer going to seed. He had the long lope of a countryman, Armagh or Tyrone maybe. This rotund character had chosen to display his beer-gut to best advantage by wearing a green T-shirt with yellow stripes which bore the legend: 'Boston Fenians welcome the Belfast Irish, 1970'.

Alan wondered if people up the Falls, faced with such eccentricity, would be impressed by his patriotic fervour, or just murmur Belfast's favourite put-down: 'Wud ye luk at the cut of yer man!'

This sartorial triumph stopped suddenly, and pointed an accusing finger.

'Have I not seen you in pubs about the Falls? Who the fuck are ye? What the hell are ye doin' up here? Ye haven't been fallyin' us, have ye?'

He drew menacingly close. One of the dogs growled, sensing its master's anger.

In moments of stress, people often slew off personalities accumulated over a lifetime and assume again their habits of long ago. Alan adopted an aggressive tone he hadn't used since he was eighteen. Brian noticed his accent thickened, echoing uncannily the big man's tone.

'Who the hell's asking? Since when have I had to seek anybody's say-so before I walk the hills of my own city? Or where I have a drink? They call them *public* houses, y'know.'

Alan stuck out his chin, the way he used to stick it out at Linfield supporters on Saturday afternoons. In those days he would say he was neutral – he didn't care who beat Linfield.

Today his protagonist was ready to respond, but the shorter man waved him down, and spoke more quietly.

'Listen, friend, I suspect from your boys' voices that ye've been livin' away from Belfast for a while. Well, nowadays people here have to be a bit aware of what's going on. A few fellas've been found on this hill with holes in the back o' their heads. Now me and m'friend are politically active, so the UDA and UVF think we're legitimate targets. That's what makes us worry when a stranger we've seen drinking in the Irish Volunteer turns up on the Cave Hill.'

As Alan looked at him, a puzzled frown crossed his face. He wondered if this shorter man resembled a slimmer photograph he'd seen in police headquarters. If so, he was a significant IRA leader.

Alan thought quickly. For months, he'd been trying to make contact with real IRA men, rather than the fringe characters he chatted to in pubs, or the Sinn Fein front men who were MI6's only Republican contacts. He decided to take a chance, though he wished his sons hadn't been with him.

'Well, since you're curious, I'm Alan Houston, and I'm Labour Party adviser to Charles Corbett, the secretary of state. He's not satisfied with the kind of indirect contacts he's had with Republicans through the Security Service. He recruited me because I was born here, to see if I could do any better. About getting peace, y'know. Perhaps you can help me?'

His heart raced as he saw their startled reactions, realised what a crazy, unjustified risk he was taking, with his sons' safety and his own. And after his row with Mary about security! They were in a remote place, too. Both men were in poor physical shape, but if the encounter turned nasty, and they had to make a run for it, he suspected the Alsatians would be the least of their troubles. These men might have guns.

The two looked at each other. One of the dogs sniffed at Peter's hand. The boy seemed close to tears. At last the quieter man spoke.

'Even supposing we did know anything about the matters you're referring to, Mr Houston – which, by the by, I'm not saying we do – how would you want us to contact you? In the back streets off the Falls, y'know, we're not exactly on Stormount's invitation lists.' (Alan noted the self-conscious mispronunciation.)

A thrill ran down his spine. At last he'd got a real bite.

He dug into the pocket of his jacket, and found a supermarket receipt. He wrote on this, and handed it to the shorter man.

'That's the number of my private line at Stormont. Will you give me a call there, on Monday?'

'Aye, well I'll consult others, and I'll probably phone you, though not as soon as Monday, I'd reckon. These things take time.'

Alan looked him in the eyes, and heard coming from his own mouth an expression of enthusiasm from the vocabulary of his youth.

'Stickin' out,' said the secretary of state's political adviser.

The Republican replied in kind. 'Dead on,' he said, with the first, tentative smile Alan had seen on his face.

The rain that had threatened began to fall, but Alan was elated. If this did produce a meeting, he would be speaking to people he understood, and who understood him. Each would know viscerally what the other side was on about. That'd be a start, an advance on talks between Sinn Fein smoothies and some graduate of the British spy school in Beirut.

As the clouds released a downpour, the two groups parted. Alan, Brian and Peter hurried on in silence. They took shelter on a route through the forest. Brian spoke, in a hushed, anxious voice.

'Who *were* they? Do you think they'll have us followed, to see where you live? Isn't it foolish to get involved with people like that?'

Alan spoke slowly and with care. 'Listen, boys, I'm sorry you were with me when I bumped into those two. They may only be another pair of gombeen men, who think they're closer to the IRA leadership than they really are.'

Then he explained what his job in Belfast really involved. Charles Corbett hoped for an IRA ceasefire, so Alan was trying to open negotiations. Charles himself, as an elected politician and a minister of the crown, couldn't talk to people the law said were criminals.

'That's a job for somebody like me, if I can get close to them. This morning may be a long shot, but it's the best prospect I've encountered so far. I had to take it. Sorry if it alarmed you.'

Peter shuddered.

'What a scary pair of hoods! And their language wasn't fit for Sunday school, was it? What do you think Mum will say when we tell her?'

Alan and Brian looked at each other, thinking of the furious scene on Boxing Day. Brian told his younger brother that this was not an incident he thought they ought to trouble their mother with.

Alan smiled. 'I think that's probably wise, Peter, old son, if it's all right with you? Your mother worries too much.'

Peter nodded uncertainly.

[17]

The secretary of state for Northern Ireland was smiling today. He was back from the suburban halls of Stormont to the place he loved best, the House of Commons. Since his wife had died of cancer, he felt more at home here than anywhere else. The MPs bustling about the Members' Lobby, the policemen and badge messengers who guarded the doors and kept the mail and messages flowing, the journalists pursuing their trails – they were all a substitute family. The Corbetts hadn't been able to have children.

Charles had been invited to see the Prime Minister in his room behind the Speaker's Chair – for a New Year chat, the private secretary said. Tom Sanderson, who had been surprised to reach the top job in his late sixties, was ostentatiously relaxing into it. His private office had surreptitious side-bets on which new prime ministerial mannerism would appear each week. Today he kept putting his stubby fingers together in a judicial pose. His face was almost beatific, apart from occasional twitches of anxiety, when the corners of his mouth resumed their instinctive turn downward.

'Sit down, Charles, sit down. Thought we'd better have a talk. Now in January, party conference may seem a long way off, but I can foresee stormy months ahead over Ireland.'

Charles felt deflated. This meeting wasn't to be about the paper he had submitted on unemployment. The Old Boy was dodging him on that.

'I've never doubted there'll be storms, Prime Minister, but what in particular had you in mind?'

It soon emerged that the tempests Tom Sanderson was perplexed about had nothing to do with people being killed or maimed in Belfast

71

or Derry. It was hostile resolutions from constituency Labour parties that worried him.

'I'm particularly bothered about our civil rights lobby, Charles. Geoffrey Lawther, QC, is now taking an interest in your department. Getting a big airing in our so-called friendly press, he is.'

Charles flushed with anger.

'My principal aim just now. Prime Minister, is to preserve people's civil right not to be murdered, knee-capped or punished with a spiked baseball bat. Does Lawther think we should just leave the UDA to kill an innocent Catholic every time the Provos murder an RUC man?'

'Don't become rhetorical, Charles. It's a law of political nature that those who don't have responsibility don't behave responsibly. The actions of what Lawther would call "Crown servants" are all he's interested in. That means everybody from the Prime Minister to the lowliest part-time policeman. What have the IRA or the UDA to do with him?'

Charles rose, and began to pace the room.

'You'll remember what Baldwin said about Beaverbrook and Northcliffe – I think he pinched it from his cousin, Rudyard Kipling? "Power without responsibility, the prerogative of the harlot of every age." To apply that to people like Lawther is unfair to harlots.'

The Prime Minister waved him into his chair.

'Charles, Charles! Don't raise your blood pressure – I can't afford to lose you just yet.' He grinned mischievously. 'Maybe later, but not just yet. Take a word of advice from a veteran in this rough old trade of ours. We *are* politicians, not priests. Our job is to survive, and do the best we can. That's the Damon Runyon principle of politics. Try taking a stiff helping of pragmatism with your corn-flakes tomorrow morning.'

Charles grimaced, but he knew the futility of quarrelling with Tom Sanderson. Prime Ministers always have the last word – until the moment, that is, when their backs become vulnerable to a political stiletto. Sanderson couldn't afford to sack his Northern Ireland Secretary just now. But was he malicious enough to isolate him in cabinet? That would be fatal to Charles's political standing.

The Prime Minister tapped his pen on the desk.

'If we asked Geoffrey Lawther what he would do, the answer would be to get out of Ireland. That's what a lot of our members would say too. As I recall, Charles, I told you something like this when I sent you to Stormont.'

'People who say that, Prime Minister, rarely consider the probable result. Murder and sectarian abuse would spread to the whole of Ireland, perhaps into Scotland as well.'

Charles wondered if he dared give Sanderson a semi-philosophical lecture on the dangers of pandering to orange-and-green politics. The Old Man was notoriously touchy about being patronised by subordinates who were better educated than himself. If they were that clever, Tom Sanderson thought, why hadn't they got where he was? Charles decided to be brave.

'Please listen, Prime Minister. Since you sent me to Belfast, I've been thinking a lot about nationalism. Not just Irish nationalism, but the Ulster nationalism that Unionists have welded on to their original decision to remain British. What strikes me is how anachronistic *any* nationalism now seems.'

The Prime Minister frowned. He was really too experienced for a political lecture from this youngster.

'There's still a lot of it about, Charles. The foreign secretary bends my ear about it every time we have a tête à tête. Nationalism in the Middle East, nationalism in the Balkans, in Asia, you name it. Feel free to tell me why it's out of date – I like to be be educated by you younger chaps. But do keep it brief.'

Charles said nationalism had some logic during the many millennia when most people rarely moved from the place where they were born. It represented the ancient human instinct for mutual support, spreading from families to neighbourhoods. 'Community' some people called it. But since nationalism had gone mad in this century, it had provoked international slaughter, from the Somme to the Holocaust. Now it was simply irrelevant.

'Mass migrations have brought millions of people far from their home countries, to escape persecution or to find a better life. The old nation-states may make laws to deter immigration, but they simply won't work. The flow will go on. It's already washed away the old foundations of nationalism. I don't think we should base policy on that, in Ireland or anywhere else. It's one world nowadays, Prime Minister.'

Tom Sanderson looked at the clock. He wouldn't discuss this young man's memo on unemployment today. He knew Corbett thought he wasn't being radical enough in his economic policies. Well, sod him! He must use this conversation to bring another departmental minister to heel. Nowadays Tom Sanderson saw this as his principal role in life.

'Don't let Ulster get under your skin, Charles. I won't leave you there for too long. And yes, we'll have to do something about unemployment, perhaps with you more directly involved. Just before the next election – that would probably be best.'

Then he drew himself erect in his chair, and addressed his young colleague more formally.

'But while you're at Stormont, secretary of state, I'd just like you to concentrate on getting a ceasefire. The sooner the better. Understood? That would do a lot to quieten our Party critics.'

Charles murmured that it would also quieten the fears of decent people in Belfast, Derry, and the Ulster countryside.

The Prime Minister ignored this.

'Get me a ceasefire, Charles. I need a result.'

He picked up a file to indicate the meeting was over.

As Charles walked down the corridor, he silently instructed himself that he must 'turn the other cheek'. For an irascible man, Charles was surprisingly good at this when subordinates offended him, not so good with Prime Ministers.

As he made his way out of this building that allowed England to be called 'the Mother of Parliaments', he reflected on the weaknesses that disfigured democracy. As when politicians protecting their own backsides ignored the sufferings of people they were especially responsible for – the unemployed, the poor, the sick, those intimidated by criminals, or drug-dealers, or terrorists.

Even Charles's 'other cheek' was hurting as he contemplated Tom Sanderson's equivocation. His leader, he decided, not for the first time, was a pompous fraud.

When he climbed into the car, Big Ben was chiming three times.

Charles, as a Jew familiar with the New Testament, heard this as a cock-crow of betrayal.

[18]

It was not till February 2ND that the telephone rang in Alan's office. He had begun to think the man on the Cave Hill had decided against talking to him.

'Mr Houston? If there's anybody monitorin' this line, get him off. We get nowhere without trust, do we? And, y'know, my friends have ways of making sure our trust's not abused. OK?'

Alan fought down his irritation at being threatened. He was excited – this just *might* be a breakthrough.

'Shall we proceed, Mr . . . er . . . I'm sorry, I don't have your name.'

'No need for names at this stage, Mr Houston. I'm the older of the two men you and your sons met up on the Hill just after Christmas. Nice-looking pair of lads, if I may say so.'

Alan almost choked at the bizarre politeness. This might have been a guest visiting for the first time in the English Home Counties. But this same voice had probably said to some poor creature: 'Say your prayers – this is it,' before carrying out the execution ordered by the Army Council, or perhaps just decided by the voice itself.

Alan thought he had better murmur thanks for the compliment to his sons. Then he said, 'You know what I'm after. I'd like to meet you and your associates to discuss a ceasefire. Can that be arranged?'

There was a dry laugh at the other end of the line.

'I didn't ring up *just* to admire your family, y'know, Mr Houston. My associates think a meeting might be worthwhile. But just us two, for a start. Tomorrow mornin' would suit me fine – no use hangin' about. I'll pick you up at eleven in a wee café called Joe's. Near the bottom of Upper Donegall Street, just a hundred yards down from the chapel, but on the other side. Don't be late. And come on yer own. We'll be watchin'.'

Suddenly the line went dead. This man didn't believe in unnecessary courtesies. Alan picked up the phone again, and spoke to the secretary of state's private office. Bill Simpson told him the boss's helicopter was just arriving from Aldergrove airport.

Alan looked out of his own window, and saw the Stormont crows perform the alarmed squawking and scattering with which they always greeted the arrival of a helicopter. These birds, or their ancestors, had endured such disturbance since Direct Rule began five years ago, but they still seemed indignant at their changed environment.

Just like the Unionists, really.

Alan returned to earth.

'Listen, Bill, I need to see him ASAP Alone.'

'Do my best, Alan, but the PUS is with him. You know Dick – never likes the S of S to spend much time with the natives.'

After his drunken display at dinner, Dick had been working hard to build bridges with Charles. He made no such effort with Alan, having decided, evidently, that he was an enemy. Alan reflected that the IRA weren't the only people who thought of 'the Long War'. The British civil service were past masters. While the Provos used Semtex, the Sir Richards employed a well-crafted position paper, or a discreet lunch at the Reform. He must watch his back.

Ten minutes later, Charles called him in. Without looking up, he shouted his greetings.

'Morning, comrade, have a nice, restful weekend? I've got loads of work for you. The PM says he needs a result here. Distant rumble of autumn conference time!'

Alan couldn't contain his excitement over his own news.

'Charles, I've something to tell you that may be very important. Of course, it may be a false trail, but I want your agreement that I follow it up.'

'Right, you've caught my attention all right, and thankfully diverted me from my ungrateful chief. Shoot! If that's not careless talk in these parts.'

Alan retailed his encounter on the Cave Hill and that morning's phone call.

'The police files have pictures of these two – Liam Hughes and Sean O'Brien, if I'm right. They're active IRA leaders all right.'

'D'you reckon they are people who could deliver a ceasefire?'

'Not sure whether any individual could. Surprisingly, the IRA's riddled with bureaucracy. But these men are hard enough cases to be listened to in the IRA, better than the politicos that MI6 talks to.'

Alan explained his rule-of-thumb. As soon as an IRA leader was quoted in the newspapers, he mattered less in 'the armed struggle'. If Sinn Fein emissaries conceded too much, they might be murdered by their own side.

'That's what happened to Michael Collins. They thought he didn't use a long enough spoon to sup with Lloyd George. Collins won independence for the part of Ireland that wanted it, but that didn't save his life.'

The mention of murder reminded Charles to worry about Alan's safety.

'You did tell your protection people the three of you were going walkies in this remote spot?'

Alan shook his head.

'Then regard yourself as told off. I don't want to lose you, and we certainly ought not to take risks with your boys. Don't do it again, d'ye hear?'

'But what about the meeting I've been offered?'

After much thoughtful drumming on the desk, Charles said Alan ought to go, because this looked like the best chance of a breakthrough they'd seen so far. But he mustn't place himself, possibly even his family, in danger. What could be done to minimise this?

Since his row with Mary, Alan had thought a lot about security. His conclusion was clear.

'Frankly, nothing. The security people would like us to put Peter in an English boarding school, but that's not on.'

'You really ought to think again about that, Alan. If anything happened to the boy, you'd be devastated. Boarding education's not so terrible. Not exactly the happiest days of my life, but still . . .'

Today Alan Houston's mind was not focused on his family's security. His political nose told him that if the Prime Minister didn't get a ceasefire, he'd start playing again with thoughts of British withdrawal. Alan had put his personal safety right to the back of his mind. He might suspect he was a physical coward, but at least he was a single-minded coward.

Charles could have been eavesdropping on his thoughts.

'What about your own safety?'

Alan said if any protection people accompanied him the IRA would abort the meeting. This was the nearest to a chink of light they'd seen. He must test it.

Charles turned his mind to what Alan's objective should be. The IRA would want to talk politics, he said, but he wanted to talk about a ceasefire.

'If they'll stop killing people, and promise never to begin again, we'll talk politics all right. But no illusions this time. Tell them I'm not offering to capitulate. So no more using talks as propaganda. No more posturing at the White House or the Faniel Hall in Boston. No more playing London, Dublin and Washington against each other. Or the Unionists and the Nationalists. Or the Tories and ourselves. No divide and rule. Just find out if they're serious, and if they're not, tell them to sod off.'

Charles had a tendency, when angry, to dissolve into minor obscenities. Alan smiled.

'In view of the callous attitude of our friends towards unhelpful intermediaries, Secretary of State, would you advise me to express any "failure to agree" in *precisely* those terms? I'm sure the FO could think of something more diplomatic.'

Charles laughed, and said they must talk again that evening. They ought to keep everybody else in the dark. Dick and Diana were going to dinner at the General's residence, so he and Alan could have a long session to work out tactics.

It was almost seven o'clock before Alan found time to telephone Mary. She was dressing for a party being given by a Unionist MP, Angus Dunluce, who lived a few miles from them.

'I'm afraid I can't make it, Mary. Something has come up. I really am sorry at having to call off. Dunluce seems the most reasonable of the Unionists, and I want to cultivate him.'

Mary felt he was really apologising to their host, rather than to her. This unhappy view was confirmed by his next remark.

'Mary, you will go yourself, won't you? I really don't want to offend him. Would you apologise for me, service-of-the-Queen kind of thing? You'll enjoy yourself.'

His wife looked down at her long blue dress, her party shoes, the varnish she had just applied to her nails. She spoke through gritted teeth.

'Yes, I'll go. But don't expect me to enjoy myself.'

[19]

Mary suspected she'd need more to drink than the breathalyser tolerated, so she called a taxi. Alan had a nerve, asking her to go to this party alone, and offering no reason for his absence, except the usual, 'work'. She wondered if he was just 'talking about terrorism' with Diana. To Mary, that phrase was becoming a *Private Eye* cliché, like 'talking about Ugandan affairs'. This was what a few months in Ulster had done to the Houstons' long love affair.

Mary hadn't expected to find the company enthralling, and she didn't. The first group she joined was dominated by a handsome, contralto-voiced woman, Susan Newhouse, who was married to an English don at the university. She told Mary her husband had been teaching at Oxford, but she'd persuaded him to move to Belfast.

'What was wrong with Oxford?'

'As a city, nothing, quite pleasant really. But golf is my addiction, and the courses were too tame. Expensive as well.'

Susan's other addiction, Mary soon discovered, was gossip. She pulled from an infallible mental filing-system a series of wounding tales about women known to others in that company. Mary didn't want to know any of them. Drifting from group to group, she accepted several refills from the Dunluces' son, an eager youth of fifteen who took too literally his father's admonition to keep people's glasses topped up.

Soon she found herself standing alone, in that bleak moment at large parties when it becomes apparent there is *nobody* present worth talking to. Just then, she heard a voice that wasn't local saying, 'Would I be wildly wrong if I guessed you weren't enjoying yourself?'

He was tall and slim, almost ascetic, yet with an amusing face. As she wrinkled her nose in agreement, he offered a further insight.

'My belief is that you're wishing you were tucked up in bed with a good book. If that's right, I can only say I'd happily join you.'

Mary laughed, and said if he meant in bed, he was being presumptuous. She supposed some might call that flirtatious.

He said he was called Colin, and quickly fetched them fresh glasses of wine. It was probably Mary's fourth, but who was counting? The party brightened up. Mary felt enough at home with a fellow exile to review the eccentricities of the other guests. Unfortunately – well, at the time she thought it unfortunate – she plunged into an acerbic account of Susan Newhouse's talent as a gossip.

Colin, grinning conspiratorially, led her into an alcove.

'Madam, what I have to reveal may disturb your Anglo-Saxon *sang froid*, and we Anglo-Saxons must stick together. Hower, as the old comedians used to say: "That's no lady, that's my wife, boom, boom."'

Mary began to apologise, but Colin assured her she wasn't telling him anything he didn't already know. His wife was both a boor and a bore. The wine must have removed Mary's inhibitions. She said lightly that she wouldn't go as far as that about her own husband, though his idiosyncracies were beginning to strain her tolerance.

'Ask me in a month or so, and I might promote him to the "boor and bore" category.'

After that, they introduced themselves properly. Colin Newhouse taught English literature at Queen's. He was a Londoner, increasingly unhappy about living in Northern Ireland and furious that Susan had persuaded him to abandon Oxford. He was amusingly dismissive of his Belfast tutorial groups. For too many students, he claimed, literary merit wasn't the criterion of excellence, but a perverse view of politics. Half the group only seemed interested in novelists or poets who were Irish and Nationalist, or rather 'cradle-Catholic', as he'd learned to call an anguished generation of agnostic Catholic writers. The other half were interested in British and, to a lesser extent, world literature but, unlike their classmates, they instinctively lost interest if the writer had an 'O' at the beginning of his surname.

'I've had trouble doing justice to both Liam O'Shakespeare and William John Shakespeare.'

Their hosts' son bounced over to tell Mary a taxi had called to collect her. Colin asked if he could cadge a lift – take her taxi on to his home, he added, rather too hastily.

Mary raised one quizzical eyebrow. This was a difficult trick to pull off. In the sixth form, she and two friends had spent hours practising it. Only she could avoid a tremor in the other eyebrow. Weeks later Mary learned that Colin thought this provocative. Perhaps she meant him to.

She asked how his wife was getting home. He said she had a club championship the next day, so she wasn't drinking alcohol, and had driven herself to the party. She wouldn't expect him to wait for her. Susan was clearly enjoying herself, and from many previous occasions she would know he wasn't.

'I think you might say that Susan and I are semi-detached.'

When they reached the Houstons' house, Mary didn't ask Colin to come in. Peter's bedroom light was still on, and she could see the babysitter through the windows of the living-room. The silly girl had been so enthralled by an idiot television programme that she'd forgotten to draw the curtains. Mary made a mental note to tick her off.

Colin said he'd telephone soon. She replied that it would be nice to talk again. Then she brushed his cheek with a kiss and went into the house.

[20]

Alan Houston walked into Joe's Café just before eleven. He'd already examined people on the opposite side of the street. No obvious lookouts, but then the Provos had been staking out buildings for years.

The café had steamed-up windows and an atmosphere of decrepitude. Behind the tea urn stood a man in scruffy shirt with soiled cuffs. The eponymous Joe? He cocked an enquiring head.

'Tea or coffee?'

Alan looked about him.

'I was meeting a friend,' he said uncertainly.

'Would that be Liam Hughes?'

Alan's thoughts raced back to the picture in police headquarters. So the man on the Cave Hill *was* Liam Hughes, one of the most important figures on the military wing of Republicanism.

'I don't actually know his name – we've just arranged to meet here.'

'Aye, well I suspect Liam's your acquaintance, mister. Before he went to the Gents he ordered coffees for you and hisself. There they are, on his usual table in the corner. Backs to the wall, that's our Liam. He's a sketch, that fella, eh?'

Joe clearly took Alan to be a Republican sympathiser. This exploded one Belfast myth: you couldn't tell Prods or Micks by how far apart their eyes were.

Alan sat down at a table with two cups of milky coffee. He'd have preferred black – to steady his nerves, he felt irrationally – but this was no time to be pernickety.

Within a minute the shorter man from the Cave Hill joined him, and stuck out his hand.

'Good mornin', Mr Houston, I'm Liam Hughes.'

He wore the same old-fashioned corduroy trousers and Donegal tweed sports jacket, with an open-necked shirt, olive green this time. Wrinkles at the side of eyes and mouth suggested a sense of humour. His hands were stubby and muscular.

As they drank their coffee, Liam Hughes asked Alan for assurances he wasn't being trailed.

'The RUC know perfectly well who I am and where I live. But I don't see any reason to help them follow me home.'

Alan asked in surprise if they were going to Hughes's home.

'Aye, sure we are. My wife'll give us a more substantial elevenses than Joe. You must still be enough of a Belfastman to enjoy the odd snack between meals? Come on, I've got my car just around the corner – illegally parked, you'll not be surprised to hear.'

This was the first time Alan had seen him smile. When Liam Hughes smiled, his whole face lit up. If Alan hadn't known his record, he'd have classed him as a happy-go-lucky, grandfatherly figure, with a penchant for making quiet little jokes, and laughing at other people's.

Liam *was* a grandfather. His two daughters and one son had given their parents four grandchildren so far, all under three years old. Liam doted on these infants and was much softer towards them than he'd been when his own children were small. But at that time, of course, he had been a front-line terrorist.

Liam Hughes had been born into the Movement. His father, now dead, was a Socialist Republican councillor just after the war, and his elder brother, Ruari, was an active IRA volunteer in the campaign that lasted, spasmodically, from 1956 till 1962. Ruari had had to leave in a hurry – for Boston, via Dublin – when an informer helped the police penetrate his unit. A sister was also a volunteer, and in one perilous operation had been used to conceal a rifle in her pram. The man who fired the rifle she spirited away was her brother Liam.

So old school friends, from a huddle of streets on the Falls Road that were 100 per cent Republican, envied him. They might all do their bit for the Cause, but Liam was different, of the Republican blood royal – though they wouldn't have put it like that.

Now Liam was a planner. His earlier role hadn't left him enough energy, perhaps enough tenderness, to deal easily with children. He had been afraid of what tenderness might do to his operational efficiency. So he'd been an absentee father. Had Alan but known, he and Liam had this much in common: they both felt guilty about neglecting their children.

On his second time round, as a grandparent, Liam was a dab hand, according to his wife, at changing nappies and giving babies their bottles. His elder daughter reckoned he had a better knack of getting a fractious child to sleep than any woman she knew. Liam attributed this to his musical prowess. He had a huge repertoire of folk music – English, Welsh and Scottish, as well as Irish – and sang till the children dozed over. He claimed modestly that the babies slept to escape the boredom of his voice.

Though now high in the IRA leadership, Liam Hughes had decisively changed his attitudes. In his heart he was on the peace wing of Republicanism, though he kept this to himself. He hadn't told anyone, not even his wife and he hadn't moved over to work in Sinn Fein, because he knew that would reduce his influence. He remained on the Army Council, but he was a surreptitious peacenik.

The principal reason for the change was his growing family. He could not bear the thought that the Troubles might last into his grandchildren's generation. A few years ago his son, an IRA Volunteer aged seventeen, had only just missed blowing himself up. Nowadays, Liam sometimes looked at an elfin, blue-eyed youngster on his lap, and murmured to himself: 'No, God, not him, not them!'

Sometimes late at night he thought about his own time on active service, and occasionally that made him weep. The memory that came to him most often was of television images of a Yorkshire soldier's funeral. Liam couldn't be sure whether it was his bullet or one from another man's rifle that had killed the English soldier. The flag-draped coffin and the smart regimental bearer party were not what troubled him, but a distraught widow and two weeping children. It was then that he wondered whether the age-old grievances of Irish Republicans made all the suffering worthwhile.

Liam drove Alan up the Falls Road, to the pleasant suburbs on the Western saucer of hills that surround Belfast. Soon they were in the front room of a small semi-detached house. What struck Alan was the opulence of the carpets, furniture and fittings – not bad for a man in his early fifties who said he'd been on the dole since he left school. There were two telephones, with different numbers. This subscriber clearly needed to be reachable in a hurry.

Liam saw Alan looking at a Celtic cross made from stained wood.

'Perhaps not the most beautiful object ye've ever seen, Mr Houston, but let's say it has sentimental value for me. It was made by a friend of mine, unjustly banged up in Long Kesh.'

At that moment, a woman Alan assumed to be Mrs Hughes arrived with a tray. He rose politely, expecting Liam would introduce her. He made no move to do this, and his wife never raised her eyes to either man, simply placing the tray on the table and leaving silently. The feminist revolution had evidently not reached the higher ranks of the Provisionals. Fleetingly Alan thought how Mary might have reacted if he'd ignored her in this Sheikh-like manner. Hurled the tray at his head, perhaps?

It was a very Belfast kind of elevenses: a large pot of tea, covered by a knitted cosy; biscuits with sweet icing; some lavish cream cakes that wouldn't have disgraced afternoon tea at the Ritz, but looked indigestible to Alan so early in the day.

'Eat up,' Liam Hughes urged him, and set a firm example himself. Alan did his best, wondering if this was an obscure rite of initiation, like the innumerable pints of bitter he'd once drunk at a London dockers' union meeting, when in pursuit of a Labour council nomination.

Liam's talk was courteous, and occasionally witty enough to make Alan laugh. But he fenced when Alan tried to discuss terrorism. As Charles had foreseen, Liam wanted to talk only about politics, not military matters. But despite his own late night doubts, he made no pretence of believing violence was unacceptable. He quoted a Republican from an earlier age, William O'Brien, who maintained that violence was the only way to secure a hearing for moderation. Liam himself, he assured Alan, was a believer in moderation, but . . . well, there you were.

Once he said if the British would only go home, Irishmen could settle their differences in a few weeks. Alan reminded him gently of a problem Republicans found difficult to get their heads round: that there were about a million people in the North-Eastern corner of Ireland who, for better or worse, *felt* themselves to be British.

For the only time in their conversation, Liam flared up.

'If they feel that fuckin' British, they'd better go back to Britain.'

Alan struggled not to follow this flight of fancy. If the Protestants went home to Britain, after four centuries or thereabouts in Ireland, what about the English descendants of the Pilgrim Fathers? Their migration was more recent than the Ulster one. Should they return from America? Not to mention the Germans, Italians, Russians, Scandinavians, Jews of the Diaspora, Afro-Americans, brought in chains from their own continent?

And, oh yes, the Irish-Americans? Prods and Micks? Denuding the Eastern seaboard cities and Chicago of their Irish ghettoes, emptying the Appalachians of their hill-billies, and leaving the American Indians to get on with a simple life rudely interrupted from the arrival of the *Mayflower* onward?

Alan silently counselled himself against such a discussion with Liam. He dragged the conversation back to how talks about a ceasefire might be set up. After a couple of hours, they'd made some progress. He promised to report back to his boss. Liam said he, too, would talk to his friends.

Then he offered to drive Alan back to the city centre.

'I don't suppose yer security handlers would be ecstatic to have ye wanderin' around the Glen Road on yer own.'

Alan said he hadn't told them he was coming, and wondered whether Liam believed him. When they emerged from the house, Liam fell to his knees, and looked carefully under his car. He noticed Alan's surprise.

'It's not just coppers and soldiers that get blown up, y'know, Alan. Apart from any nefarious activities your secret army might have in mind, we have the INLA to worry about. They don't like us either.'

Alan nodded. If he had nursed any doubt whether he'd been talking to someone significant in the IRA hierarchy, this worry disappeared. With a thrill of excitement, he said to himself that his luck had turned.

So it had, in a way. Alan Houston was too elated to worry about what he was getting into.

[21]

Alan didn't tell Mary what had kept him away from the Dunluces' party. Would their lives have turned out differently if she had known he was trying to negotiate an IRA ceasefire? Even a couple as close as the Houstons can brew their potions in separate test tubes, and assume the two will never interact. The long evening that Alan spent with Charles Corbett planning tactics for his meeting with Liam Hughes was the evening when Mary met Colin Newhouse.

Mary was slowly settling to life in Ulster. The arrival of spring produced a crop of invitations that were more like the political and media thrashes she used to enjoy in London. The General gave drinks at Army Headquarters in Lisburn. The Chief Constable was host at his office in the Belfast suburbs. The BBC Controller buttered up the local Establishment at a buffet lunch.

On 17 March, St Patrick's Day, Charles held a reception for 300 at the old Governor's Residence in Hillsborough and Mary met Diana for the first time. To Alan's relief they seemed to get on well; Mary found Diana much more amusing company than most other women she'd encountered here. After Alan introduced them, he left to talk to a local politician, while the two women swapped complaints about the narrowness of social life in Belfast. Mary had been accumulating illustrations.

'Have you noticed that the men and women at most parties gravitate to opposite sides of the room? Could they be under-cover Sikhs?'

Diana laughed. 'Don't complain, Mary. I've found that the men here talk almost exclusively about sport and making money. They're seriously uninteresting.'

Mary didn't think Diana would ever become such an intimate as Grizelda Atkinson, her only close friend in Ulster, but she did have charm. She was also quite beautiful, in a haughty Scots way. In fact, Mary was almost as impressed by Alan's colleague as he seemed to be. She even suspected she might agree more often about local politics with this apparently sensible woman than with her husband.

Mary had heard from Alan, in trivial detail, of his bruising arguments with Diana. Once, he told her, Diana had said to him: 'The trouble with your method of debate, Alan, is that you make your opponent feel personally responsible for the heat-death of the universe.'

'She got you bang to rights, didn't she?'

Mary's doubts about Diana lay outside politics. Alan had once told her he had advised Diana not to waste her time on the public service. She was better fitted to be one of those incisive QCs in a telly soap, intimidating witnesses with her piercing blue eyes. Now that Mary had met this formidable woman, she could see that this would have pleased her. Perhaps it was meant to.

Diana certainly waved her aggressive charm around her like a claymore. Earlier in the party Mary had observed her flirting with a senior army man. Was she doing the same with Alan? Political disagreements between them didn't matter a damn. Ideas never mattered as much between a man and a woman as personal chemistry. After a long interval, Mary was rediscovering this truth for herself. But she dismissed musings about Colin, and concentrated on what she thought of Diana. For all the intelligence and charm, if she had been asked to sum her up in a single word, it would have been 'predatory'. On the way home she was to mention this casually to Alan. He seemed surprised, but soon began to talk about a politician he had met for the first time that evening. Personalities were not Alan's abiding interest.

On the other hand, Diana liked Mary, with the admiration of an analytical mind. A few years older than herself perhaps, but she still looked after her appearance, and retained a sexual glow. She was wearing a simple dark blue dress that Diana judged just right to bring out the colour of her eyes. Well-groomed fair hair, good figure, an intelligent woman who talked interestingly about pictures, music and books. Strange match for her rough-hewn husband.

'You must have been thrilled by that brilliant coup of Alan's?'

Mary looked puzzled.

'I mean, establishing direct contact with the IRA, even having tea and buns in Liam Hughes's parlour.'

'Liam Hughes?' Mary echoed, her face reddening. She realised how few of the names in Alan's new world meant anything to her. Diana said Liam was a leading IRA figure, possibly Chief of Staff. The Government had never managed to make contact with him before.

'Whatever Liam says, goes. Already we've noticed a let-up in the violence, a kind of informal ceasefire. We're hoping to get serious talks going for the first time. Of course, it's sickening that tit-for-tat killings and punishment beatings go on, but that's just Provos and Loyalists doing what comes naturally. Some progress at last! Your husband's quite a goer.'

Uncomfortably Mary nodded assent. Diana could see that Alan had not told her about his clandestine activities. Was he just being over-zealous about security? Or did this confirm what she suspected, that the Houstons' marriage was not in good shape?

Diana looked out from under her long eyelashes. 'Don't worry, Mary, these politicos have secrecy on their brains. Charles was so hush-hush about the rendezvous with Liam Hughes that he told Dick and me that Alan had a migraine. I ask you! Your husband's not a sensitive enough plant for that particular ailment, is he?'

When the Houstons got home after the reception Mary asked about the contacts with the IRA. Alan began to explain that he couldn't tell her about Liam Hughes until the Prime Minister made up his mind. Since then, he'd meant to find time –

Mary interrupted. 'Political *ingenue* though I may be, Alan, I *had* noticed the absence from the telly news of our nightly bombs. Didn't you think of claiming responsibility? Using "a recognised code-word", naturally, before the IRA got in first.'

Alan considered this a sick joke, but he suspected he might be losing his sense of humour, so he said nothing.

[22]

As the weeks passed, Alan Houston wondered which was having the rougher ride, his relationship with his wife or his peace talks. Mary was more aloof than ever. She looked bleakly across the breakfast table one morning, after he had come home around midnight for the third time in succession.

'When you arrive an hour and more after I've gone to bed, it plays havoc with my sleep. Last night I was awake . . . oh, for a couple of hours, and I'm exhausted this morning. Hadn't you better move into the other bedroom?'

'You were sleeping soundly enough between two and three, while I was tossing about. In fact you were breathing deeply, almost snoring, I'd say.'

A more sensitive husband would have avoided this line of argument. It is a fact well known to every middle-aged wife that while men sleep soundly, they don't. Vice-versa with husbands. By ignoring Mary's suggestion Alan contrived to stay in the marital bed, though in an increasingly icy atmosphere.

In the weeks that followed his meeting with Liam Hughes, politics had also turned sour for Alan. He was surprised not to have heard from Liam. What had the IRA thought of his proposal for talks about a ceasefire? By the end of that long conversation in Liam's sitting-room they had been using Christian names. Now Liam was ignoring him. Alan decided to telephone.

Only at the third attempt did Liam's wife reluctantly bring him to the phone. He was guarded, but made it clear that he himself was not to be involved in any talks about a ceasefire. Liam spoke in circumlocutions. He implied, without actually saying so, that British officials in London had already been in touch with the IRA.

Alan stumbled into expressing his anxieties about such contacts. Afterwards he worried about this indiscretion. It was only months later that he was to admit to himself that he now felt closer to this IRA terrorist than to some of those who worked for Her Majesty's Government.

'What I fear, Liam, is that people who don't understand how delicate this all is might balls up what we've started.'

Liam was interested to learn that the British bureaucratic machine was leaving Alan out of the loop. The Brits never ceased to mystify him, an assiduous observer of his enemies' idiosyncracies. Of course, if you'd worked with the Provisionals' Army Council, nothing about human organisations ought to surprise you. All sorts of people played their own games. Still, he'd better be careful about what he said to Houston.

'Ach, don't worry, Alan, arrangements are being made all right. That's really all I can say.'

Alan suspected Liam had *appointed* the IRA negotiators, holding himself in reserve. He devoted most of his own time to telephoning various Whitehall offices, trying to find out what was going on. Finally Alan reached the same conclusion as Liam: that his Whitehall contacts were deliberately keeping him in the dark. In early April, he spoke to Charles.

'I'm fed up kicking my heels about Stormont, not knowing what's happening behind our backs. My phone call with Liam has left me more uneasy. What can we do about it, Charles?'

'Don't worry,' Charles advised him, in an uncanny echo of Liam. 'You've made the essential breakthrough. The Whitehall machine was bound to kick in because the PM has to authorise any detailed contact with terrorists, but when it gets to serious talking about politics, we'll be able to throw our weight around.'

It was the newspapers that made Alan twitchy. Again, Charles told him to relax. 'You, more than anyone, ought to know that when there's no genuine information journalists make it up.'

'Yes, but there must be something behind all these news stories and editorials in the London papers. To quote two truisms, you can't make bricks without straw and there's no smoke without fire.'

Alan also noticed that Dick was more secretive than usual and he commented on this to Diana.

'I suspect our revered Permanent Secretary is sitting at the centre of this whole web, pulling the strings, without too much reference to Charles.'

She smiled knowingly. Diana had her own sources of information and she was not about to share these with Alan, or anybody else.

What lay behind the eccentric press coverage was a new appointment Dick had made. He had sent on gardening leave an honest but plodding Ulsterman who was the department's chief press officer, and was now operating through a smoothie seconded from a London public relations agency. Alan decided that this man was probably responsible for the most authoritative-sounding article.

This said that the talks would eventually move beyond terrorism to politics, that the Irish Government, perhaps even the Americans, would be brought in to help and that there would eventually be a new Downing Street Declaration. This would replace Harold Wilson's Downing Street Declaration, right at the start of the Troubles, which had said firmly: 'The border is not an issue.'

By contrast, the author of the article said, with an inspired flourish: 'The new Declaration will make the Irish border look no more relevant than that between England and Wales.'

When an agitated Alan took the cutting in to Charles, he responded wearily. 'I can't envisage an Offa's Dyke running through Crossmaglen or the Bandit Country. The IRA would blow the Dyke up, as a residual symbol of imperialism.'

The Secretary of State's complacency was misplaced, for he too was being side-lined, although this was not because the Prime Minister had decided it should be so. Tom Sanderson might exercise a subtle tyranny over his ministers, but he did believe in ministerial government, reckoning that men and women who had to win votes every four or five years were better judges of public affairs than civil servants, however clever and experienced.

This, however, was not the view of Sir Richard Heston, as his diatribe at Charles's first dinner at Stormont had revealed and, more significantly, it was a proposition that had simply never occurred, as more than a theory, to Dick's titular boss, the cabinet secretary, Sir Philip Radley.

Even Dick was in awe of Sir Philip, who had a mind like a razor and who, unlike Dick, looked every inch a mandarin: immaculately tailored, carefully cut grey hair, anguished forehead, decisive spectacles.

Both these servants of the state knew that ministers came and ministers went, that parties were elected and then defeated, but that through everything the permanent civil service must keep the country on a sensible track, secure in its alliances, not offending other countries unnecessarily, keeping the extravagances of politicians under firm control.

Sir Philip and Sir Richard, like colleagues at the Foreign Office, the Treasury, and in embassies in Washington and Dublin, had their own long-standing views of what should be done about Ireland. The Prime Minister and his cabinet were mere passing objects on their permanent landscape.

[23]

Members of the Northern Ireland Committee of the Cabinet filed in for their meeting an hour before the full weekly Cabinet was due to assemble.

When they were seated – five ministers in almost identical grey suits, with the cabinet secretary Sir Philip Radley, in an even greyer one – Tom Sanderson raised his eyes from his red folder, embossed with the royal coat of arms. He looked across to his Northern Ireland secretary, and raised an eyebrow as an invitation to present his report.

Charles said that since he'd told colleagues about Alan Houston's breakthrough in his talk with Liam Hughes, the IRA had gone silent.

'When Houston spoke to Hughes on the phone recently, he found him enigmatic. There were assurances that talks about a ceasefire would be set up all right. There were also hints which I found surprising that British government representatives had already been in touch with the IRA Army Council. I'd be interested if colleagues can throw any light on this.'

He looked at the foreign secretary. Ralph Coates had come into the Labour Party from the Diplomatic Service, where he had finished up as trade attaché in Moscow. Charles often wondered if he had really been MI6's man in the embassy, for his nominal post there was a step aside from a bright diplomatic career. Soon after returning from Russia, Coates had left the foreign service to seek a Labour parliamentary seat. Everyone had been surprised when the PM plucked him from back-bench obscurity to be foreign secretary. Tom Sanderson had reached an age where he did not worry much about party opinion.

Coates smoothed his silver-grey hair.

'Yes, I think I can assist the Northern Ireland secretary. Our people – you, Prime Minister, will know which service I encompass in that phrase – have been in touch with Irish Republicans over several years, as part of their normal task of keeping an eye on enemies of our country. Also looking for clues as to what might wean them from their barbarous ways.'

Across the cabinet table, Charles fumed silently. How bloody condescending! The foreign secretary did not read these thoughts. Sensitivity to colleagues' feelings was not Ralph's most obvious talent.

'When we heard of the activities of the political adviser at the Northern Ireland Office, it seemed prudent to renew those contacts, and get more formal meetings under way, which we have now done.'

Charles exploded.

'Did it not occur to the foreign office to consult Alan Houston and me before these contacts were made? Judging by the nonsense appearing in the newspapers, somebody in Whitehall is feeding out tendentious rumours about likely outcomes. Heightened expectations among Republicans are dangerous. They might wreck what Houston has so far achieved. Let's remember that he has reached proper IRA men, the people who make bombs and shoot people, not just those shady Sinn Fein politicians MI6 has always talked to.'

Charles might have become even more rhetorical if the Prime Minister hadn't called on the defence secretary at that moment.

Robert Frazer was an ambitious man, sedulously keeping his nose clean. His hope was that he would succeed the foreign secretary, in the unhappy event of Ralph tripping up over his department's ambiguous policies in the Falklands, or Hong Kong, or Rhodesia. So he said what he thought the PM would like him to say.

'If we start worrying about stories in the newspapers, Prime Minister, we'll never get any business done. I think the Northern Ireland secretary risks being overly departmental. What matters, surely, is to get some kind of Irish settlement on the road. I almost said "any kind of Irish settlement". I must tell colleagues that among my own friends in Washington, I detect growing irritation at the way the whole business is dragging on. I believe they represent a wider international impatience.'

At the mention of Washington, the chancellor, who was worried that he might have to go to the IMF for another credit facility, growled his approval of what Defence had said. Anyhow, he didn't feel he owed Charles Corbett any favours, after the whingeing he'd done about unemployment.

Charles was gathering himself for a riposte when the Prime Minister, looking at the clock, said they had better adjourn, to allow him time to go over the agenda for cabinet with Sir Philip. Perhaps Charles would wait behind for a moment? He'd call the others back in ten minutes.

When the room cleared, Tom Sanderson picked a paper from his file. Charles noticed that it was signed in red ink, revealing to him that it had been drafted by the man with this eccentric affectation, the cabinet secretary. Tom Sanderson, too, found himself subtly coerced by the sheer brain-power and swiftness in decision of his most senior adviser.

When he addressed Charles, the Prime Minister did not read directly from Radley's paper, but he did keep referring to it as he spoke.

'Charles, I'd better tell you that the FO will have to be the lead department in these negotiations. It makes sense. They have at their finger-tips the expertise in doing deals with terrorists, for years and years, all over Africa and Asia. They also have their links with useful posts in Dublin and Washington, and of course their ... er, their special resource. Incidentally, I'd be obliged if you didn't talk out loud about MI6, even in this room. On that subject, least said really is soonest mended.'

Charles began to protest, but the PM waved him down.

'Must get this cleared up before cabinet. Of course the FO will lean on your department for advice, about local political consequences of any deal. Advisory, that's the role I see for the NIO. And doubtless Alan Houston will have a useful part to play there.'

Philip Radley suppressed a smile. He knew how much advice the Foreign Office would accept from that quarter. He and Dick Heston had privately agreed that Charles had been misguided to have a native Ulsterman involved in such a delicate area of UK policy. This was what had inspired him to make his note for the Prime Minister unusually prescriptive. Mustn't give the old boy any excuse for bottling out of a confrontation with Corbett.

The full Cabinet proved to be a rubber-stamp for what the PM had said to Charles, and what the mandarins had previously decided. Tom Sanderson introduced the item himself, reporting the appointment of the Foreign Office as lead department in negotiations as 'what has been agreed'. This left those ministers not in the know to deduce that this was a formal decision of the cabinet's Northern Ireland Committee. A few looked quizzically at Charles. It was not like him to avoid a fight.

Charles was smarting after his private dressing-down, but he had a politician's instinct not to kick against the pricks. There would be wider battles to be fought, and *amour propre* must not entice him into unwinnable ones against other, more powerful, Whitehall departments. But he wondered about the role of the cabinet secretary, and of his own permanent secretary, whom he was finding less and less trustworthy.

After Charles had told his political adviser about the defeat in cabinet, Dick Heston's secretiveness continued to irritate them both. Two weeks after the Foreign Office had officially begun their talks with the Republicans, the permanent secretary reported enigmatically to the morning meeting at Stormont.

'From what I'm told, negotiations are proceeding smoothly. This time we might well get a result. A favourable result, I suspect.'

Charles Corbett noted this as another example of Sir Richard's independent activities, but he said nothing. The permanent secretary's bland report provoked Alan into a quarrel, however. When the meeting broke up he went uninvited into Dick's room. Dispensing with preliminaries, Alan spat out what was troubling him.

'What exactly do you mean, Dick, by "a favourable result"?'

'I don't mean it will necessarily delight the Grand Orange Lodge.'

Alan reddened, but he held himself in.

'Doesn't it offend your professional dignity that these talks, set up by your department – by me, in fact – are now taken over by those masters of ambiguity in the FO, with God knows what consequences?'

'Not at all. Professional diplomats are the best people to conduct professional diplomacy. HMG is negotiating with people from a neighbouring nation. The Foreign Office, or their intelligence operatives, are the appropriate people to do that. I'm content to rely on their expertise and judgement.'

Alan exploded. 'They're not talking to Irish government representatives, for heaven's sake. They're talking to the Provisional IRA. Who elected them? The elected representatives of our neighbouring nation sit in Dail Eireann, and form the only government the Foreign Office ought to be talking to.'

Dick looked smugger than ever.

'This conversation is going nowhere. I'll have to get on with my work.'

He noisily opened his file and began to sign letters.

If Alan had persusaded Diana to confide in him, she could have revealed what lay behind the rumours. But she told nobody at Stormont what she knew, because she had now gone freelance on policy. She had not accepted transfer to the domestic civil service just to be an elevated clerk. Diana saw Whitehall as a miracle that happened by mirrors. She believed in her right and duty to influence it, for the better.

Diana had dined in London with Howard Considine, a man she'd had a brief affair with in her Foreign Office days. She used to quote to her brother a memory-prompting tip about the names of the American Congress's foreign policy committees: 'Congressmen have *affairs*, but Senators have *relations*.' She'd never intended to turn Howard into a relationship.

He now worked for MI6, as she herself had done in what she called The Days Before the Fall. Considine claimed he had surreptitiously been talking to Republicans for years. She guessed this really meant Sinn Fein.

Diana took a dislike to her old friend, who had developed a mid-life need to grope under cover of the table-cloth. She regarded her ex-lovers as cold kale anyhow. So she was disenchanted enough to wonder who had told Howard to insinuate himself into the current talks. Perhaps he was in some private enterprise mission outside the main negotiations. MI6 had always been a law unto itself, even though the taxpayer footed the bills.

Because Diana thought Ireland was at a historic turning-point, she had started a diary. After this dinner, she wrote a long entry.

24 May: I was nearly as astonished by the tale Howard's telling Republicans as by his romantic proclivities. I'll record this as accurately as I can, though it's difficult to concentrate on diplomatic detail when you're trying to remove a hand from your thigh, without seeming unfriendly.

Howard maintains that Republicans can get much of what they want – a promise of some kind of united Ireland within fifteen or twenty years – if they only convince the Unionists they'll have a marvellous role in such a set-up. That means offering those power-starved leaders of the Prods a revived share in the spoils of government: ministries, ambassadorships, and so on, but emanating from Dublin rather than London.

Hypothetically true perhaps. The Unionist *leaders* are boringly ambitious, in a petty kind of way. They hate not having the trappings of office, however nugatory. But I fear earthy rank-and-file Unionists are as little likely to be convinced by such a scheme as by a plan for an Irish expeditionary force to Mars, manned jointly by the Provos and the UDA.

What made Howard's bluster more credible, however, is something I've been involved in myself. Earlier this month Dick sent me to London to act as note-taker at a very hush-hush meeting between the Cabinet Secretary and his opposite number from Dublin. Upstairs room at the Reform Club, with the hall porter having to smuggle me in through the staff entrance. Security or rules forbidding women? I didn't dare to ask.

The Irishman, previously their Ambassador in Washington, came out with a line totally consistent with what Howard told me. He seemed to assume the final communiqué from these talks will convert Irish unity into a foreseeable possibility. More surprising, Sir Philip didn't openly disagree with that. Just tapped his pen on his pad with worldly-wise condescension. I'm not sure Charles or Alan will be happy with the outcome of their initiative, assuming there ever is one – which, on past experience, I doubt. It's usually 'all smoke and no fire' out here.

I keep asking myself why I'm so concerned about the shock Alan Houston has coming to him, particularly as this new political line suits me well enough. The answer is simple. He's taken great personal risks to bring peace to his native patch. Unlike the rest of us, he's emotionally involved. And Alan may be putting his family in danger.

I suspect also that he's wrecking his marriage. When I met his Mary, she was suffering rather noisily the effects of 24-hours-a-day politics on her home life. I wouldn't be at all surprised to hear she was reaching for her lawyer. I wonder could she cite HMG as co-respondent?

Apart from all that, I'm growing fond of young Mr Houston.

[24]

Mary had not heard from Colin Newhouse since their encounter at the Dunluces' party and this surprised her; he had seemed so eager that evening. None the less, her morale had improved. The crop of political receptions made a change from her perpetual round of suburban parties. Her sharp rebuke to Alan after the Hillsborough reception had changed his behaviour. He now seemed to realise how ludicrous his secrecy about the Liam Hughes affair had been and how careless it had been to let her hear the story from Diana. He also recognised, belatedly, that Mary was uneasy about Diana. Quite unnecessarily, he huffed to himself.

Mary assumed that Alan was over-compensating for his previous absenteeism but slowly he revealed why he had more time at home: the Foreign Office had taken over contacts with the IRA and Alan had little to do except grow frustrated. Mary, unfortunately, did not find this a flattering reason for him to spend more time with her. When he complained that Stormont was being kept in the dark, she was less than sympathetic, observing with a raised eyebrow: 'Surely Diana should be able to tell you what her old colleagues in the Foreign Office are up to. That first night you had dinner with her in London, you told me she was a member of MI6.'

'*Was* is the operative word. She seems to be totally out of that loop nowadays.'

Alan thought it prudent not to mention what Charles had told him about Diana's Czech affair. He still did not understand how shrewd his wife was about human nature. The reason Mary was teasing him was that she judged Diana would never be open with him. She might know things, but she would not reveal them unless she saw some advantage.

To feed Alan's worry, Dick Heston's tame PR man was planting more strange stories in Fleet Street, and the Dublin newspapers showed that the Irish Government was briefing journalists along similar lines.

'Why do they bother, Mary? Dublin journalism boasts so many would-be Padraig Pearses and Maud Gonnes manquées that any official briefing is otiose. The journalists spin their convoluted webs and disappear up their own orifices. I wonder whether readers in the Republic pay much attention, or do they just turn to runners-and-riders at Leopardstown?'

Mary tried to look interested, but her mind drifted away to race horses. Anyhow she wasn't sure who Maud Gonne was. She could see Alan was trying to revive an old intimacy through their habit of workplace gossip. He didn't seem to notice that this was a one-way process. She felt like screaming: 'I don't have a bloody job to talk about, you stupid oaf.'

She was angry that he had made no effort to put her in touch with the local art world, as he had promised. There had been an infuriating incident at the General's party, when she had seen the museum director across the room, and was aching for Alan to introduce her.

But where was her husband when she needed him? Talking to the army Number Two about security in West Belfast – a subject they discussed twice a week anyhow. By the time she kicked him on the ankle, the director and his wife were saying goodbye to their hosts, and it was too late.

As the weeks passed, she began to wish that Colin would telephone. Alan's dutiful efforts to tell her his non-news about politics had begun to pall. Perhaps this was because Mary found Ulster politics about as fascinating as watching paint dry. But perhaps it was also because Alan himself was beginning to pall for her. In those first fateful months of his new job their marriage had finally lost its sparkle.

Marriages don't often break down in a blaze of adultery and betrayal; in most cases, talk of a 'guilty party' is simplistic. Mary thought a phrase from the Road Traffic Act would be more appropriate to her case: Alan was driving their marriage 'without due care and attention'.

In late May Colin telephoned. He had been away from home a great deal, he didn't say where. Would she like to have lunch the next day? Mary said she would. No reason for mentioning this to Alan; it would just be a pleasant outing.

This was the first time in twenty years of marriage that Mary had deceived him.

[25]

Three weeks after his cabinet defeat, Charles Corbett called Alan into his room. He looked grave as he told his private secretary they mustn't be interrupted.

'I've had a private talk with the PM. He's now as worried as you are.'

'A bit late! May I ask why?'

'Scared our negotiators are being outmanoeuvred.'

'How terribly unpredictable that was! Charles, the FO's negotiating tactics are bound to go wrong, because they don't understand terrorism. Posturing over diplomatic niceties is dangerous. We're sitting on a volcano. And do you know why?'

The Northern Ireland Secretary wished Alan was not so tangential, because he wanted to ask him to undertake a difficult task. But Charles Corbett was wise as well as clever. He knew when not to interrupt.

Alan went back to first principles, as he was inclined to do. He said Charles's predecessor had been crazy to allow the IRA and the Loyalist paramilitaries to control their ghettoes. Doubtless he saw the middle classes were doing nicely, with plenty of subsidies about, and their own savings invested well away from Ulster.

'The losers in these Troubles are working-class families, both Prods and Micks. The paramilitary bully-boys swagger round their streets, and when they're not recruiting their youngsters, they're selling them drugs, or beating them up for not doing what they're told. These are families who've been out of work for three generations, Charles. That's where the recruits for the IRA and the UDA come from. But they'd care less about flags if they'd any hope of getting a job.'

Charles filed that thought away, as most ideas with a time-span of more than a month get filed away in Whitehall. He would have to do something about unemployment, if the Troubles ever gave him half a chance. But his problem was more immediate: he told Alan what had caused Tom Sanderson's panic.

'To start with, he now accepts the Provos *needed* to run down their campaign. Too many of their people have been killed or are serving long gaol sentences, and Loyalist paramilitaries have been murdering too many Catholics.'

Alan spoke bitterly. 'I could have told the PM that months ago, Charles. But because some spook or FO Noddy puts it in a report, it gets believed.'

'Point taken. It's an ugly fact we in government would prefer to ignore, but the Loyalist thugs have contributed to the IRA's change in mood. Decent Catholics are frightened, fed up with the Troubles, fed up with us – the Government, Army, RUC – for not being able to protect them. But they're also fed up with the Provos, who haven't protected them either. So the IRA's strategy was unsustainable – Mao's pool of support and all that.'

'That doesn't quite explain why Tom Sanderson's worried.'

Charles said neither he nor the Prime Minister could square this intelligence assessment of IRA difficulties with a change of tone in reports to their Cabinet Committee. At first these had assumed that government negotiators held most of the cards. But recently the team had begun to produce early drafts of some future communiqué, which gave a strong whiff of the IRA's demands.

'I told the Cabinet Committee the Provos were being allowed to behave like Montgomery at Luneburg Heath in 1945 – they'd fought their enemy to a standstill, and just needed to dictate terms. That riled the foreign secretary, but the Prime Minister was with me. He revealed to me that he's given the cabinet secretary a bollocking for pursuing an independent policy, probably with the collusion of Dick.'

When Alan asked what would happen next, Charles shuffled his papers.

'That's where you come in again, Alan, if you're willing.'

Alan waited.

'Old Tom has concluded it isn't only the Irish who say things just to please whoever they're talking to. He wants to know just what half-promises our envoys are making.'

'And my role?'

'This may seem like a funny way to run a railway, but we want you to reopen your private line to Liam Hughes, and find out what our people are saying to the IRA.'

Alan counted ten before he spoke.

'I once met an old American who'd been all through the Pacific War. He told me about an encounter in the wilds of Iwo Jima with a Doughboy from Brooklyn. This man's truck had broken down, and he had no hope of getting spares so, mopping the sweat from his brow, he gave his judgement on his generals: "In my opinion, buddy, they oughta sub-contract this goddam war to General Motors."'

Charles laughed nervously. Alan was glaring at him again.

'You're not telling me the Government intends to rely on an IRA man to reveal to us our own negotiating stance? Wouldn't it be better to kick ass in Whitehall?'

Charles raised his hand.

'All right, it's unconventional, but the PM says we also need to know what the IRA's bottom line is. We're not likely to get *that* information from our own people, are we?'

Alan shrugged his shoulders, and said he couldn't promise Liam would be frank with him.

Having secured Alan's agreement, Charles again warned him about his personal safety. Alan said he was more worried about his family than himself. He would tell them to be careful.

But back in his own office, that wasn't what he thought about at all. An exciting truth was sinking in. He was back at the centre of the most thrilling political drama he would ever witness. Alan Houston intended to enjoy it.

It was a pity he had grumbling anxiety on the home front – not so much about the security that Charles always felt duty-bound to mention – more the uneasy state of his marriage. At least if he pulled off this second meeting with Liam, he'd have a lot more to talk to Mary about in the evenings. Alan had learned his lesson about secrecy.

But had he learned other lessons? Since that Boxing Day shouting-match with Mary he had done nothing about security, because he couldn't believe the risks were real. But he decided now that when he got a spare moment he would ask the man with the toothbrush moustache whether there was anything the authorities could suggest about Mary, Peter, even Brian at Cambridge. That might mollify his wife.

Alan Houston was by nature an optimist. He soon found himself thinking that perhaps he was just being neurotic about Mary's distant manner and, for now, he'd better concentrate on the meeting he had to arrange with Liam. He could easily sort out personal problems later, he told himself. After all, Mary was scarcely the type of woman to run off with some Belfast toyboy.

[26]

Mary was startled that the pub they met in that first lunchtime was only half a mile from Alan's boyhood home. She would have felt less guilty if Colin hadn't chosen the Antrim Road. Still, there was a beautiful view over the Lough. On a day like this, with spring leaves fresh on the Cave Hill's trees, and the sea sparkling in bright sunshine, she could see why Alan kept raving about the place.

The voice of conscience might say she was deceiving him, but Mary did not see her embryo relationship with Colin Newhouse like that, not in the least. This was simply a pleasant man with interests and opinions that had nothing to do with Northern Ireland. It was the kind of alternative company she badly needed.

Colin was wittily eloquent about the intellectual inadequacies of most of his colleagues at the university, and the fact that few in his Senior Common Room had ever moved away from their home university.

'God, the parochialism that surrounds me, Mary! I feel like a reluctant novitiate in an enclosed order. By the way, don't repeat that phrase to your husband, or he'll think I'm a covert Papist.'

Mary wished he hadn't said that. It made her feel disloyal.

'People like Alan don't have any hang-up about Catholics. It's politics he's obsessed by, that and leftish economic thinking.'

'Did you tell him about our meeting?'

Mary's reply seemed to him needlessly sharp.

'For heaven's sake, I told him we'd met at the Dunluces' drinks. Alan was more interested in your political views than in social chit-chat. Surely even in this place two English people can talk about the arts over a drink without its being misinterpreted?'

Colin raised his eyebrows and smiled.

'Never underestimate the public's appetite for gossip, my dear, especially in backwaters like this. Reminds me of an old university friend of mine who works for one of the Sunday tabloids. He reckons you can get by in journalism if you stick to three or four well-tried story lines. His favourites begin: "Tongues were wagging in this sleepy Blankshire village tonight, as . . ." Then you tell the sub-editors to take local news agency copy for the alleged facts.'

They talked about the films Colin had seen, a couple at the university film society that week, the rest on his recent visit to London. When Mary complained she had no chance to see anything but general releases, Colin suggested she should come to the film society with him.

In the next few weeks they did this several times. If Alan phoned to say he would be home that evening, Mary told him she had arranged to go to the cinema. Alan, who had other things on his mind again, assumed she was going with Grizelda Atkinson.

Usually Mary agreed to have a drink afterwards, but she had absorbed what Colin said about gossip, and insisted on going to a pub well away from the university. The web of acquaintance in middle-class Ulster was small.

Colin intended to leave Northern Ireland as soon as he had found a suitable academic post elsewhere, preferably back in Oxford. His wife, Susan, did not figure in those plans. Mary, if she could be persuaded, did.

Diana was keeping her eye on the Houstons' marriage, principally through her conversations with Alan. Since meeting Mary, she found the subject more interesting – purely as a student of human nature. She often wondered how Alan fitted into Mary's family background.

He had never totally shed his youthful Marxism. Funny, then, that he should marry a filly from a military family whose views, according to his occasional funny anecdotes, were conventional Home Counties Tory, with an admixture of hunting, shooting and fishing. On visits to his in-laws, did Alan just bite his tongue on his socialist views, or did he let them all hang out and risk Mary's father suffering an apoplexy?

Diana had a friend at the university, a Scottish physics lecturer. He mentioned to her Mary's visits to the Film Society.

'She and Dr Newhouse appear to be very close,' he said.

Talking to Alan, Diana approached the subject tangentially.

'I'm getting fed up with not having any free time. It's claustrophobic up here – we never seem to talk about anything except politics. I used to know a lot about films, but I never see any nowadays. A friend at Queen's was telling me they get out-of-the-run movies there – apparently the Film Society's well run, by an English don called Newhouse.'

Alan showed little interest, so Diana didn't pursue the subject. Perhaps he knew about Mary's friendship with Colin, perhaps not. There was no reason yet why she should tell him. But she would keep the Alan-and-Mary file in her mind open.

[27]

Are all men self-obsessed? Mary wondered. They were certainly less interested in human relations than women. For while Mary was considering the future of their marriage, she didn't think Alan saw anything amiss. The truth was that Alan was worried about their marriage too, but his forthcoming talk with Liam had temporarily driven everything else from his mind.

He told Mary what Charles had asked him to do, but even his rhetorical exuberance – 'the British Government has to ask an IRA man what its own envoys are saying!' – passed over Mary's head. For her thoughts were elsewhere as well.

Alan had again found it difficult to contact Liam. It was several days before his call was returned. When Alan suggested they meet the following day, Liam sounded reluctant.

'Y'see, Alan, our organisation's been conducting these negotiations through carefully selected spokesmen. To tell ye the truth, I helped pick them meself. Our Army Council wouldn't want me operating in any kinda freelance fashion.'

Alan knew Liam was a senior figure on the Army Council. He took a risk.

'Look, Liam, I'm pretty certain these talks are getting bogged down.'

There was a long silence at the other end of the line. Alan Houston sounded as if he had something important to say. Liam chuckled.

'Well, I've always thought they might need the two of us before they're done. So maybe a chat wouldn't do no harm. But it'd better be in my favourite drinking club on the Falls, so's everybody can see us.'

When he put the phone down, Liam cursed under his breath. With the informal ceasefire still on, he had been hoping to get away the next day, for a bit of fishing in a lough in the hills above Belfast. Impossible to get any reliable time off in this job nowadays, he thought, like any over-worked business executive.

'Mind you,' Liam said to his silent wife, 'you aren't guaranteed peace anywhere these days. This place is goin' to the dogs. When me and Gerry Fogarty went to this same wee lough a month ago, a mob of noisy teenagers was ejiting about – swimmin' and splashin'.'

Mrs Hughes nodded her head in sympathy.

'Aye, but d'ye know, Martha, none of them had a dally on them. Boys *and* girls. Even when they seen Gerry and me, a couple of oul' fellas, the girls made no attempt to cover theirselves.'

Liam was a law-and-order Republican.

'Some fellas I know would have given the lads a bloody good hiding.'

Later that day, Alan found something new to worry about. At Charles's morning meeting the general officer commanding reported a punishment attack in the New Lodge, a hard Provisional area near where Alan was born. An army patrol had found a teenager lying on a street corner.

'He crawled out from a back alleyway, both his legs broken. He was losing a lot of blood from a deep cut on his head. If the soldiers hadn't got him to hospital quickly, he would have died.'

What shocked Alan was that the General talked about this brutality without indignation, as if it were the law of the jungle. Alan still couldn't accept that the streets he grew up in were a jungle. What was the point of talking about a ceasefire if this sort of thing was still going to happen? He decided to make his own enquiries.

He telephoned a friend in the Mater Infirmorum Hospital.

'Aye, a baseball bat job,' said the doctor, as if he were describing a common ailment like appendicitis. 'Joe Rooney, aged sixteen. They casually battered his head against a brick wall as well. I wish these thugs could get into their thick skulls that most human skulls aren't all that thick. The head wound could have killed him. Even his leg injuries mean he might spend the rest of his life on sticks, poor wee bugger.'

That afternoon Alan went to the hospital. He took cigarettes and chocolate, but Joe Rooney suspected he was police, and would talk only about football. His one comment on his injuries was to complain he'd heard one of the soldiers saying 'This lad's probably a Provie bastard.' Likely enough, Alan thought, but he wondered if Joe knew that the squaddies had saved his life.

On his way out, one of the nuns gestured him into the nurses' room.

'I don't know why I'm talking to you, Mr Houston, and you with the British Government. Our priest has told us our only duty here's to care for the sick, and keep our eyes, ears and mouths shut. He said to care for any religion, or none – civilian, soldier, policeman, even B Specials when they were still going. But what's been done to young Joe has left me sick, sore and tired of the Provies. It was them did it all right, Mr Houston.'

'How do you know that, Sister?'

She said the man who'd come in to see Joe as soon as he recovered consciousness was not a relative, as he claimed, but a big shot in the IRA.

'Sure he was one of the internees you let out of Long Kesh. My sister says he's a chancer, into drugs and ivry sort of divilment. She read in *Republican News* he'd been IRA Intelligence Officer in there. I wish to God you'd kept him in, sir. Joe nearly died. And yer man was in here to warn him to keep his mouth shut.'

Alan had to promise the nun not to tell any of this to the police. There was nothing they could have done anyhow, without Joe Rooney's cooperation.

As he left, the nun said: 'I just wanted somebody at Stormont to understand that this lull in the bombing isn't the whole story.'

Alan wished she could have told this to the cabinet's Northern Ireland Committee. He was angered by what Joe's beating horribly confirmed about life in the ghettoes.

He knew he ought to calm down before facing Mary. After his driver dropped him he sat on the garden bench for five minutes. It was pleasantly cool under the willow tree. Mary had left the curtains undrawn, and the lights were on. Mozart was seeping out from the tape-deck. Unobserved, Alan watched his wife. She'd been ironing and listening to the music. He smiled when she began to sort out his accumulation of old newspapers.

As Alan watched the beautiful, natural, calm woman he'd married twenty years before, he remembered how much he had loved her. Past tense? He wasn't sure. It was true that he found her more lovable nowadays like this, with the volume turned down. That steered them clear of rows.

But they didn't have a row that night – quite the contrary. Alan told Mary why he was worried about the meeting he'd arranged with Liam for the following day. He described Joe Rooney's narrow escape from death. She was horrified, sympathising with his anxiety.

He said sadly, 'I'd better face the facts: unless Liam hands me a miracle tomorrow, my peace initiative is falling apart.' Then, his defences down, Alan told his wife how much he still cared for her and, pouring out a torrent of guilt about not devoting more time to her and the family since they came to Ulster, he apologised endlessly. Mary felt sorry for him and they drifted into making love. She had often had Alan when he was more passionate, but never when he was more considerate. Her own passion surprised her.

Afterwards, as Alan's deep breathing turned into a quiet snore, Mary lay awake, a puzzled frown creasing her brow.

[28]

Liam Hughes had invested his Republican street-cred in winning a political deal. The Cause had gained a lot since his encounter with Alan Houston on the Cave Hill. Even the hard-liners were beginning to admit that the Armalite was not Ireland's only weapon.

As he supped stout in the club, he felt pleased to be seeing Alan again. Liam couldn't think of him just as 'a Brit-loving Quisling', the description Sean favoured. Alan Houston had taken risks to push these talks forward. Liam had heard whispers his marriage was in trouble. His wife being English couldn't help.

When Alan entered the club, housed in an old warehouse, he looked at the bare wooden floor, the Republican symbols on the walls, and sat down on the hard chair Liam pulled up for him. Liam said sardonically he hoped the surroundings weren't too grim. Alan smiled.

'No, no, I've been in several UDA and UVF places that were even more austere. Their pictures were different, all ladders and stars instead of Tricolours and Celtic crosses.'

Liam ordered him a pint, and said the talks with British representatives were going better than he'd expected.

'Our fellas think it's easier to talk to the true Brits, those perfect English gentlemen, with their stiff upper lips and rolled umbrellas stuck up their arseholes. Oh yes, and their lovely Oxford accents.' (Unlike the native English, Liam gave the second syllable in 'Oxford' its full phonetic value.) 'Better than dealing with hard oul' Prods from the same stubborn stock as ourselves.'

Alan thought Liam's comment contained a germ of truth. Neither of them came from a blood strain that found compromise easy. But he believed that what they had in common mattered more than the difference in their religions.

'My kind of Presbyterian thinks Christianity is about loving your neighbour, Liam, not hating Catholics – or Protestants for that matter. That's cowboys and Indians stuff.'

Alan thought he'd better remind Liam that if he were ever to get a united Ireland he would eventually have to negotiate with the Unionists. Liam nodded. He didn't care to mention that if a united Ireland came in his lifetime, which seemed unlikely, he would get as far away from Belfast as possible – Kerry, say, or even his brother's in Boston. Liam did not believe a change-over would be bloodless. Some Protestant thugs made even Sean look like a recruit for the Legion of Mary.

Only as their talk went into a second pint did Liam twig what Charles Corbett's adviser was after. He had been told to find out how high the IRA was pitching its hopes. Who had instructed him to do this? Probably not just Corbett. Liam was an avid reader of political commentary in British newspapers, and he detected the hand of the Prime Minister, Tom Sanderson.

He had been wondering for a few days whether the people his side's envoys were meeting spoke with the full authority of Her Britannic Majesty. The reports of what that slimy MI6 man Considine had said made him sound more Republican than Liam himself. He wished to God the Brits would get their act together. No bloody discipline!

As Liam reached this disobliging conclusion about the ancient enemy, Sean arrived, accompanied by the ubiquitous Cathal. The Alsatian, which Alan had not liked much on the Cave Hill, seemed even more boisterous in this confined space. He leaped up on Alan, and Sean took his time before shouting, 'Down, Cathal.'

'Hello, Sean,' said Liam, as the barman delivered another pint. 'Mr Houston here doesn't seem as cheerful about our talks as we've been.'

Alan noticed that Liam didn't use his first name except when they were alone. Sean looked puzzled and angry.

'But our envoys have been telling me how helpful the Brits have been.'

Sean clearly fancied himself as a mimic, and slipped into the most spurious simulation of 'posh' English Alan had ever heard.

'Nice fellas, see the Paddies' point of view, an' all that. "We understand the sweep of history, old boy, hear the ebb-tide of empire, like every other empire before us." So orfully, orfully sensible, don't y'think?'

Alan said that was not how he read the situation.

'Don't close your eyes to the realities of democratic politics. The British Government can't order people to knuckle under to Dublin, any more than they can make you knuckle under to Stormont.'

Alan added sadly that if when Republicans spoke about peace, they really meant victory, there wasn't a hope in hell of a settlement. If recent history taught anything, it was that people must be persuaded to compromise.

'That includes your people, Liam.'

Sean erupted. 'Listen, Mr Houston,' he said in a low voice. 'Just you listen. We've all got a lot invested in these talks, not least your good self.'

Alan smiled at this piece of secretarial college politeness. But his smile soon evaporated as Sean continued.

'If anything goes wrong, and we don't get what we're entitled to, the IRA won't just blame Downing Street or the Crown forces. You're closer to yer man at Stormont, Charles fuckin' Corbett, than anybody else. If this all falls apart, we'll mind where you come from, you and your family.'

The two glared at each other. Liam saw that Sean had missed the political point. The British envoys had obviously gone beyond their brief, and their ultimate boss was pulling back. Anyhow, it was stupid of Sean to threaten Houston's family. Nobody would want to hurt those young lads they'd met on the Cave Hill. What would be the point, except blind vengeance? And that wasn't the business Liam Hughes was in, because somebody might do the same to his family.

Alan tried to concentrate on what Liam was saying, but he couldn't wipe Sean's outburst from his mind. He had seen a police file about this former Commanding Officer of the Tyrone IRA. In a shoot-out at a border barracks, Sean's unit had killed a Green Finch, a twenty-year-old part-time woman soldier in the Ulster Defence Regiment. Sean was a ruthless terrorist, while Liam, despite his past, had the makings of a politician.

Liam could have augmented Alan's knowledge of the border incident. Sean's number two had described to him the stunned atmosphere when the young Volunteers learned that one of them had killed an Irish girl no older than themselves. Sean, squatting among them in the IRA's safe house, saw his duty. Their morale needed to be stiffened.

'Listen to me, lads. My only hope is that she was pregnant, so that we'll have got two of the fuckers.'

While Liam digested what Alan had told him, Sean and Alan continued their quarrel. Alan asked about the beating of Joe Rooney.

'That evil wee runt!' Sean exclaimed. 'He was a drug-dealer, on his own account. I'm sorry our lads didn't top him.'

Alan lost his temper.

'You sound like one of Hitler's thugs in the thirties.'

'I've no particular hang-up about Hitler, on the principle that England's difficulty is Ireland's opportunity, and your enemy's enemy is your friend.'

'Six million Jews didn't find him much of a friend,' said Alan quietly.

'Aye, well, maybe the Yids got what was coming to them.'

This was too much for Liam, who aroused himself to rebuke Sean for mindless bigotry. 'You oughta join the soddin' Orange Order, Sean.'

Alan was surprised when Sean accepted this insult without complaint. Liam's authority seemed to prevail, perhaps over everybody else's.

Liam's thoughts were reaching a gloomy conclusion. Alan Houston's hard line today *did* mean it was the British Prime Minister himself who was pulling the rug from under his government's intermediaries. They'd gone further than Tom Sanderson wanted to go.

When he voiced this suspicion, Alan's response was careful.

Republicans should not assume Britain spoke with a single voice, even that of the Whitehall establishment. The harsh notes on the British side were not just the few Belfast accents. (He looked at Sean as he said this.) The IRA would be wise to look for deals that would help their own people, and everybody else as well.

Liam shook his head sadly.

'God, how I'd like this struggle to be over! But can't you understand how hard it's been for the IRA even to suspend its campaign, never mind ending it? Too many of our people have been killed and banged up and brutalised for me or anybody else to convince the Army Council we've got to forget our war aims.'

Liam now suspected that the Brits wanted a compromise he couldn't deliver. So he decided he must give their emissary the hardest possible version of what his terms would be.

'If you're asking what would make us call a formal ceasefire, it's a bankable promise of a united Ireland. And not too far off.'

[29]

Later Liam wondered if he ought to have given Alan Houston protection on his lonely walk down the Falls to the city centre. Sean was muttering that somebody should arrange a 'head job', but then Sean was so full of bombast this was like ordering his fourth pint of Guinness (which he had just done). The real danger came from the wilder youngsters who might have recognised Houston, and would want to rough him up. Liam was too angry to suggest an escort, Alan too proud to ask for one. Liam concluded that at least the political adviser did have guts.

He could not shake off his gloom. This peace initiative had run into the sand because the Brits could not control their envoys, who seemed to follow their own hunches. Thinking of what he would have to report to the Army Council, a phrase from the Western films he'd loved as a boy floated into Liam's mind: 'White man speak with forked tongue.' He'd have a job convincing the harder men on the Army Council not to restart the campaign, even though they knew it was getting nowhere.

Alan Houston's dilemma was the mirror-image of Liam Hughes's. He would have to tell Charles that the talks he'd engineered had failed. British negotiators had raised IRA expectations so high that even a sane man like Liam did not believe he could lower them to rational levels.

But what should he tell Mary? After Sean's threatening words he would have to warn her at once about personal security. He hoped she would take it calmly.

The conversation got off on the wrong foot. Mary noticed that Alan had been drinking and began her familiar complaint about neglecting the family. To his astonishment, she seemed at first to have forgotten that he was meeting Liam that evening. Since Mary had begun seeing Colin Newhouse her retention of details from her husband's political conversation was briefer than before.

Phrases from Liam's and Sean's conversations competed with each other in Alan's head: 'Nice-looking pair of lads, if I may say so,' and 'If this all falls apart, we'll mind where you come from, you and your family.' He blurted out more of this to Mary than was wise.

He warned her of the new dangers, urged her to take more precautions, both for herself and Peter. Vary her routes, when driving to her usual shops or friends' houses, pick Peter up from school as often as she could, always if possible. Alan hesitated.

'I wonder if we should think again about this boarding school idea.'

It was this change of mind that ignited Mary's naked fear for Peter – Alan *must* be scared. She kept silent for several minutes. Then the dam broke. He had never seen anything like it before, from his rational, once loving wife.

'Sixteen bloody ninety!' Mary screamed at him. 'King fucking Billy! United sodding Ireland! Who gives a bugger? Like that Ulster poet said, nobody cares whose flag flies on their benighted castles. Why the hell have you brought us to this awful place? What on earth do you think you're achieving?'

'At this moment, I think I'm achieving very little. Nothing in fact.'

Alan was looking for sympathy, like last night. When things had gone wrong in the past – jobs he'd failed to get, newspaper scoops that had eluded him, pieces to camera that looked embarrassing on the video later – she had offered a ready shoulder to lean on. What Wordsworth called 'those little, unremembered acts of kindness and of love' – that was Mary. Long ago it was this instinctive kindness which had first made him love her.

But now Mary had no sympathy to spare, except for herself and her children. If he thought it was as hopeless as that, she shouted, why was he endangering himself, Peter, her, maybe even Brian at university. The thought of Brian provoked a fresh outburst.

'What security is there at Cambridge, for heaven's sake? You remember Brian's talk with the head of his college?'

He waited for the flood of words to subside. Then, for the first time in their marriage, he walked out on her without saying a word. Alan had no particular objective in mind, not leaving for ever, or anything dramatic like that, not knowing what he was going to do, just wanting to be on his own. He walked aimlessly for an hour, and when he returned they didn't even say goodnight. That was the first time this had happened since they'd married twenty years before.

Mary was preparing for bed. Alan decided not to provoke a further outburst so he slept in the guest room. In the limbo between wakefulness and sleep, his mind drifted back to their love-making the previous night. That might have happened in another world.

His wife, on her own, did what she found herself doing more often nowadays, thinking seriously about her future.

It was in this mood that Alan and Mary Houston faced the most challenging day of their lives.

[30]

The next morning Charles asked Dick Heston and Diana into his room to hear Alan's bleak news. They had run into the buffers. Who knew how soon the IRA would start bombing and shooting again? Charles was more angry than they had seen him.

'The people who leaked nonsense to the media that fanned up IRA expectations ought to feel ashamed. But they probably don't, because people are operating on conflicting agendas. I suppose that's how government always works.'

'Even in matters of life and death?' Alan asked bitterly.

'Yes, even then.'

Dick smiled at this weary response. Not far below his surface lay a streak of malice. His look said: 'I've seen all this coming.' He proposed they begin at once a fundamental review of their strategy. Charles ruled this out, with a brusqueness that bordered on the rude. He no longer trusted his permanent secretary.

'We all need time for reflection.'

When they broke up, Diana followed Alan into his room, and put her hand on his shoulder.

'Sorry to see you so down in the mouth, Alan. You got further than anybody else, and you deserved a better result. But I don't think churning it over on your own will help. Has the time come for our long-awaited Awayday?'

Alan remembered Diana's suggestion that they should go off on their own to hammer out ideas, in a way that was never possible in the office. He had put her off until Mary had settled in. After last night, that seemed less significant.

Diana ran through possible subjects.

'Item: What do we do now? Item: Whether I want to carry on here. Big Item: Whether we think Charles will. Personal Item: Whether you should.'

Out of the blue she asked how his marriage was surviving the shocks.

Alan thought for almost a minute before speaking.

'*Comme ci, comme ça.*'

'That was a long time in gestation. Time for our Awayday! I promise at least to be better company than Liam Hughes, or his cuddly chum Sean.'

It was sunny as they sped down the ceremonial drive that fell for a mile from the parliament building at Stormont. Just as they turned on to the main road, a Republican intermediary was telephoning Howard Considine in his London flat. The IRA had acted within twenty-four hours of Liam's angry outburst to Alan. The intermediary said that the informal truce was going to end: the British had been playing tricks. Military operations would resume.

Considine was not surprised, though he just stopped himself saying this to the caller. He looked angrily in the mirror. It was the Prime Minister who had scuppered his efforts. He knew these had the backing of the most influential people in Whitehall, not to mention Washington. Politicians!

In that age before pagers and mobile phones, Alan and Diana were able to proceed on their Awayday, oblivious of a development that would transform his life.

They drove along the Antrim Coast Road, built as employment relief during the potato famines of the mid-nineteenth century. For miles there was nothing but a dry stone wall and shingle or sand between Alan's car and the North Channel. On the hillier road in the far north-eastern corner of Ireland, the scenery became more dramatic. Cliffs fell abruptly to their right, with the sparkling sea and the coast of Scotland beyond. To their left, thousands of sheep clung dizzyingly to the slopes. Yellow whin gave colour to the bleak basalt rock.

They talked politics over lunch in a hotel at the Giant's Causeway, but mostly they relaxed after recent strains, relished each other's company. Later they walked along the cliffs.

Although this was a golden day, the wind dispelled any Mediterranean idyll. The waves far below must have been six feet high. They broke over flat rocks like soap suds. Diana had brought field glasses, and stopped to look at cormorants and shags on the cliff faces. They lay face-down on the grassy path's edge to study the Causeway itself. Around them were clumps of harebells, thistles and bachelor's buttonhole.

It was difficult to judge which piece of distant land was in Scotland or in Ireland. Alan said a common fallacy was that this narrow sea was a barrier, when often it was a bridge. The sixteenth century Scots settlers in Antrim used to take their boats home to Scotland for church services.

'Do you ever wish they'd stayed there?' Diana asked. Alan decided to treat this as a rhetorical question. Glasgow's communal relations hadn't been a stunning success either, had they?

Then they gossiped, mostly about Dick. Alan regarded Diana and Dick as the closest of allies. He told her that Charles and he had wondered whether she would marry him, once they escaped from the claustrophobic quarters at Stormont. Diana shook her head. She had decided she could only get hurt in a permanent relationship with this deeply unhappy man.

'Mind you, I was consciously using Dick's liking for . . . for country matters to get my own ideas about Irish policy accepted.'

Alan blinked at her frankness, and said he hadn't thought civil service colleagues discussed their Option Papers in bed. More in memoranda. Diana laughed.

'Civil servants, especially those of us nurtured by the security service, are not unlike politicians – highly intelligent and highly sexed.'

Then Diana began to complain about the difficulty a woman had to exert any real influence in public affairs.

'The truth is, for all the liberal prating of politicians, they really don't believe we ought to be involved, except as glorified tea-ladies. Have you never wondered, Alan, why I'm working at Stormont when I was once a Foreign Office diplomat?'

Alan tried to look surprised. Clearly Diana did not know he had been told about her Czech affair.

'Well, years ago there was a minor incident in my personal life. They used it as an excuse to stop me serving abroad again. Do you think they would have done that to a man? Of course not! So I thought, "Well, damn them." I decided the only way to have satisfaction out of whatever duties they gave me was to make sure I was in control, whatever pompous males might think.'

She bit her lip in recollected anger. She supposed Alan, with all his class prejudices, thought hers was a privileged childhood, among all those Scottish lairds and deer? Well, it hadn't seemed like that at the time.

'I was a frightened little girl, quite lacking in self-confidence. I really had to push myself to go for the Foreign Service examination, rather than just staying in my shell. But when I got into diplomacy, I loved the work. So when that career was stolen from me, I reacted, maybe overreacted. If you've decided I'm a toughie, Alan, don't blame me. Blame the anti-woman culture of our public service.'

As they paused to admire the Mull of Kintyre, sticking out from the Scottish mist, Diana was still thinking feminist thoughts. For heaven's sake, wasn't the sovereign they were all supposed to serve a woman? Her indignation welled up again. Even the conspiracy of men who ran Britain could not stop the hereditary principle from producing an occasional queen.

'And haven't the last two of those done well?' she said, with a sudden, frivolous grin.

But Diana was confident the politicians would never let a woman become prime minister. The Tories would get rid of poor little Thatcher long before that ever arose. Alan said he wasn't so sure about that. Diana was not to be diverted from the personal part of her theme.

'The Corbett-Houston axis showed signs of thwarting my machiavellian schemes at Stormont. I thought a lot about how to get round that road-block. I'd gladly have bedded you, Alan, if I'd thought I could have penetrated – pardon the solecism! – your Presbyterian inhibitions. And not just for political reasons. You are quite fanciable, in a dour sort of way.'

Alan flushed and said huffily that people like her were wrong to assume that Christians, even Presbyterians, were obsessed by sex and sin. That was not his kind of religion.

'You seem to believe the idea behind the seventh commandment was just something first thought of three millennia or so ago, by a follower of a Middle-Eastern god.'

'Heavens, Alan, I didn't mean to offend your religious susceptibilities.'

He waved this aside.

'I've no more idea than you how it came to be written down, by Moses or somebody else, but it's no more than a codification of common sense in human relations. They don't work without trust. A contemporary humanist who doesn't believe in either God or marriage might express it in more modern style: "Don't cheat on your partners, otherwise they'll cheat on you. And both will lose the peace of mind that distinguishes love from screwing around."'

Diana wryly commented on his elegance of expression, and said the publisher of some new translation of the Bible ought to hire him. But she had a more serious intent.

'I accept the sense of that, provided a marriage really does bring peace of mind. But what if a wife can't make allowance for the strains a career imposes?'

Alan frowned, then emitted a long sigh.

'Or a husband is too obsessed by his career to notice his wife is falling out of love with him?'

'That too, Alan, though I doubt that you're exclusively to blame. Big bust-up last night, I assume?'

He nodded miserably, and they walked on in silence. At last Diana spoke.

'May I resume our academic discussion of extra-marital sex? What if quarrels within a marriage become a nightmare? Is an affair still unthinkable to you?'

Alan considered this to be less academic than *ad hominem*. He smiled at Diana, and found that he didn't mind. For all his troubles, he felt more light-hearted than at any time since he'd come to Stormont.

'Do I detect a suggestion of what's vulgarly called a little bit on the side?'

Diana said brusquely that she was certainly not proposing they should go for a roll in the hay, like a pair of teenagers, but she did happen to have with her the keys of a cottage in the Glens, which her spookish FO colleagues used.

'I still maintain my contacts in that world, Alan.'

He mentally played back dozens of conversations with her, wondering which pieces of her information or argument came from sources that he now distrusted profoundly.

But it was not only Alan Houston's political curiosity that was now aroused. As he looked at Diana – her long hair falling towards the striking bosom that had intrigued him when they first met, her sparkling, intelligent eyes, her infectious smile – he felt a rising desire he now rarely experienced with Mary. Was it curiosity or desire that prompted his next question? Alan was no longer in the mood to judge. He just knew he wanted this conversation to go on.

'You're not telling me you bed IRA men to obtain intelligence?'

This stung Diana.

'What do you think I am? Going abroad to lie for your country is a duty we diplomats accept cheerfully. Lying down over here, and thinking of England – or in my case Scotland – doesn't come into it. What we do with paramilitary thugs at our cottage, you chump, is *question them*. Sometimes rigorously enough for their fingernails to fall out.'

They walked on in silence. Then she smiled, drew a bunch of keys from her pocket, and said quietly: 'It's in Glendun, a glorious valley! Like to see it? No strings attached.'

Slowly Alan nodded his head.

As they turned to walk back to the car, he saw a man hurrying up the hill. When he came to within a hundred yards of them, Diana slipped her hand free from Alan's.

'It's a policeman. It almost looks as if he's come to speak to us. I let Dick's private office know roughly where we'd be.'

The man arrived, red in the face and breathless.

'Mr Alan Houston?'

Alan nodded.

'I'm Sergeant Bruce, RUC Portballintrae. It's bad news, I'm afraid, sir. Your son Peter's been kidnapped. We believe it's the IRA.'

Alan's head sang.

'Oh, God! Not Peter. Please, not Peter.'

Diana grabbed his arm, then turned back to the policeman.

'Let's get down to your station, Sergeant. I need to make phone calls. Perhaps you could arrange an escort to get us back to Stormont as quickly as possible.'

'We'll certainly need to do that, Ma'am. I can see you haven't heard that the IRA are resuming their campaign. This kidnapping is their first action. You're both high risk as well. Anyhow, I'm sorry to give Mr Houston such a shock. I'll find a drop of something to steady him when we get down below.'

[31]

Mary was forty minutes late arriving at the school. Since Christmas, when she first heard about security warnings, she had never once failed to be at the gates to meet Peter.

'But remember, cars sometimes break down,' she had told him. 'So if I'm more than ten minutes late, you'd better go home on the bus.'

That day, the day after Alan warned her about Sean's threats, she was very late. When she did reach the school, the road was crowded with police cars and a policeman told her that a boy had been kidnapped. Even before the headteacher broke the news to her, she knew it was Peter.

He had been walking from the school gates to the bus stop when two men pushed him into the back of a car. Another boy who was only thirty yards away saw what happened and heard Peter's shouts. As the car sped away, he ran back into the school to raise the alarm. He remembered the registration number. Later police found the car burnt out in West Belfast.

An hour after the kidnap, a man using what the jargon described as 'a recognised code word' telephoned the *Evening Chronicle*. He was formally announcing the end of the informal ceasefire – the same news Howard Considine had heard from his contact a few hours earlier. This caller also said that the Provisional IRA were holding Peter as a hostage and they would reveal later their terms for his safety.

The newspaper's switchboard operator was experienced in this bizarre world of terrorist calls. She had taken down several previous IRA statements, signed with its traditional pseudonym, P. O'Neill. This middle-aged woman, who spent most of her waking hours worrying about her policeman husband, found this custom less intriguing than visiting journalists did. P. O'Neill had made announcements that led to bereavement for too many of her friends. She hated the play-acting brutality of it all.

She told the police that after reading his formal statement the caller had suddenly lost his temper. He yelled at her, and though she couldn't swear to the exact words, she was sure of their import.

'This boy's father's the Quisling who sabotaged Ireland's best chance of freedom in a thousand years. Let him sweat a bit! And if he wants his son back alive, he'd better persuade his English masters to do exactly what we say.'

Then he had hung up.

Mary was driven to Stormont Castle in a police car. She told the RUC detective who went with her that she had been held up by queues at an army check-point. The oath witnesses take in court requires them to tell 'the truth, the whole truth, and nothing but the truth'. Few of us, in ordinary life, find the first and third clauses difficult. What many stumble over is 'the whole truth'. Doesn't a white lie often make life run more smoothly?

In Mary's case, the whole truth was that even without a check-point she would have been half an hour late arriving to meet Peter, having spent a long lunch-time in a country pub with Colin Newhouse.

When she had telephoned Colin just after breakfast, she was still smarting from her row with her husband.

'I need to talk to you, talk seriously I mean.'

Over a lunch lasting three hours they talked about the state of their marriages, Mary admitting that hers was on the rocks. They didn't decide anything about the future. Mary was not an impulsive person: she had never intended to cross the Rubicon that day, she just wanted to look to see what was on the farther shore.

Colin did know what he wanted. He told her again that his marriage and his academic job in Belfast had both run out of steam, and he was determined to return to England. He would like her to join him. Mary smiled uncertainly. He went to get them another drink and they talked on.

Afterwards, as Colin watched her walk away across the pub's car

134

park, he believed she would agree to live with him. When she'd kissed him, she had put her arms round his neck, which showed far more commitment than anything she had done before. Then he heard her murmur in his ear: 'I'll be in touch, Colin, very soon indeed. I'm nearly at the end of my tether too.'

Their kiss was a lingering one, and it was not just Colin who prolonged it. Mary knew in her heart that this was a lovers' kiss.

Bill Simpson, the principal private secretary, was giving Mary a cup of tea when Alan arrived at Stormont. She almost spilled it as she ran into his arms and burst into tears. She might no longer love her husband, but they had created this child together. At that moment Mary felt the whole burden of responsibility for having lost Peter. Later she would blame Alan's job, but for now Mary could only think that when she should have been protecting her child, she had been with Colin Newhouse.

The first coherent words she spoke were to repeat the half-truth that the army road-block had held her up. The next was about her elder son.

'I've phoned Brian, he's catching the next plane. The police are picking him up at Aldergrove, and they'll bring him here. I wanted him with me. You think they can keep *him* safe, don't you?'

As Alan reassured her, he thought how odd it was that she relied so much now on their elder son, still only eighteen. He supposed this was a sign of how far their marriage had deteriorated. Alan shuddered. He had lost his younger son and was in the process of losing his wife. His world was falling apart. He felt more alone than ever.

These people around him – Charles, Dick, Diana, Bill Simpson, the police and army officers, some of whom he regarded as friends, not just colleagues – might appear anguished by what was happening to him and Mary. Their compassion was genuine, but when they went home tonight, they would be able to sleep, and to think dispassion-ately about the kidnapping. A great gulf divided them from him.

Alan winced. Peter had fallen into a gulf, perhaps for ever.

When Alan and Mary were taken into Charles Corbett's room, Dick Heston was also there. Diana had remained in her own office. She told

Charles she ought to stay by her phone, to keep in touch with the police. He thought that was wise – Charles was not as olympian as he appeared, and knew that Diana would not be Mary's most comfortable companion at this moment.

The conversation was confused. Reassurance from Charles and Dick, anxious questions from Mary, which neither of them could answer. Dick explained that until the IRA telephoned its demands, they did not know many answers. But they were confident they would get Peter back. Alan, like a doctor who contracts a fatal disease, knew too much about terrorism for his own peace of mind, so he kept silent.

What made him speak at last was Mary's final question. She recalled that Alan had once told her a chilling story from the earliest stages of the IRA campaign. Several businessmen had been kidnapped, in one case murdered. Harold Wilson's cabinet had discussed what they would do if one of their own number, a minister, were taken hostage. The unanimous decision was that they 'would have to let him go'.

'They said they couldn't pay Danegeld,' Mary sobbed.

Alan looked shattered.

'But that was the cabinet, Mary. It was a reasonable decision for them to take about themselves, and a brave one, but it didn't concern a twelve-year-old boy. They wouldn't have said that about their families. No government would.'

Nobody else spoke. Even in Mary's anguish her sensitive nose picked up the scent of political animals keeping their options open. As soon as Brian arrived she said she would like to go home. Charles embraced her.

'Yes, get what rest you can, my dear. We all feel for you. Everything that can be done will be done. Everything – I can promise you that.'

She thanked him, and soon they were in a police car – manned today, she noticed, by two plain-clothes men. As it bowled down the ceremonial avenue from Stormont, a desperate thought came to Mary.

'This is what remains of my family. Us three, in the back of a police car. I ought to face the truth – Peter's gone. I'll never see him again.'

[32]

Alan persuaded her to take a sleeping-pill. Without comment, he moved back into their bedroom. He couldn't risk taking a pill himself; he had asked Charles to make sure he was told any further news, and he wanted to be alert. No phone call came.

Alan succeeded only in dozing fitfully. He kept wondering how Peter was being treated. From time to time a guilty question inserted itself: when the sergeant came puffing up the cliffs at the Causeway, what point had his relationship with Diana reached?

Alan wanted to believe he'd only been satisfying his curiosity about what safe houses looked like. But as he tossed on the bed, trying not to waken Mary, truth whispered in his ear. He had been about to mark the end of his marriage by breaking the vows he had taken twenty years before.

As the night hours dragged on, Alan Houston despised himself for thinking about his sexual wanderings, when he should have been thinking only about Peter's safety. But Peter's safety was now beyond his control, beyond the control of everybody except the ruthless men who held him.

He still felt disloyal – not to Mary, for whom he felt less and less loyalty – disloyal to Peter, poor, innocent Peter, wherever in Ireland he was tonight, Peter, who thought his parents' marriage was eternal, as long as an afternoon in the cricket field.

Once or twice when Mary whimpered in her sleep he put his arm around her. Without wakening she moved away. Mary, deep in her drugged sleep, was in a similar state to Alan's. She couldn't get the problems of Peter and of Colin Newhouse disentangled in her troubled subconscious. Her husband did not come into her dreams that night; he hadn't been there for some time.

Just after four, when the first glimmers of dawn showed around the curtains, Alan went quietly downstairs to make tea. As he sat warming his hands on the beaker, he reached the same conclusion as Mary's the previous evening. Peter was unlikely to be released alive.

He stood at the window gazing out into the garden. It was one of the longest days of the year. The early sun filtered through the willow tree, and the birds began to sing. Nature was unfeelingly cheerful.

His thoughts were invaded by memories of the death-bed of a friend who had lived to be ninety-two. Almost forty years before, his son had been killed in a road accident, and though he'd had a full life, he had never ceased to grieve. As the old man sank into the mists of death, he murmured to Alan, 'I've always railed against the fates for bringing our deaths in the wrong order.'

Alan now saw what he meant. It seemed so little to ask of God that he keep the generations in their appropriate places in the queue for the exit.

Raddled by sleeplessness and fear, he felt even more sorry for himself. There were times when you were on your own, totally. Some profound emotions just couldn't be shared. He supposed it would be like that at the very end of life. Somebody would hold the dying hand for a time, but then the loneliness of pain would take over, the agony of death. Nobody had stayed around long enough to tell us about that. Assuredly, nobody could share it.

And at the last, oblivion. Unless there was something afterwards, which he hoped there might be. Alan dropped into a cramped doze in his armchair. As he slept, he dreamt that the man greeting him at the pearly gates, as in a thousand cartoons, was St Peter. It was the name that wakened him.

'Not my own lovely Peter, please God, not that. I can't bear Peter dying.'

Soon he was churning over his thoughts of the night. He had not been concerned then about immortality so much as immorality. Alan Houston's puritanism was catching up with him, at the most vulnerable moment of his life.

Mary and Brian came down, and the three of them had what breakfast they could manage. As they were finishing, the doorbell rang. It was Edward Mason, an old clergyman who had known Alan's family since long before he was born. His visit today could be embarrassing. Mary was agnostic, and she had never met Edward before. She was also distressed beyond belief. Alan feared she might resent his arrival.

Edward Mason had a domed grey head that reminded Mary of John Reith, the first head of the BBC. He'd been a tall man in his younger days, but was stooped with age, his face lined with the constant pain of his arthritis. His brown eyes were compassionate.

As he came through the door Edward spread out his arms, grasped Mary and Alan's hands in each of his, and murmured that this was no time for religiosity. He had just come to show his love and concern. If they wanted him to say a prayer, he would gladly do so, but he didn't mind. They all knew what they wanted God to do. To Alan's surprise, Mary murmured that she would like him to pray with them. So they all stood around, Alan and Mary holding each other, Brian looking lost and devastated, while Edward spoke of their love, their hope and their fears. Then he embraced Alan and Mary, shook hands with Brian and left.

Alan and Mary didn't speak about him after he'd gone but separately each thought the same, as people who have been married a long time often do. They both wondered whether, if he had been a Catholic priest rather than a Presbyterian minister, they would have wanted him to take their confession.

There had been a time when the Houstons loved each other so much that they discussed coincidences like that. Now they could not even enjoy the support of shared pain. Their intimacy had eroded, slowly at first, but now irretrievably.

The agent of that erosion was mutual deceit. Even their family's tragedy could not raise the curtain that now hung between Mary and Alan, heavy as velvet, impenetrable as steel.

[33]

That afternoon the IRA's terms were telephoned to the *Evening Chronicle*. They were holding Peter Houston hostage for one of their men who was mortally ill in Wormwood Scrubs. They wanted him transferred to a prison in Northern Ireland. There was no hint about what would happen if the government refused.

Prisoners had been moved for humanitarian reasons before. In this case, however, medical reports from the prison said that Tommy Hughes – Liam's cousin, it soon emerged – might not be as ill as he pretended. The doctors needed time and further tests. After an arms raid in Berkshire, Hughes had been given twenty years at the Old Bailey. This long sentence was one of the IRA disasters which had caused Liam and others to think about a ceasefire.

The Government's problem was stark: if Hughes really was dying they could allow him back to Ulster, but they didn't want a dangerous terrorist who was not seriously ill to be transferred just to make escape easier, or so that he could benefit from Stormont's more generous parole.

This first telephone demand was worrying, but clear. Charles authorised his press office to release the IRA's terms to the media. He hoped this would avoid wild speculation, which might make the task of freeing Peter more difficult. However, it did not work out like that.

The next day brought a second call purporting to give the IRA's terms. This message, telephoned to the BBC in Belfast, no longer linked the demand to transfer Tommy Hughes with the kidnapping. Peter Houston was not even mentioned. Instead, the caller said if the authorities did not move Hughes, the IRA would bomb the London Underground.

When Charles was told of this threat, he closed his eyes and shuddered. An attack on the extensive tube system was almost impossible to guard against. It had been a recurrent nightmare ever since the Troubles began.

The BBC switchboard had standing instructions to turn on a tape-recorder a soon as anyone claimed to represent a terrorist organisation, so the RUC Special Branch was able to hear a full voice recording. The caller sounded eccentric, and there was no code word. The police decided the message was not genuine, and Charles Corbett agreed. He asked the BBC Controller for Northern Ireland not to raise public alarm by broadcasting a threat that seemed to be a hoax.

Although this second telephone call was not announced, veiled hints began to appear in London newspapers. After a few days of garbled stories, Roger Corfield approached the Controller. Roger remained the same effervescent reporter who had shared the Houstons' first breakfast-time in Belfast. Because he worked for Network News in London, he did not often meet the Controller. Now he high-hatted this grey functionary. The Controller had no news experience, having risen through Music and Arts. Roger's approach was insidious.

'I'm afraid the Head of News in London will get very upset if he hears BBCNI seems to be censoring information the public's got a right to know.'

Roger subtly added that HON – the BBC delights in acronyms – might feel impelled to complain to the Board of Management, even the Governors.

Broadcasting House in Belfast no longer enjoyed much independence – 'nothing like as much as those spiky Jocks', as the Director-General had once said, in a period of turbulence with the colleagues in Glasgow. The Troubles had put Belfast in a client relationship with London. In face of Roger's bullying, the Controller was not about to stand on his dignity. Surely now that rumours had appeared in some newspapers, the Corporation was freed of any obligation to secrecy? He agreed that Roger should prepare a story for the *Nine O'Clock News*.

When Diana warned Charles he gave a weary sigh. He had noted a pattern in press coverage of IRA statements. No sooner had one organisation received the first phone call, backed by the code word, than alternative theses began to be aired. These were not blatant journalistic manufactures. There was always a source of some kind, though often no more reliable than 'friends of the Prince of Wales'.

Charles considered editors very odd characters.

'They make a sanctimonious fuss about the lobby system at Westminster, implying that the Number Ten spokesman is force-feeding their lazy political correspondents like so many Périgord geese. Yet when their man in Belfast hears "exclusively" some implausible rumour, they salivate like Pavlovian dogs.'

He said editors' normal scepticism fell into disuse in stories about Ulster. They suspended disbelief, as in any imaginative art. After all, neither the IRA nor the government was likely to sue for libel.

Roger Corfield thought himself much better informed than his local colleagues, who broadcast only on Ulster programmes. After his story appeared on the News and was followed up by the other media, Roger telephoned Diana.

'I feel it my duty to warn the Government through you, Diana, that this threat to the London Underground ought to be taken seriously.'

Diana laughed.

'I might have guessed, Roger. So it was you who leaked that phone call the BBC received to a few newspaper chums, and then persuaded the poor old Controller you must follow up these leaks. What a trooper!'

Roger hotly denied this, but quickly resumed his urgent warning.

'Listen, Diana, I've been picking up hints about bombing the tube from my Republican contacts for . . . oh, a month or more.'

Diana said that wasn't what the police or army thought. Corfield snorted.

'If the Paddies act dozily over this one, Scotland Yard may dismiss it. They're far too inclined to accept that the RUC know their own patch. But a few of us hacks are deeper into that particular muckheap than PC Prod.'

When Diana told Charles about this conversation, he shoved his spectacles angrily on to his brow.

'Just after I came here I had a similarly earnest warning from

Corfield. He told me, in a hushed voice, that Loyalist paramilitaries planned to assassinate me or one of my junior ministers, just because we were Labour. Seemed a bit unfair, that. Have you noticed, Diana, how confused the hacks get when allocating Right and Left labels to people over here? Anyhow, the RUC and Security people advised me to forget it, and we remain unassassinated.'

Charles acknowledged that Roger Corfield didn't lack contacts, zeal, or self-confidence. His imagination was over-developed, but he was a good broadcaster and amusing company, if you had plenty of time. 'I must confess, however, that I find it difficult to take young Mr Corfield quite at his own valuation.'

He knew, of course, that it was dangerous for a politician to take any public interest in which reporter editors chose to cover their actions. But he worried about it all the same.

'How can the public make any sense of what I'm trying to do in Belfast if it's reported by conspiracy theorists and prima donnas? Don't the BBC need a bright young man to make New Zealand less boring?'

The final straw for Charles that day was a call from the Prime Minister.

'Ye gods, Charles, London Transport plan to start random body-searches at tube stations tomorrow. With the shrewd judgement for which that management is noted, these'll probably begin at Oxford Circus during evening rush-hour. That'll cause chaos, and make the public even more fed up with Ulster.'

Charles said he shared the police belief that the London Underground plot was fantasy. The Prime Minister's reply was impatient.

'Yes, yes, I'm sure the young lad *is* their real bargaining counter, that the Underground threat *is* fantasy. But it's a fantasy that's appeared on the *Nine O'Clock News*, so the Great British Public will believe it's true. And the London section of the GBP will kick me. So I have no alternative but to kick you, Charles. Extract digit, old boy, right? Get a grip on this kidnap business. I'll give you whatever help you need with the Home Office about transferring the prisoner – never my favourite department, that.'

As Tom Sanderson banged the phone down, Charles thought, not for the first time, that politics was an ungrateful sod of a profession. It was several minutes before he took in that the Prime Minister had promised him vital help. Detached as Tom sometimes seemed, he knew his government's only objective must be to restore Peter Houston to his parents before the IRA did something dreadful to him. Therefore Tommy Hughes would have to be moved. The Prime Minister knew he must pay Danegeld, whatever the home secretary said.

[34]

Diana organised a meeting of a dozen journalists. She played them the tape of the telephone call threatening the London Underground, and a senior policeman pointed out the deficiencies of the story. Charles hoped this would convince the media that the threat was not serious. In Roger Corfield's case this proved to be a forlorn hope. He had already persuaded the *Late Night Special* programme to take a report from him. He'd given this a working title of which he was proud, 'The Disaster Scenario'.

As they dispersed, Sam McCluskey drew Diana aside. 'I know who that caller is, but I don't know where my duty lies.'

Within a couple of minutes, Sam was facing Charles Corbett and Dick Heston. Charles asked if he was quite sure he recognised the voice on the tape.

'I needn't tell you, Sam, it could have serious consequences for him. And, of course, if he *is* speaking for the IRA, identifying him could have serious consequences for you. I feel obliged to say that, just in case you have any doubts.'

'Thanks,' said Sam drily, 'but doubts about who he is are not my problem. Or doubts about his membership of the IRA, who wouldn't touch him with a barge-pole.'

He then described events four or five years before, when he had been a lecturer at Queen's University. The man whose voice he'd heard on the tape had belonged briefly to his tutorial group. His subject was 'the methodology of political studies', which Sam described as his feeble attempt to inject some honesty into political thinking and writing by the young. With most of his students he had felt that at least something rubbed off, even in a place like Belfast,

145

where they all arrived, from seventeen and a quarter upwards, with their prejudices in full muscular development.

'But this man was something different. He wasn't simply a convinced Republican – perhaps about a third of the group were that, just as most of the rest were Unionists. He was also deep into fantasy. He didn't buy just the ready-made fantasies that the propaganda machines peddled. He invented his own – and he had a fertile imagination.'

After other students complained that this garrulous misfit was wasting their time, Sam took him aside and suggested that, since he seemed to have interests far removed from Sam's teaching on methodology, he might be attending a class that would be useless to him.

'He took the hint and didn't come back. Soon after that he left Queen's. I've heard he's scraping a living in London as a journalistic tipster. I've seen his by-line, though just once, in the *Irish Times*.'

Dick Heston asked, 'What's his name, Sam?'

'Look, I can't put a former student of mine in trouble with the police just because the bloody fool indulges in escapades like this. Can't you accept that this phone call was the act of an inadequate? It's just the kind of nonsense that might divert the police from getting young Houston out.'

Charles nodded. This was precisely what he feared. But Dick cut in to say that MI5 had traced the phone call to a box in Shepherd's Bush. Sam had just confirmed that his student was now in London. Didn't that prove that MI5 were wiser than the police in taking the threat seriously?

Charles was about to disagree, but Dick interrupted him with a sonorous declaration.

'Secretary of State, I must advise you, now that Mr McCluskey has told us this, we can't just leave it there. The media are already running with the story. You've heard about Corfield's "Disaster Scenario"? If anything did happen on the Underground we'd be left swinging in the wind.'

Charles winced. The media again, stopping him taking common-sense decisions! He thanked Sam for his information, and said he'd have to think it over. When Sam had gone, Charles turned on Dick with ill-concealed irritation.

'Let me tell you, Permanent Secretary, what's bugging me. We need like a hole in the head a great stand-off over confidentiality of sources with the whole media confraternity. Of course, it's not a classical journalist's case – after all, McCluskey was an academic at the time. But any suspicion that we're abusing Press ethics will set the whole tribe off, in London as well as Belfast. Result: diversion of effort from our single, overwhelming duty, to free Peter Houston.'

Dick remained firm. The police must at least ask McCluskey who the man threatening the Underground system was. Charles finally agreed, but said it must be done carefully. He would speak to the Chief Constable himself. Dick frowned. He liked to keep contacts with police and army under his personal control.

The interrogation took place the next day, in the editor's office of the *Chronicle*. To the mature, all policemen look younger every year. But this was the youngest Detective Constable either McCluskey or Fred Hargreaves had ever seen. Even his aspirant black moustache couldn't conceal his extreme youth. He was dressed in a suit for the occasion. Sam guessed he would normally wear a wind-cheater. When Fred said he would like to be present, 'as a sort of prisoner's friend', the Constable laughed.

'I seem to have left my handcuffs back in the station, sir.'

He obeyed to the letter his instructions not to be heavy-handed, writing meticulously into his notebook everything Sam said. The key points were his belief that he recognised the voice, and his views on the caller's character.

When the policeman asked politely for the phone-caller's name, Sam said he couldn't give it, and cited the journalists' code of conduct, as applied to his academic years. Hargreaves thought he did this in such a confused and unconvincing manner that, if repeated in a witness-box during any contempt of court case, it would cut the legs from under his defence counsel.

The young detective took the refusal calmly.

'Ah, well sir, as you'll understand that's well above my level of competence. Pity you can't give me the name. If I went back with something the secretary of state himself couldn't find out, it would do my promotion prospects no end of good, so it would.'

He smiled again, and waited. Then he snapped his notebook closed.

'Well, if you won't, you won't. But from listening to his phone call a few times, and from your description of his personality, I'd guess that it's Eamonn Murphy, the so-called journalist who lives in West London.'

Fred looked furtively at Sam, but neither of them spoke. The policeman smiled and began to reminisce. About a year ago the Metropolitan Police in Shepherd's Bush had taken to telephoning each time an informant told them the latest mad tale Eamonn was recounting in the pubs.

'On one occasion, he'd been to Dublin, and a friend on the IRA's Army Council said they were going to snatch the Prime Minister from Chequers, by helicopter, if you please. Another time he'd received a call from Boston, and the Irish-American connection had organised dissident CIA men to help smuggle arms into Lough Swilly.'

Unbelievable as these reports had seemed, Special Branch at first went through the motions of checking them out with informers. Now Eamonn Murphy had become a joke between the RUC and the Met.

'We tell them they ought to nick him for wasting police time. After this one, I wouldn't be surprised if they dumped him back on us, under the Prevention of Terrorism Act. Though in his case it ought to be the Prevention of Daft Rumours Act.'

After he left, Fred looked quizzically at Sam, who nodded his head.

Later, a deflated Dick received the RUC's reasons for saying that the London Underground story was baseless. Charles nodded when he was told.

'That's not what's worrying me any more, Dick. I've just received a horrifying report from the chief constable. Special Branch have heard on their grapevine that Peter's kidnapping is not simply a lever to get Tommy Hughes transferred. The IRA want that all right, but they also want to punish his father, whatever that means. They blame Alan for the sudden souring of their discussions with Government go-betweens.'

Diana burst out indignantly: 'But that's monstrously unfair to Alan. He bust a gut to get these talks going.'

Charles nodded. Of course the IRA was overestimating Alan's influence, compared to that of the PM. But this report did have frightening implications. He dreaded to think what they meant by punishing the father.

'Peter Houston's been in their hands for more than a week. We've got to get him free before something awful happens. We must just hope Tommy Hughes is still the key to that, though nobody can be sure. This is certainly more important than nonsenses about the tube.'

[35]

The next day Charles suggested Alan should come in and have a talk.

'Would you like to bring Mary?'

'I don't think she's up to it yet. Her mood's very low.'

As soon as Alan entered Stormont Castle, Charles's private secretary, Bill Simpson, grasped his hand in mute sympathy. Alan's response was grim.

'You've been through something like this, Bill, when they murdered your father. I think they'll do the same to Peter.'

Simpson shuddered and said he hoped that wouldn't happen. Alan must not despair – Charles was putting extreme pressure on everybody to make sure Peter was freed.

As they entered the secretary of state's office, Bill told his boss that the chief constable, Bob Harbinson, had just warned him of a security development. He would speak to Charles when he had details.

Alan started, and said it must be news about Peter. Bad news, his expression said. Charles intervened at once.

'No, it won't be about that. I'm expecting a report from a police stake-out on the Shankill. Bob thinks they may be on to an arms dump.'

Alan sat back, content that nothing dreadful had happened to his son. Charles wondered what it must be like to suspect every phone call was an announcement of disaster.

Charles intended this meeting only as a diversion from Alan's worries, a sign that the Houstons' dreadful plight was not forgotten. But he decided to begin with the one piece of good news he had.

'I'm cautiously optimistic that we'll get Tommy Hughes transferred to the Maze. The PM's now on our side against the Home Office. I've got all sorts of reservations about the Old Man, but he does get the big decisions right.'

Alan looked relieved, though Charles warned him they could not be sure it would lead to Peter's immediate release. He had expected that Alan would arrive armed with questions about what was being done to release his son. He had prepared himself to put the best possible gloss on what was happening, which was very little. The police, army and intelligence units had still failed to pick up any hint of where the boy was being held. Charles was nonplussed when Alan sat slumped in his chair, saying nothing, leaving his chief to fill the vacuum. What on earth could he talk about in such circumstances, something that wouldn't seem utterly insensitive?

After leaving a gap that seemed interminable, Charles blundered into political gossip. He knew that Alan, like every other political animal, was intrigued by Tom Sanderson's complex personality. So in near-panic he decided to end the agonising silence by revealing his true feelings about his boss. None of them was flattering. They were peppered with anecdote.

'Have I ever told you what Tom said when he asked me to take on this job? In his most half-witted manner, our revered leader asked whether I was a Protestant Jew or a Catholic Jew. I gathered it was a joke he'd been told in the Division Lobby by an Ulster Unionist. That figures – what a bunch of plodders!'

The PM was really trying to find out whether Charles had any deep prejudices about religion that would get in the way of being effective in Northern Ireland.

Just then, Bill Simpson came in again.

'I've been listening on the police wavelength. There's been a car chase down near the Border in South Armagh. Are you content to wait for Bob Harbinson's call, or will I get them on the line right away?'

Charles suspected this incident might involve Peter Houston after all, but with his mind full of the report about the IRA's determination to punish Alan, he played for time. No use causing premature alarm.

'Thanks, Bill, but I'll wait for Bob's call. He'll be busy.'

He looked across at Alan, who had scarcely reacted to the interruption. Charles was relieved, though surprised, that his adviser had not made the connection with Peter. Alan had scarcely moved in his chair since he sat down. His thoughts must be miles away. Charles did not know what to do, so in despair he returned to his story.

'When the PM asked this footling question about my Jewishness, I took it at face value, and replied solemnly that I was "Liberal Synagogue, non-practising".'

He had then given the PM his disillusioned view of religion by quoting from *King Lear*:

As flies to wanton boys are we to the gods,
They kill us for their sport.

And that, he said, looking to see if Alan would react, was not a bad slogan for a British Minister plunged into the most theological bog – the Middle East perhaps excepted – in this agnostic world.

In as much as Charles had any plan for this conversation, he had hoped that his philosophical coat-trailing would arouse Alan from this impossible reverie. At last, with a sigh, he rose to the bait.

'I know agnostics still think of themselves as intellectually adventurous, Charles, and it might have been true in Darwin's time, but agnosticism's now the fashionable view.'

Now that he was momentarily aroused, Alan drifted into an aggressive lecture that Charles was happy not to interrupt.

'It's not a theological bog here. It's a sectarian bog. That's different, and worse. I was brought up on the liberal and rational wing of Belfast Nonconformity, and I do get irritated by non-believers who shadow-box with an enemy they've invented for their own delight. They conjure up people who believe in the literal truth of the scriptures, down to the last burnt sacrifice. People who've never given a thought to *The Origin of Species*, never suffered a moment of Tennyson's honest doubt.'

Charles was so relieved to have found a way of breaking the corrosive silence of their first meeting since the kidnapping that he decided he must keep this strange conversation going. So he said mischievously that he'd concluded from the press that Christianity was either about Protestants and Catholics in Belfast; or about Rangers and

Celtic in Glasgow; or whether the C of E ought to have women priests; and whether Catholic priests ought to take vows of celibacy; and if they did, whether they should bother keeping them. And, oh yes, whether the C of E ought to allow homosexual clergy.

'What I can't understand, Alan, is why people like you insist on ignoring these sectarian and sexual delights, and bring in all this grown-up stuff – about the nature of the universe, the conflict between good and evil, the divinity of Jesus, and whether science has said the last word about Creation. News editors simply don't understand it.'

Alan smiled ruefully. He found it difficult to concentrate on this discussion, but he knew Charles was doing the best he could to help him through an impossible afternoon.

'Of course news editors don't understand religion. The practical side of Christianity is meant to be love for your fellow man, doing for others what you would like them to do for you. That's not news, though maybe it was two thousand years ago. Anyhow, there's precious little love around in Ireland nowadays, as I'm discovering.'

Charles was relieved when the red telephone on his desk rang. There was anxiety in his voice as he greeted Bob Harbinson. Alan started. He had just realised that the car chase might involve his son. Charles ended the call abruptly.

'Mustn't keep you, Bob. Phone me back when you hear anything more. Anything.'

He swung his chair round to face Alan again.

'The RUC caught a glimpse of Peter in the back of a car near the border. At least, the observer is sure it was him, though the driver thought it might be a young girl. They first noticed the car doing a noisy U-turn at an army road-block. They're still in pursuit.'

His political adviser's face had drained of blood, and he looked despairingly out of the window.

'It's good news, Alan – it proves Peter's alive.'

Alan winced. This was the first time, after endless phone conversations, that Charles had acknowledged his son might not survive. He aroused himself to speak.

'But they haven't got him back yet, Charles? Where is the car heading for? Are the police likely to catch it, without a crash or a shoot-out? Did Bob say how Peter looked?'

Charles shook his head. The chief constable had only had the first flashes from the patrol.

'Do you want to telephone Mary?'

Charles focused on practicalities, rather than let Alan drift into painful speculation about Peter's fate. But the reply was a shake of the head.

'This'll only put the wind up her, like it's frightened me. We'd better wait for more definite news. I can't face talking to her yet.'

Then he slowly confessed to Charles that for months now Mary and he had been drifting apart. Their marriage was all but on the rocks.

'Result of your coming to Ulster, I suppose?'

Charles was not as oblivious of the lives of the people who worked for him as his aloof manner suggested. At his encounters with Mary he'd concluded that Alan's job was not giving *her* much satisfaction. Perhaps, one way or another, Alan himself was not satisfying her either. Charles felt a moment of guilt about how hard he was working his adviser. But this passed quickly. He hadn't reached his level in politics without a streak of ruthlessness.

Alan confirmed that his marital troubles had begun because Mary resented having to live in Ulster and the disruption of her career. But now he felt that both she and Brian blamed him for what had happened to Peter.

'She thinks I've neglected her and the family. She hates it here, says the people she mixes with bore her. She may also think I'm getting too close to Diana. She may be right about that.'

Charles didn't comment. Bill Simpson brought in a slip of paper. Charles read it, frowned, and then said, 'A message from the chief constable. There's been some sort of altercation with the Gardai on the border. Bob's checking it out personally. He'll be back to us ASAP, but it may be an hour or more. I think you'd better stay with me, don't you, Alan?'

[36]

Charles glanced pityingly at the pale, lined face of his political adviser, and knew they were in for a harrowing hour. If Alan churned over the unknowable while they waited for news, he could only hurt himself. They'd just have to talk about something entirely different, however insensitive that seemed.

'Do you know what first made me like the House of Commons? It was the beer, the best in London. Being a Yorkshireman, I'm something of a connoisseur.'

Alan tried to show interest. Charles was doing his best. But he wondered what was happening on the border. Or maybe it was all over . . .

When he refocused, Charles was still speaking. In the mid-fifties, when he'd become an MP, the Labour Party had fewer members from the law, school-teaching and the universities, far more trade unionists, especially miners. These working-men were always complaining about the quality of the beer served in Commons' bars. Eventually an exasperated catering manager invited them to make alternative suggestions.

'At last one old fellow from South Wales, a cross between a prop-forward and a pit-prop, addressed this sophisticated restaurateur.

'"Look, boyo, we don't want no more of this London piss, see? We want Miners' Federation Bitter, like in our clubs." And ever since, Tory MPs who wouldn't easily distinguish between Nye Bevan and the devil incarnate happily sup up their Fed like the miners.'

They laughed at the story. Alan was trying hard to attend to this inconsequential chatter. But still the telephone didn't ring, and Charles judged they would need something more substantial than MPs' drinking habits to stop his adviser relapsing into harmful imaginings.

'Despite all my study, and all your instruction, Alan, people in Northern Ireland still puzzle me. Why is it that a province so outwardly religious displays so little of the Christian charity you've been talking about? Why do people in places with no pretensions to holiness show more tolerance of their fellow beings?'

'That offends me too, Charles. There's too much hell-fire, Old Testament, hate-your-enemy religion, and too little of the gospel of love. That's equally true of appalling missioners who frighten Catholic youngsters, and of the crazier Protestant fundamentalists.'

Alan's attention lapsed, and Charles knew he was wondering why the chief constable's inquiry was taking so long. At that moment, the red telephone jangled the silence.

'What news, Bob?' Charles said, as he picked up the receiver. Then his face clouded over, and Alan's hands tightened on the arms of his chair. There must have been a shoot-out. Had Peter been killed?

Charles saw the signs of panic, and immediately said, half as a question to Harbinson, half in assurance to Alan: 'So they've got away? But no shooting?'

As Bob Harbinson began his account of what was happening, Charles told him he'd ask Alan to listen in on the extension. The chief constable said his patrol was almost on the tail of the IRA car when they reached the Garda check-point on the Armagh-Monaghan border. The guard on duty began to question the driver of the first car.

'Apparently he kept looking through the window at the small boy in the back seat, between two other men. By the way, both my constables are now convinced this was Peter.'

Alan's bewildered mind still wasn't sure whether this was good or bad news. Now at last they knew where his son was. But what were his chances of survival?

The chief constable said another guard had stopped the RUC car thirty yards back. He began a bantering conversation, but they shouted they were in hot pursuit of an IRA kidnap squad.

'My men jumped out and ran up the road to the border post, just as a Garda sergeant emerged from the wooden hut. When he saw the

RUC uniforms he pushed his subordinate aside, and waved the IRA car through. It sped into the Republic.'

Charles exploded in anger. Bob Harbinson murmured his regrets that they hadn't managed to free Peter straightaway. He assured Alan that his son had looked well, though frightened. He would come across to Stormont to tell them about a talk he'd had with the Garda Commissioner. Some of what had been said was too sensitive for the telephone.

When he put down the receiver, Charles suggested they ought now to pass on what information they had to Mary, otherwise she might hear a garbled report on the tea-time news. He was surprised Alan was not straining to make the call. This, after all, was the first sighting of their child since he was kidnapped. Sensing Alan's reluctance to face an unpleasant conversation, he said, 'Would you like me to tell her what we know so far?' Alan nodded gloomily.

At first Mary was elated that the policemen had seen Peter. But when she heard that he had been whisked off into the Republic, and that the RUC had not been able to continue the chase, she became at once indignant and tearful.

'The Israelis wouldn't have taken much notice of the border, would they? Anyhow, aren't the Irish supposed to be our allies in the fight against terrorism?'

Charles calmed her down, saying that after they had seen the chief constable, Alan would be home soon with up-to-date news. He thought her response was chilly. His political adviser had not exaggerated. To say he and his wife had drifted apart was an under-statement.

During the telephone call Alan put his head in his hands. His breath came in rapid gasps. Charles saw he was close to breaking down. How on earth could he avert this, put in the fifteen minutes till the chief constable arrived?

'Stay as calm as you can, Alan. Probably best if I just keep talking. You won't mind if I make it a monologue?'

Alan nodded miserably.

'The only time I've regretted losing all religious conviction was when my mother died of cancer last year. I dreaded the weekly visits, when I brought her gifts she'd never use, and talked about trivia. Seemed a futile way for two people who once loved each other to spend their last times together.'

What made it worse was that, coming from an Orthodox Jewish family, he had 'married out'. Although his wonderful wife had died a year before, even on her death-bed his mother hadn't been able to conceal her disapproval of a woman she had refused to meet.

Charles dropped into silent reflection for several minutes. Then he spoke suddenly, almost urgently.

'There's all the difference in the world, Alan, between my agnosticism and the indifferentism of thoughtless people. I think I can claim to be an intellectual. I just find – *found*, when I was trying ineffectually to comfort my dying mother – that I could get no further than the word "incomprehensible". I'm not saying "I don't care", but, reluctantly: "I *can't* know." Does that make some sort of sense?'

Alan nodded again. How much he was hearing of all this, Charles did not know. He talked on about his mother: she had chosen to leave hospital and die at home, in the country farmhouse she and his late father had bought after they escaped from the Nazis just before the war.

'It was like something out of a Victorian novel. My two sisters were there, of course, but also my mother's brother and sister, and a couple of cousins I'd never met before. Jews are almost as engrossed by the rituals of death as the Irish.'

At the end, just his two sisters and himself were in her room. His mother's breathing was by now shallow and noisy. All any of them could think to do was to stroke her cheeks with their fingers, or wipe the spume that quickly accumulated on her lips. Life at such times, near one's original roots in parents and family, seemed to happen in bright colours. The images remained on your mind's eye for ever.

Charles sat silent for a time. Then he spoke in a stronger voice.

'Strangely, when she died I felt *released* – from Freud's super-ego I suppose. It was as if she had been looking over my shoulder all those years of my childhood, youth and manhood. Now she was gone and I was sad, but I was glad. Glad, naturally, not to have to go for those weary, meaningless talks, which I could see she hated as much as I did. But glad also that a relationship which had run out of sap had ended.'

He was revealing more about himself than he'd ever done before. Alan knew he ought to respond. Dragging himself away from his own thoughts, he said:

'If only we could free ourselves from guilt!'

Charles smiled sadly.

'An American academic once said to me that Ireland's problem is that both Catholics and Protestants have an over-developed capacity for guilt. I told him if he wanted to know about real guilt, he ought to dig into the soul of a Jewish agnostic.'

That day Charles had learned about the reasons for his adviser's bad conscience. As he finished his story, Alan was attentive enough to appreciate that he was being told his feeling of guilt was not unique. Charles, he concluded, was one of the few politicians he knew who was not obsessed with politics, but nurtured ideas that had nothing to do with the Public Sector Borrowing Requirement, or money supply, or even the SDLP.

The two men were sitting in silence when Bill Simpson showed Bob Harbinson into the room. The chief constable was flushed and angry.

[37]

Bob Harbinson had talked at length with the Garda Commissioner. Michael O'Connor had only been in his job a few months, but his opposite number said he was straight as a die and hadn't prevaricated about the bizarre happenings at the border.

'It seems everybody in the Garda Síochána knows the sergeant involved is an IRA sympathiser. I asked why he was sent to such a sensitive post? The previous minister was the sergeant's cousin, so when he applied to go to this Republican village – to sort out his dead father's estate, he said – the Minister thought that sounded fine. So did the then commissioner, who was a lickspittle. By the way, another cousin keeps the local pub, which is a rendezvous for Provisionals from miles around.'

When Harbinson showed his surprise, O'Connor hadn't minced his words about the difficulties of his job. Did Bob know that all promotions above the rank of inspector had to be approved by the cabinet, and that some police officers were regarded as Fianna Fail men, others as Fine Gael?

'Michael himself stayed non-party, but he only got to the top by good luck. He was put in charge of Dublin traffic when a huge row broke out about imminent gridlock. He managed to sort that out, so the politicians were grateful. They appointed him Commissioner over the heads of more senior men who'd burnt their fingers on the political aspects of terrorism.'

Charles exploded.

'And what does that slippery phrase mean?'

'It means that senior Garda officers do only as much to help us as they think their government really wants. That's the truth behind all

Dublin's windy assurances at Downing Street summits about co-operation against terrorism.'

Alan asked if any more was known about Peter's whereabouts. Bob Harbinson said the RUC men had definitely seen him in the IRA car that drove into the Republic.

'So Peter could be anywhere in Ireland by now?'

The chief constable said it wasn't as bad as that. As soon as the commissioner was alerted he'd ordered road-blocks on all roads. They hoped the kidnap party was confined to a small area on the southern side of the border.

'Of course, that's hill country spotted with small farms. The IRA men wouldn't have much difficulty getting shelter and help, either on their side of the border or ours. South Armagh's the most virulent Provo area in the North.'

Bob Harbinson had read a lot about the political history of South Armagh.

'It's been stirring trouble for ages. I hear the Anti-Partition League there wrote to Clement Attlee during the Berlin Airlift, warning him that Crossmaglen wouldn't support him in a Third World War.'

Charles laughed.

'So that's why we didn't drop the Bomb on Moscow.'

The chief constable noticed that Alan seemed dejected by his discouraging analysis, so he tried to comfort him.

'At least you know that Peter's alive.'

It was the second time Alan had suffered the shock of this remark. There was worse to come. The chief constable turned to Charles.

'By the way, you remember that report from my Special Branch? The rumour that one reason the IRA kidnapped Peter was to punish his father for the breakdown of the talks? Well, they now tell me that's without foundation, their informant maintains they misunderstood what he said.'

Charles shuddered at this indiscretion. Bob was a good policeman, but not the most sensitive of men. Apparently it hadn't occurred to him that Charles would keep that report from an already devasted father. Alan was hearing about this threat for the first time, and he barely noticed the denial. This fitted in too neatly to what the IRA had said twice already – in the original phone call to the *Chronicle*, and in Sean's personal threats to his family.

Alan was stricken by guilt. Peter was being held hostage not just for some tactical advantage to the IRA, but because of his own political activities.

Charles telephoned the minister for justice in Dublin. He began coolly, adopting the self-conscious bonhomie which was customary in London-Dublin conversations. He took in Daithe O Suilleabhain's explanation with mounting rage. It was that the RUC had no right to come storming up to the border, expecting to be allowed to stop vehicles that were legitimately travelling into the Republic. If they had suspicions about the car, they ought to have telephoned ahead – to Dublin, rather than the local station, because all such matters must be handled at political level.

'Come on, Daithe, even you can't expect policemen to act so slowly when they know a car contains a kidnapped youngster? I assume you've heard this boy's the son of Alan Houston, who's been working the shirt off his back to get peace?'

The voice at the other end of the phone droned on. Charles had noticed before that O Suilleabhain's talk was gusty with grandiloquent phrases which turned out to mean little. He had schooled himself to suffer this in uncomplaining boredom, so long as the subject was the historic wrongs of England's involvement in Ireland. But over life and death matters Charles's tolerance was thinner.

Harbinson and Alan were astonished to see his face contort grotesquely. Charles knew he mustn't say out loud what he felt about the Irish minister. Much less offensive words than those in his mind might provoke recall of ambassadors. So instead the secretary of state for Northern Ireland held the phone away from him, crooked one arm in a simian gesture, pretending to scratch his armpit, and simultaneously raised the other, as if he would swing from the chandelier.

When he returned his ear to the phone, the monologue from Dublin was beginning to abate. Charles spoke coldly.

'Doubtless you *will* want to report to the Taoiseach, as I will to my Prime Minister. Apart from the overwhelming priority of finding young Peter Houston, about which we've had some assurances from the Gardai, I don't think the incident at the border can just be left there. Perhaps this is an occasion when *you* might wish to conduct one of those public inquiries you're always demanding from us. Think about it, Davy.'

When he banged the phone down, Charles looked to Alan, expecting he'd be pleased at the robustness of his boss's response.

But Alan's thoughts were not on politics, but on his small, frightened son, held hostage somewhere in the Republic.

[38]

It was eight o'clock, and Alan had not arrived home yet. He had simply not been able to face talking to Mary, and had lingered on for a drink with Charles and Bob Harbinson. They both saw that Alan's speculation about Peter's possible whereabouts was going round in circles. Eventually Charles reminded him that his wife was waiting for him.

Mary's mood about Peter swung between anger and anxiety. This was now grinding down her spirit. She was angry that the RUC had been so close, and yet had not rescued him. She was also angry at herself for not having been more gracious when Charles telephoned.

Above all, she was furious with Alan. Furious that he had become such a coward in their marriage that he hadn't even the guts to phone her with news about their lost son. God knows, Charles had enough to do, trying to get Peter freed and seeking peace in Ireland, without having to take over duties any proper husband and father would have carried out.

She was also angry at Alan's lateness, though she didn't believe he would have anything more cheerful to tell her. Yes, Peter was alive, but the two police forces had let him slip through their fingers. Those murderous thugs might kill him at any moment, or he might be caught in cross-fire when the police or army thought they had cornered the IRA gang. In her heart, Mary did not believe her child would survive.

She was expecting Alan to arrive home about six o'clock. By eight she concluded he was ploughing over the old ground of politics and terrorism with Charles, or Dick, or Diana. Typical! It was her child, not Diana's.

Mary could not stand being alone a moment longer, so she telephoned Grizelda. No reply. In despair, she called Colin's home. Susan answered and was effusive in her sympathy. Fleetingly, Mary wondered why Susan thought she was calling her husband. Not that she cared. So far as the egregious Susan was concerned, Mary did not feel at all like a home-breaker.

When Colin heard what a state she was in he said he would pick her up at once. They went to a pub in Bangor. Its customers were watching television, so they were not disturbed. Colin was the right person to keep her company that evening – sympathetic, but not emotionally involved. Mary remembered that he had not met Peter. She gave a shudder. Probably he never would.

Although Colin knew and cared little about the Troubles, he tried to steer her logically away from the belief that the IRA would kill Peter. He took her hand in his.

'The bad publicity that would shower down on them, in America as well as in Britain, would be too devastating to contemplate. Remember, Mary, these guys are dedicated propagandists as well as terrorists.'

Once she had a glass of wine in her hand, Mary slipped into complaints about Alan. She said it was time to admit she had not been in love with him for a long time. This was not just a result of Peter's kidnapping and her belief that it had happened because Alan had neglected security. (Mary by now had buried her own guilt deep in her subconscious.)

'Quite simply, I'm bored with him. He used to be such fun. No more.'

Colin nodded sympathetically, though he could not decide whether this meant Mary was in love with him. Neither, as it happened, could Mary. She kept hearing in her head a dreaded word, 'rebound'. In her teens, this was a snare girls used to warn each other about, as they navigated the perplexing friendships of youth. She told herself that Colin and she had already discovered they shared many interests – books, pictures and music, for a start. He had catholic tastes in all three.

More important, he had an instinctive understanding of women. Or perhaps she meant of one woman. In either case, this was a quality that Mary found lacking in Alan. But when Colin tried to talk about the future, Mary bridled.

'I'm incapable of thinking or feeling anything until I have Peter safely in my arms again.' She looked down into her glass, and added bleakly, 'Though I don't believe I ever will.'

Colin again argued against despair, and succeeded enough for Mary to reveal that she might be offered a job in London. The Director of the Tate Gallery had telephoned to say that her old chief in the Impressionists' Department was off ill. Nobody was sure how serious it was, but he was near to retirement and might go early. The Director wanted to know about Mary's availability.

'Poor man, he was bending over backwards to be tactful, asking endlessly about Peter and the kidnapping, before mentioning what he'd called for. Unfortunately, at the crucial point he fumbled his words.

'"We'd wait, of course, until your son's kidnapping is ... resolved. It's just that we'd need to know whether you'd be interested if – I mean, of course, *when* he's freed. Or would your husband's job tie you down to living there indefinitely?"'

Mary said she'd told him she would be interested and available. They agreed to talk again when she had further news about Peter. Colin congratulated her. He said he himself was even more determined to return to England. Belfast had been a mistake. Vacancies that would suit him were due in London and Bristol, conceivably at Oxford too. He had talked to Susan. She had no intention of going with him, which was what he had hoped. He looked expectantly at Mary.

'Colin, I really can't discuss our future tonight. Can't you see how distressed I am?'

They sat in silence. Eventually Colin touched her cheek with his finger, breaking into her thoughts.

'Time I took you home.'

When Mary turned her key in the front door shortly before eleven, Alan rushed into the hall and hugged her with relief. She quickly disengaged herself.

'Where on earth have you been, Mary? I got here about nine, and

166

I've been frantic ever since, thinking the IRA had got you too. I phoned round the neighbours, and put a call in to RUC headquarters.'

When Mary saw his distress she felt contrite. But that mood quickly passed when the telephone rang, and Alan embarked on a long conversation with Diana. Mary swept into the kitchen, and made herself a cup of coffee. As she passed through the hall, her husband was discussing some forthcoming television programme about the IRA wanting to blow up the London Underground. Charles had said this was a nonsensical rumour, so she couldn't see why they were wasting time on it. She concluded that he and Diana just liked talking to each other – at all hours of day and night.

When Alan eventually ended the phone call, he asked where Mary had been earlier, and whether she hadn't thought it foolish to leave the house? She could not resist her riposte.

'I was meeting a friend. As for leaving the house unoccupied, haven't you noticed we no longer need a babysitter?'

When she saw Alan's look, she was sorry she had said this. He was so close to tears that she broke down herself. Peter was his child too, a baby he had idolised and still loved. Alan took her in his arms, as if the past six months had not happened.

But so far as Mary was concerned, they had happened. She and Alan had crossed bridges they never could recross. Before they went to bed, Alan began to tell her about his telephone conversation with Diana. Mary icily interrupted him.

'In the circumstances, might she not have left her thoughts on forthcoming BBC television programmes until tomorrow at the office?'

Alan looked pained.

'The call wasn't just about the television programme, Mary. Diana phoned with good news for us. She was just asking me whether she should give the BBC advance warning about it. Tomorrow evening, Tommy Hughes will be transferred from Wormwood Scrubs to the Maze.'

What Alan did not say was that it was now more than six hours since Charles had given him advance warning of this sliver of good news. He couldn't bring himself to tell Mary why he hadn't telephoned to tell her this. It was because of security.

[39]

But did Tommy Hughes's transfer mean Peter would be freed?

Last night Alan had put a cheerful spin on the news that he was to be moved. That was for Mary's benefit. Today, as he was driven to Stormont, he was less sure. As the time for the prisoner transfer approached, Alan faced a chilling truth: what happened to Peter would soon be decided. He was gripped by doubt. Was the chief constable right in dismissing this report that what the IRA really wanted was revenge against himself?

Alan hoped someone at Stormont would talk him out of his neurotic thoughts. But the talk there was not directly about Peter; instead the morning meeting was buzzing with opinions about that evening's *Late Night Special* programme. Diana led the discussion.

'The BBC are going ape. Roger Corfield has convinced himself that the threat to the London tube is the IRA's real bargaining counter to secure Tommy Hughes's transfer. Hugh Seabrooke's flying here to chair a Belfast/Dublin/London chit-chat about effects on the ceasefire talks.'

Seabrooke was the programme's star presenter, and his involvement produced gossip about the BBC from all round the table. Charles cut this short.

'In my experience, dear comrades, speculation about what the gods of the media may or may not do is a work of supererogation. Like another well-regarded deity, they move in a mysterious way their wonders to perform.'

Later he confirmed to Alan, Dick and Diana that the home secretary's announcement about Hughes would come in a written answer to a planted question late in the evening, when he was safely in the Maze.

'Keep that within this room. I could do without a Sinn Fein celebration at the prison gates.'

Diana was the first to react.

'What reason will HMG give for the transfer?'

'The Home Office spokesman will imply that Hughes has a grave illness, though the prison doctors now know he doesn't have cancer, but a duodenal that's easily treatable.'

Alan said that reporters were bound to link the transfer to the London Underground threat. Suddenly he looked miserable.

'A few might even ask about any link to Peter's release, but I wouldn't bet on that.'

Charles assured Alan that his son's release was the sole reason for moving Tommy Hughes. But the Home Office could cast a useful fog over that fact by not rubbishing the Underground threat too vigorously. Phrases like 'We can neither confirm nor deny' would be freely sprayed around.

'But are we sure they intend to free Peter at once, or even soon?'

Charles took a long time to reply.

'Hard as it is for you to take, the answer has to be "no". I still hope we'll get him out soon, but the effect of this mega-production on the threat to the London Underground does worry me. The furore might make the IRA think we'll concede more if they leave both threats hanging over our heads. That's why this morning I would cheerfully strangle every single member of the BBC Board of Management.'

Dick frowned, and said he was being unreasonable. The BBC had to follow up rumours like this.

Ever since Charles had concluded that his permanent secretary was plotting with the cabinet secretary to create policy behind his back, he had become less tolerant of him. Now his irritation overflowed. Rumours, he said angrily, were part of the problem. If Dick really wanted to know what was wrong with the media's treatment of Ireland, it was that they were awash with rumours and opinion, rather than reporting. Broadcasters and journalists here gave people in

England no help in *imagining* what it was like to have your life wrecked by terrorism.

'George Eliot once said that the whole point of art and literature – and I suppose that includes the media – is to help us perceive imaginatively why others feel differently from ourselves.'

Dick was not to be diverted into literary criticism. He said George Eliot hadn't borne the responsibility to stop the Irish quarrel wrecking the peace of the United Kingdom. This was a row Charles was happy to continue.

'If you can't see beyond parochial pettiness to the universal issue, Dick, you're less acute than I've always thought. If we allow terrorists – whether Loyalists or Republicans doesn't matter – if we let them have their way, we undermine democratic government everywhere. In twenty years' time people all over the world with supposed grievances will be kidnapping children, hijacking planes, blowing people up. In the Middle East, the Basque country, Latin America, the Balkans, maybe even the United States. I'm sorry to sound apocalyptic, but Ulster's a test-tube for democracy and the rule of law. Good men have to draw the line here, or we surrender everywhere.'

There was a tense silence. Dick was not impressed by his boss's claim to prescience, but judged that he must say no more.

Alan was called out to take a phone call from Mary. She sounded almost cheerful. He noticed that he and Mary see-sawed in optimism and pessimism, one up when the other was down. He determined not to spoil her mood.

'Nothing definite yet, but we hope we'll hear some news not too long after that event I told you about last night.'

'How long?' Mary asked.

'Maybe a few days. We're waiting to see what impact this evening's programme on the tube threat has.'

Mary groaned. Charles had said this threat was nonsense; why couldn't they just concentrate on Peter? Alan had no answer to that.

When he came back into the room, Diana was talking about *Late Night Special*'s requests. They would like to interview Charles. He shook his head.

'I'd have to keep mum about the prison transfer, without telling a direct lie. No interview.'

She had warned Roger Corfield this was the likely result, so he had suggested she should brief the BBC team over lunch. Charles looked at Alan.

'Do you feel up to joining that unappetising event? An ex-telly man might persuade them to keep their lunacy under some kind of control.'

Alan nodded agreement. What Charles did not make explicit was what he hoped – that Alan's presence, as father of a boy in peril of his life, might dissuade the broadcasters from dangerous speculation. Alan was willing to try anything.

Dick murmured that he had papers to deal with, and left. The others had time to waste until lunchtime. Alan's brief experience as a temporary civil servant had shattered any belief that governments control events. They are often mere spectators, waiting on the margins while everybody else – from young men with red braces in the money markets of Tokyo, Wall Street or the City of London, through media editors, to terrorist thugs – take the most important decisions. Governments can merely react to these.

So Charles had time to waste. His mind was still on the programme about the London Underground.

'These body searches on the tube the PM told me about – they're going to cause huge delays. So Mrs Smith of Ealing will worry that her Derek – who's doubtless late because he's having a furtive drink with his secretary – has been blown up on the Central Line. To hell with the BBC!'

Diana tried to argue that *Late Night Special* usually did their research thoroughly. Charles shook his head dismissively.

'I sometimes think that programme's guiding light is the Pecksniffian professor in *Lucky Jim*. D'ye remember? The research projects he supervised, Amis said, were noted for the pseudo-light they threw on non-problems. Likewise *Late Night Special*.'

Charles then asked Alan why broadcast presenters were so ill-informed, yet full of opinions. His adviser pinched himself. Was he really engaged in a debate on broadcasting minutiae while he was worried sick about Peter? But since yesterday's car-chase on the border there was no news about the kidnapping squad, so what could they talk about?

Alan forced himself to answer Charles's question. What presenters really cared about was live interviews. Yet any newspaper reporter could tell you that most enlightening information came from people who could not be quoted – 'deep throats', whether operating in a Washington garage or a remote London restaurant, whether cabinet ministers or whistle-blowers.

'Among presenters, that truism is heresy. Because if there's no live interview, the poor anchor's ego takes a battering.'

'A consummation devoutly to be wished,' Charles murmured.

The telephone rang. Alan jumped, and the colour drained from his cheeks. More than ever, he suspected every call was news about his son, probably bad news. Diana reached for the phone. The call was from Roger Corfield. The BBC team were waiting for her at the restaurant.

[40]

Hugh Seabrooke was about fifty, tall, aquiline of countenance, and with carefully cut black hair. He adopted the courtly manner of an eighteenth-century dandy, and was ostentatiously pre-feminist. When introduced to Diana, he murmured, 'Delighted you could come. FO, isn't it? I've always had a penchant for foreign affairs.'

Roger Corfield was determined Seabrooke should understand this was *his* story, the best of his career in Belfast, one that would be taken up by the newspapers, get the programme talked about, maybe put a bit of ginger into the cease-fire negotiations. But Seabrooke was equally determined to take control of this lunch, and he was a compulsive talker.

'The way I see our show is that the studio discussion is the only bit that really matters.'

Corfield scowled. He *knew* his filmed report was the important section. Seabrooke rumbled on, twiddling his thick-rimmed spectacles.

'Television discussions on Ireland usually don't get anywhere, because they're never properly chaired. Tonight we'll have an IRA man from Dublin – not Sinn Fein, genuine Army Council, though he'll insist on appearing back to camera, of course.'

Alan murmured he'd be surprised if any police or intelligence officer, North or South, would fail to recognise any of the big players, even from the back. Their voices were all known. Seabrooke brushed this aside.

'I intend to put him on the spot about what the hell they mean by these outrageous threats to London commuters.'

The grinding of Corfield's teeth became audible.

'It doesn't take a genius to answer that. Tommy Hughes will get home to the Maze because ministers don't relish the prospect of bombs on the tube.'

Alan knew he was talking to a closed mind, but he had to try.

'Don't forget humanitarian factors, Roger. Seriously ill prisoners have been transferred before. Anyhow, we regard this London tube threat as a fantasy. The police know the crazy who made the phone call. He lives in London, and the IRA wouldn't give him the time of day.'

Roger retorted that this wasn't what James Butler of MI5 believed. In Roger's view his judgement was better than that of the thicks in the RUC or the Met. Anyhow, he added smugly, they would soon see whether HMG didn't think it prudent to move Hughes.

Alan and Diana looked at each other. He nodded, and she spoke.

'You'll need to be careful about what I'm going to tell you, because there's parliamentary privilege involved, and you know how touchy MPs can be. This mustn't come out on the *Nine O'Clock*, right? We're only alerting your programme, in strict confidence, because the information will be published shortly before you go on air.'

She paused, wondering whether to risk needling them. Then she said:

'If you didn't know about this, you'd look even more foolish than this tube story will make you anyhow.'

Corfield was about to explode, but Diana cut in.

'Do you agree to my embargo, or not?'

They looked at each other, and nodded. After all, *Late Night Special* didn't want the *Nine O'Clock News* stealing its thunder.

Diana told them about the Written Reply that would come from the Home Office at ten o'clock. Roger Corfield whooped in triumph.

'I knew it all along. They've done the deal. Quite right too! You can't risk the lives of our own people in London by refusing a small addition to Ulster's prison population. Let folk here clean up their own mess.'

Diana quietly pointed out that Hughes had committed his offences in London, and had been sentenced at the Old Bailey. Corfield would have argued about this, but Seabrooke butted in. He'd had quite enough of Roger's chatter.

'The point I'll bring out in the discussion is that the IRA never breaks its word. If HMG has decided to bring Hughes home, there'll be no bombs on the Underground, now or later. That'll be a great relief not only to your political masters, but to London businesses and their staffs.'

Hugh Seabrooke took a sip of his white wine. He'd told the waiter earlier that it must be 'extremely dry', and irritated Corfield further by insisting on tasting it himself (thus establishing that he was the host, though their producer subsequently signed the bill). Seabrooke had screwed up his face, complaining there was a suspicion of fruitiness. But he'd airily waved the waiter to pour.

'The principal question I'll pursue is this: if both the IRA and the Brits are willing to make deals over life and death issues, what's the Irish Government's attitude? We've been promised a senior minister, perhaps even the Taoiseach. The Irish *ought* to be keen to push the Brits into more meaningful talks with the Provos. But you know how woolly they can be. I certainly intend to make them talk turkey tonight.'

Inwardly, Alan groaned. This was a prime example of television presenters' ignorance, just what Charles had been complaining about. Seabrooke was pointing himself 180 degrees in the wrong direction. The Irish Minister would not need any encouragement to take a cheap political trick against the Brits.

The producer was a thoughtful young woman called Anne Cobbold, who had not so far taken part in the discussion. Diana had identified her as an oasis of sense in a desert of male vanity.

'I wonder whether we may not be jumping too many fences at once. Perhaps I should find out on the phone what the Provos' man in Dublin intends to say about the London Underground plot. That might give us a get-out, just in case we need one.'

Hugh frowned at her.

'Oh, no, my love, do me a favour! Do you think I'm going to allow chummy from the IRA to squirm out from under the threats that have sprung the barbarous Mr Hughes from the Scrubs? I'm paid my no doubt excessive salary to prevent these slime-balls getting away with porkies like that, and tonight I intend to earn it.'

As the presenter leaned back in a haze of self-satisfaction, Alan reflected on Seabrooke's personality. He was an intelligent man, but so consumed by self-love that he no longer gave himself space to think straight. What made him cloudier than usual today was his internal rivalry with Roger Corfield. Alan hoped that Anne Cobbold would manage to talk some sense into them both.

The lunch dragged on, and Diana noticed that they had drunk two bottles of expensive wine, and were well down a third. She was glad the BBC, not the Government, was picking up the bill. Dick could be puritanical about expenses.

Roger Corfield was trying, not too subtly, to remind Seabrooke that he was ignorant of the background to this programme.

'Out here you constantly have to remind yourself that the Irish are different.'

Diana found Roger amusing in small doses, but she now decided he needed taking down a peg.

'You remind me of those people who used to say "some of my best friends are Jews, but ..." That became unfashionable after the Holocaust, Roger, so I'd advise you not to pursue your theory that people in Ireland are a different breed. Under this kind of strain, whether they live in the Bogside or the Shankill, they're always going to behave worse than people in Cheltenham or Harrogate. What do you expect?'

Hugh Seabrooke was bored with further discussion of the Ulster character. He began paying Diana heavy-handed compliments, suggesting she could come along and see the show from the gallery, perhaps have a bite of smoked salmon and a glass of champagne at his hotel afterwards. Diana said tartly that the BBC's activities that evening would keep her working late.

The programme was a predictable shambles. When the threat to the London Underground was put to the IRA man, he ignored the question, and spouted familiar propaganda about British duplicity in the talks. Seabrooke ineffectually tried to interrupt. The presenter's repeated interjections of 'But what about the London tube?' came to sound like the chorus in a Greek drama. The IRA man inexorably repeated both new and age-old grievances. The junior minister from

Dublin had nothing much to say, even if Hugh hadn't constantly interrupted him.

Alan was at home watching the broadcast with Mary. He felt uneasy. Distracted by the lunchtime wrangle, he had omitted to talk directly about Peter. Political obsessiveness again! The BBC people had expressed their sympathy, but Alan knew that neither Seabrooke nor Corfield would have listened to an appeal. He wished now he had told them bluntly they were imperilling his son's life, and walked out of their jolly lunch party. Alan felt more alone than ever, and more fearful that Peter would not be released.

At Stormont Charles, Dick and Diana were gloomily watching the familiar rushed interviews. Dick was now in less charitable mood towards the BBC.

'Broadcasting research apparently shows that no viewer can attend to the same voice for more than thirty seconds. That's why producers invite in the massed bands of the Highland Division.'

When it was over, Charles took a long draw at his whiskey, and gave his conclusion. 'Television current affairs has about as much connection with Platonic truth and beauty as Goebbels's *Völkischer Beobachter* used to have.'

But, he added, looking on a brighter side, a man or woman on a galloping horse – which roughly represented the posture of most viewers of this programme – would conclude (a) that the British Government, in order to save London commuters, had done a deal to let Tommy Hughes home; (b) that this was a necessary decision, though it was a pity they couldn't simultaneously have hanged the entire IRA Army Council.

As for attempts to free Peter Houston, they might conclude, as HMG's press officers were at this moment loyally arguing, that this had little or nothing to do with the transfer of the IRA bomber.

'And the sober fact is that this farrago of lies and nonsense will do us more good than harm. To tell the truth would have been more politically embarrassing. The downside is that the IRA know the truth all right, know they've got another kind of ruthless blackmail to which we're vulnerable.'

The next morning, Diana told Alan about the romantic end to her evening. Hugh Seabrooke had telephoned. They had a brief discussion of the programme, bombastic on his side, evasive on hers. Then he had come to the point of his call. How about that smoked salmon and champers? They had so much to talk about, and not only about Ireland. She told him she was just about to go to bed.

'I nearly added "alone", but I thought that was too obvious an insult. The poor bastard thought a visiting presenter of *Late Night Special* has *droit de seigneur* over the peasant women employed here by Her Majesty. I hope I disabused him.'

The broadsheet London newspapers reviewed *The Disaster Scenario* favourably. There was a sequel a week later, a stone's throw from the Television Centre in London. What happened then to Eamonn Murphy, the Shepherd's Bush fantasist, was almost precisely what the young detective constable had predicted.

MI5 had driven the Special Branch inspector at Shepherd's Bush to hair-tearing distraction over the supposed plot against the Underground. He decided his nick had had enough grief from Murphy, so Eamonn was returned to Ireland, under the terms of the Prevention of Terrorism Act. No more was heard of his Disaster Scenario.

[41]

Lunchtime on the day after Tommy Hughes was transferred, and still no news about Peter. Mary had been phoning Alan's office every hour. His own anxiety fed on hers. By mid-afternoon he had convinced himself that the IRA would not release Peter at once, perhaps not ever.

When his telephone rang again, Alan prepared for a further harrowing conversation with Mary but it was a different familiar voice that spoke.

'Alan, d'ye think it would be a good idea for us to meet again?'

It was Liam. Alan's heart seemed to miss a beat. Ever since the kidnap he'd been wondering whether to telephone his personal acquaintance in the organisation that held Peter. The police said this might complicate efforts to have him released. Now he knew he must respond to Liam's advance.

'You can guess there's only one subject in my mind, Liam.'

'Aye, aye, of course, Alan, I understand that. I'm terrible sorry for your trouble. But I'm as sure as I can be that you needn't worry, y'know.'

Then Liam began his usual exercise of pretending he was only a Sinn Fein member, nothing to do with the IRA – while not disowning their actions, of course. He'd been told 'on good authority' that the prospect of his cousin Tommy dying in an English gaol had been a terrible worry to his comrades.

'Now that's settled, everything should be all right. Still, it would be helpful if we talked – about the situation generally, I mean.'

They arranged to meet at the Irish Volunteer at seven, then to go on 'somewhere else'.

As an afterthought, Liam said, 'I might need to bring Sean along.

It's obvious to me he's not your cup of tea, but I think this evening he might be helpful.'

When Alan came off the phone he considered telling the police what he was doing. Eventually he decided not to. He didn't tell Charles either, or Dick, or Diana, or even Mary. With Peter's life at stake, he preferred to act on his own. Alan Houston was normally gregarious, but at the most testing moments of life instinct made him a solitary.

The encounter at the Irish Volunteer was brief. They went on not to Liam's home, as Alan had expected, or even to the Provo drinking club, but to a boarded-up house in a side-street near the pub. As Sean's Alsatian Cathal bounded round the small house, Alan examined the almost empty room they showed him into. Apart from a bare wooden table, there were four or five chipped dining-room chairs, with ragged moquette seats.

He guessed this room was used for IRA interrogations of offending volunteers, or for holding hostage businessmen and others they used to exact ransoms. Businessmen *and others!* Alan wondered if Peter had been held here. He shuddered involuntarily.

Sean misunderstood his thoughts. 'Don't worry, Mr Houston, you're not here for *quite* the same purpose we sometimes use it for.'

Instinctively Sean sounded a harsh note. He'd never taken as much trouble as Liam to pretend he wasn't in the IRA itself. Alan wondered if Sean was one of the Nutting Squad, the men who interrogated and executed informers.

The room was more dilapidated than any Alan had ever seen. When they first came in and when Liam went to the loo, he noticed the door-hinge had a loud squeak. There was also a pervasive smell which Alan soon identified as urine.

The purpose of the meeting emerged circuitously. What Liam wanted was to reinstate the suspended political contacts between Republicans and the British Government.

What an astonishing misjudgement of human feelings! Had these people so far forgotten how ordinary people ticked that they thought he'd concentrate on anything so fatuous while they left him uncertain about where Peter was, or what was happening to him?

Angrily he said this, and much more. Hadn't the IRA promised that if Tommy Hughes was sent back to the Maze Peter would be released? Did they never keep any promises?

Liam looked embarrassed. Sean did not.

'It'll serve your son better, Mr Houston, if you calm down. It's not up to me, of course, but I'd guess he'll be released soon enough if the IRA see you're helping us get the peace talks going again.'

Alan said grimly that this amounted to double ransom – the move to the Maze for Tommy Hughes, and a promise of renewed negotiations, which he personally was not able to deliver.

'Ach, well ye can help, surely?' Sean said bitterly. 'Ye helped in buggerin' them up last time round.'

Before Alan could reply, Liam cut in. He thought they should keep the two issues separate. Of course, Peter must be released, and personally he'd little doubt he would be. The question was 'when?' He thought they – the ubiquitous 'they' which always distanced Liam from terrorism! – they would be more likely to speed it up if politics was beginning to work again.

The conversation went round in circles. Alan said that his only interest now, and the only interest of everybody from the Prime Minister down, was in getting his son freed.

'Until that happens there's not a cat in hell's chance that the Government will agree to talks. You'd also have to say your informal truce is on again. The two bombs that failed to explode last weekend weren't exactly a peace gesture, were they?'

Liam urged Alan to tell the secretary of state it would be fruitful to resume talks. Surely he could do that? Alan asked why anybody should believe it would be fruitful? The Republicans had shown again they couldn't be trusted. They weren't negotiators, they were terrorists.

'Incidentally, I remember you noticed some of the spooks your envoys met were more disposed to compromise than the British Government itself. Well, you might like to know these same characters were alone in swallowing the rumour about bombing the London Underground.'

Alan knew he was being indiscreet, but he wanted to hear what Liam and Sean would say about this. Liam responded angrily.

'Ach, get away wi' ye'. Sure nobody would believe that fuckin' nonsense.'

But Alan could see that Liam's faith in the British intermediaries was shaken. Finally Alan said that the most he could do was to report to Charles Corbett that the IRA wanted to talk again. Perhaps the Government would want to hear what they had to say, though he couldn't promise this.

'I'd have a lot better chance of succeeding, and a lot more enthusiasm for trying, if my boy was back home.'

'I can understand that, Alan. We'd better leave it there. We'll do what we can.'

On Alan's way home, he drove through the centre of Belfast, brightly lit and busy again because there had been no recent explosions or murders. But the people coming from restaurants and cinemas moved quickly and nervously. They knew peace was on a knife-edge.

He swung his car away from Sandy Row into a familiar shortcut. Suddenly Alan found himself passing the headquarters of the Ulster Unionist Party. He slowed down. The building, once the citadel of Unionist supremacy, was heavily padlocked, with grills over every window.

In Alan's youth he'd abhorred this building, not for its mundane architecture, but because of the arrogant, unyielding politics for which it stood. Now this and the headquarters of all the other parties, from Sinn Fein across to Paisley's Democratic Unionists, hid behind heavy security gates. Many had been bombed. Democratic politics was becoming the sin that dare not speak its name. Terrorism, Republican and Loyalist, had destroyed that. Why bother with votes if you could say it by planting bombs?

Or by kidnapping youngsters, and bargaining with their freedom.

[42]

Alan told Charles the following morning what Liam wanted. Charles immediately telephoned the Prime Minister. Government intermediaries were instructed to reopen their channel to hear what new the Republicans had to say. Orders were sharper this time. There was to be no talking about substance until the IRA freed Peter Houston and restored their informal ceasefire.

Alan went home early. He was reasonably hopeful, but warned Mary the IRA was trying to impose a second condition. She frowned.

'What kind of second condition? Are we going to have a lot of braggadocio from the cabinet about not paying Danegeld?'

'No, no, it's nothing like Danegeld. We've paid that already. It's just that as well as moving Tommy Hughes to the Maze, they want the Government to reopen political negotiations. But that's already being finessed. I hope we'll hear good news soon.'

Mary looked out of the window and sighed deeply. Then she said, almost in a whisper, 'More waiting.'

It was then that Alan's composure broke. Despite his suspicion that their marriage was over, he was doing all he could to help Mary through this crisis. So far, in the long, gut-wrenching days since the kidnap, he had contrived to remain calm in her presence. Now, quite suddenly, unbearable weariness engulfed him. Alan began to utter one of those perpetual quotations Mary mocked him for.

'Hope deferred maketh the heart sick' was what he tried to say, but half-way through the words stuck in his throat and he dissolved into tears.

'Sorry, my darling,' he said, not realising this was the first time in months that either of them had used their familiar endearment. 'I'm feeling the strain too.'

Also for the first time in months Mary felt genuine sympathy. She thought of embracing Alan, but found she didn't want to. So she poured him a large whiskey instead. The habits of love and care she'd developed over half-a-lifetime blinked fitfully into life, like a computer that didn't fully understand what instruction it was receiving.

As they sipped their drinks, and discussed the terrible anxiety that united them in their tattered marriage, Mary knew she needed to provide comfort for Alan, and that it wasn't available within her own heart. She also wanted comfort for herself. Some people might call it spiritual comfort. Mary settled for 'pastoral care'. A psychiatrist would have served her purpose, if there'd been one to hand. But she suspected there wasn't much demand for such therapists over here.

Mary told Alan that his friend Edward Mason had telephoned earlier. Why not invite him to come and talk to them?

What she did not say was that her phone conversation with the old clergyman was the most tolerable she'd had since the kidnapping. He had encouraged her to talk about Peter. He was not Mary's idea of a clergyman at all – didn't keep her at a distance, or seem stiff-necked, like the vicars of her youth.

The Reverend Dr Edward Mason had served his year as Moderator of the Presbyterian Assembly. He held not just the honorary doctorate which came with that office, but had an advanced degree in theology. Alan sometimes jokingly called him 'Herr Doktor Doktor'. Edward's doctoral thesis and other writings marked him out as the most profound Christian scholar in Ireland. He often lectured to Catholic academics, priests and students at their seminary in Maynooth.

He was an unorthodox Presbyterian thinker, which sometimes got him into hot water. His election as Moderator had led to demonstrations on the evening he was installed. Fundamentalists who resented his Biblical exegesis besieged the Assembly Hall.

This demonstration produced a flash of courageous tolerance from Johnny O'Neill, former editor of the *Evening Chronicle*, and a man not noted for his liberalism. Encountering a raw-faced County Antrim farm labourer with an offensive placard, O'Neill suggested, with the authority of great age, that he should 'go home, and not spoil the oul' man's big night'.

'But sor, sor!' cried the demonstrator, pursuing the retreating editor, 'this man says Jesus Christ's a bastard.'

Edward would not have accepted that gloss on his writings about the Virgin Birth, but he knew his radical scholarship had made him enemies.

Ever since the kidnapping he had privately doubted whether Peter's parents would ever see him alive again. He'd known of too many cases in these Troubles where hope had lived on for weeks, even months, and then been dashed. Sometimes a body was never found.

When Edward Mason arrived, Alan explained what Liam had told him. Edward saw that Mary was watching him, so he tried to look reassured. Then, to his surprise, she initiated a conversation about life after death.

'Since this happened to Peter, I've been thinking about what I believe in. That's not a lot, I'm afraid, but I want to be ready for whatever may happen.'

She paused, and began to weep quietly. Alan moved to put his arm around her. Edward saw Mary edge away on the sofa to elude his grasp.

She dried her eyes with the handkerchief Alan offered her, and then spoke with passion.

'I can't face the possibility of never seeing my child again, without any idea of what I believe about immortality. Even if it means accepting that it's codswallop.'

Alan looked shattered. Edward was bemused. These were not the circumstances in which he could usefully explain his faith to an intelligent, well-educated woman. Life after death wasn't the core of his beliefs anyhow, though he understood why eschatology was the only aspect of religion that mattered to Mary just now. Personally, he was more interested in how men and women treated each other on earth. He was content to leave the rest to God. Edward assumed *something* came after death, but he wouldn't know what it was until he died.

He himself moved to the sofa, and grasped Mary's hand.

'Listen, my dear, we hope and pray that what you're afraid of will never happen, that many years hence it'll be Brian and Peter who have to face the sadness of their parents' deaths.'

He hesitated, then spoke in a voice that was barely audible.

'Deaths I pray will take place in a family that has remained united down the years.'

Both Alan and Mary looked away from him and from each other. To Edward their body language carried a message of almost physical revulsion.

'If you *did* lose Peter, I'd talk to you about what immortality means to me. But that's not a good idea just now. Christianity, Mary, is a philosophy for life, as well as death. A person of your intellectual sophistication would need to take it slowly, steadily, or not at all.'

The telephone rang. It was Brian, who had returned to Cambridge the previous day. Alan told him he'd had indirect contact with Peter's captors.

'I'm hopeful he'll be released soon. But it's all tied up with political talks, so you mustn't expect it to happen at once.'

Mary and Edward heard what sounded like an explosion of anger from the other end of the phone. Alan frowned.

'I think so too, Brian. You probably regard me as a political junkie, but believe me, I've reached a point where I would happily see the whole island towed into the middle of the Atlantic and scuttled. Sadly the best way of getting Peter out does involve politics. The IRA's decided that, not me.'

Edward noticed that Mary looked crestfallen because Brian wasn't as hopeful about Alan's news. Then, with a determination that was almost tangible, she shrugged that off, and asked Edward to continue where he'd been interrupted. He was surprised, and murmured that what he was about to say might seem far from her personal worries, but it would help her to understand his earlier reticence.

'A Presbyterian minister is not a priest, in the sense that your Anglican upbringing makes you familiar with. Our ministers ought to be chary about laying down the law. Presbyterians here share the great principle of Nonconformism with the Church of Scotland, with all the Methodists, Baptists, and United Reformers in Britain, and with millions more throughout the world. It's called the Priesthood of All Believers, and it means no priest can be an intermediary between a man or woman and their God.'

Alan's and Mary's minds went back to their separate, but similar thoughts on the morning after Peter was kidnapped. Each had felt so guilty that, if Edward Mason had been a Catholic priest, they would have wanted him to hear their confessions.

Edward continued his theological dissertation with a smile playing round his lips.

'I have to admit, Mary, that during a long ministry I've encountered Presbyterians, mostly in the depths of the Irish countryside, whose dedication to the Priesthood of All Believers is tenuous. Because they've abrogated their duty to think, they allow themselves to be led by the nose by some clergyman, often of fundamentalist instincts. The sick joke is that, though politically many are virulently anti-Catholic, they remain wholly ignorant of what separates our church from Catholicism, as well as from the Anglicans. It's that we're not supposed to have a priesthood.'

The telephone rang again. Alan picked it up.

'Charles?' he said, his voice all but strangled by tension.

Mary and Edward watched closely for Alan's reaction to what he was being told. There was a long pause while Charles was speaking. Then Alan interrupted.

'But does that mean they'll release him? Without political conditions?'

Edward Mason gave Mary an encouraging smile.

After another long silence while he listened to Charles, Alan said guardedly, 'Well, it's certainly hopeful rather than gloomy. But as you can guess, Charles, Mary and I won't sleep easily until we have him back ... Yes, I know you are, I know. Thank you.'

[43]

When Alan laid the phone down he did not speak for several moments. He was not convinced Charles had any real reason to think Peter would be freed soon, or indeed at all. But for Mary's sake he determined to put on a brave face.

'You'll have gathered Peter's not free yet, but it does look better. The IRA seem satisfied with the agenda we're putting to them. Their negotiators have to report back, but our man hopes they'll recommend release.'

Mary asked whether the British intermediary was someone Alan trusted. Here was another time when he and his wife still travelled along the same mental channels. His brow furrowed.

'It's James Butler of MI5. Yes, I know I've told you he's politically dodgy, but Charles has instructed him to tell the IRA whatever's needed to free Peter. Butler's own political instincts are so different from mine, from Charles's too, that we can rely on him do that, in spades!'

Edward looked puzzled.

'I don't quite understand. Where does that lead?'

Alan said so far as he was concerned, it led to hope of the safe return of their son. After that, he would be quite prepared for any amount of cheating and going back on promises to deprive the IRA of advantage.

'I hope this doesn't shock you, Edward, but just now the secretary of state has been saying precisely that, in terms so vehement I'd hesitate to repeat them in front of either a clergyman or my wife. Charles is not disposed to be over scrupulous when it comes to playing straight with people who kidnap children.'

Edward said he had no quarrel with that, Peter's safety was

paramount. He rose to leave, saying the Houstons ought to get some sleep. Mary now felt close enough to him to say that neither Alan nor she would sleep much, so they'd be grateful if he stayed on a bit. Edward sat down again. Mary said that one thing he'd said earlier puzzled her.

'Christianity's supposed to be about loving your fellows, isn't it? Yet over here it's produced far more hatred than us English agnostics can drum up, over politics or anything else.'

She stuck her chin forward, with a hint of the aggression that Alan knew well. He noticed this was the same question Charles had put to him.

Edward told Mary she had laid her finger on the shame of Irish Christianity. Too often the churches, Protestant and Catholic, had allowed religion to become sectarianism. Sadly, that now applied to many in his own church. Presbyterians – the largest church in the North of Ireland – could once claim to be a beacon of tolerance. For example, they still offered communion to Christians of any denomination, which was more than either Catholics or Anglicans customarily did.

'Don't forget, Mary, that it was our people who first fled to America to escape religious persecution, a hundred years before Catholics left to escape the Famine. Outsiders think Protestants here have a monopoly of bigotry, but that's wrong. Exclusiveness is an essential tenet of Catholicism, though some Protestant clerics have purloined that all too willingly.'

Mary looked distracted. He wondered if this was all too distant from what concerned her. Soon she revealed what she was thinking about.

'How close are the Catholic clergy to the IRA, Edward? I'm in such despair that I've been considering an approach to the Cardinal. He might have more chance of getting Peter released than the politicians, with all their diplomatic baggage to bother about.'

Edward sat silent. He suspected that no outsider had any influence over the IRA murder squads. That was what chilled his blood. But he could not bring himself to say that to this frightened mother.

'I talk often to the Cardinal, and nobody hates what the IRA are doing more than him. Most priests won't have anything to do with them, except at confession – and what a gruesome business that must sometimes be! I'm fairly certain the Cardinal has no influence with the leadership.'

Edward was diverted to talk about Catholicism. He praised Rome's social policies. Popes had been saying sensible things about social justice ever since the encyclical *Rerum Novarum* at the end of the last century and their teaching about this heavily influenced his own thinking.

'I wish, incidentally, that people wouldn't assume that when Christians – even old Blackmouth Presbyterians like myself – chunter on about morality, we're talking about sexual morality. For me morality is about justice, at home and abroad, what we ought to do, rather than what we ought *not* to do. Good Catholics and good Presbyterians don't differ about that.'

Alan looked at his watch, then guiltily at Edward.

'Would it seem rude if I interrupted to listen to the local news headlines on the box?'

Edward waved a hand in assent, but Mary exploded. 'Well, it seems rude to me, but never mind. There's nothing on about Peter any more. They seem to have forgotten his existence. It'll just show more politicians nitpicking.'

The news contained an item about the burning of a Presbyterian church, followed by comments from Unionist and Nationalist politicians in a row over an obscure Orange march. Alan had the remote control in his hand, but Mary impatiently switched off at the set.

'In present circumstances, that's as much as I can stand of both lots posturing while my son's still a hostage.'

She looked towards Edward, who resumed his explanation of why his own church was losing its former reputation for liberalism.

'When the whole Christian world is turning towards ecumenism, we over here seem stuck in a sectarian time-warp.'

Something had gone wrong with the church's recruitment. He didn't want to sound snobbish, but previous generations of Presbyterian clergy had been drawn from the sons of professionals – ministers, doctors, lawyers, and so on – or from prosperous farming families, reasonably well educated. Anyhow, they came from homes with books. The years of the Troubles had brought into the church more young men from Protestant working-class ghettoes, whose early experience of religion came near to sectarianism.

Mary said that *was* an interesting social trend. It explained some political ranting by clergy on radio and television that had shocked her. As a failed Anglican, she said slyly, she supposed this was the downside of the Priesthood of All Believers?

Edward wryly acknowledged this.

'You only have to look at the American Bible Belt to see what monstrosities the extremes of nonconformity can produce. I don't challenge the sincerity of our young clergy; it's just that their kind of faith doesn't allow any room at all for "honest doubt", even less for intellectual speculation. Thank God we're now getting young women into the ministry who are thoughtful, able and questioning.'

Despite his vocation, he believed Christians benefited from doubt. Educated people couldn't simply subjugate their intelligences to mental comfort. Religion could only be effective if it sought to discover all it could about the facts of man's nature and his place in the world, and to live accordingly.

'Religion can seem complicated, Mary, but it all comes down to Christ's two great commandments: love God, love your neighbour as yourself. If that kind of Christianity prevailed in Ireland, the tiny differences between Protestants and Catholics wouldn't matter much. QED, I suppose.'

The telephone interrupted them again. The first call was from Brian, worried that he'd hurt his father's feelings. Alan told him to forget it, but said it was lucky he'd phoned, because Charles had given them more reason to hope that Peter might be free soon.

Edward left soon after that. A second call, from Diana, was a long one. Mary shifted unhappily in her seat when she heard that Alan's end of the conversation was not about Peter, just more politics. Diana did most of the talking.

When Alan put down the receiver, the strain showed on his face.

'She says two of the national papers tomorrow are leading with much the same story. They claim the British Government's told the

IRA it's prepared to consider fixing a date, long into the future, for withdrawal from Northern Ireland. One of them says this is to avert the threat to bomb the London Underground.'

'And the other one?'

'They say it's to ... to save Peter's life.'

Mary asked how Diana thought these stories would affect Peter's release.

'She didn't say. I think the reports are simply mischievous plants by some freelance operator, possibly one of our spooks. But they'll just confuse the IRA, and may actually delay Peter's release.'

Mary wept.

[44]

Rupert Rigby-Smith was on attachment as chief of the Northern Ireland Information Service. He was the man who had helped Dick Heston conduct his independent media policy in London. That was where he usually operated. At Stormont today he was expecting a bruising time in Charles's morning meeting. Some newspapers *had* gone just a touch OTT.

Rupert was fortyish, with smooth blonde hair, a smooth suit (purple, more or less), and extremely smooth manners. He was senior partner in a public relations consultancy called Rigby-Smith, Faulkner, Jones and Huxtable-Bryce. Such consultancies do better to have four names on the letter-head, two of them hyphenated – though the hyphens need not necessarily date from the eighteenth century.

Rupert smiled at Alan over his half-moon spectacles. He feared the political adviser might be his principal critic over the news coverage. Months ago Dick had told him that this man was a snake-in-the-grass.

Junior ministers, civil servants, and the army and police representatives were gossiping as they waited for Charles to arrive. After a particularly self-serving anecdote from Rigby-Smith, a Whitehall official laughed.

'Rupert, you are the most incorrigible name-dropper I've ever met.'

'Funny you should remark on that, old boy. The Prime Minister says just the same thing.'

For anybody innocent of the ways of the London press, that morning's papers were a revelation. The truth came in 57 varieties, and the sneaky word 'may' appeared in most headlines. The two papers

Diana had telephoned Alan about said the Government was considering fixing a date for withdrawal, but one implied this was in the mists of future time.

Elsewhere, by contrast, the Provisionals were reported to be weary of their 'Long War' and asking London for a fig-leaf that 'might' allow them to end violence for ever, without getting much in return. Another paper said more Irish terrorists 'might' be moved from English gaols. Yet another believed IRA negotiators wanted a date for the freeing of all its prisoners.

There was remarkable congruence between each paper's news report and what its recent editorials had advocated. A modern newspaper is often conducted on the comfortable principle that its wish is father to its thought, or at least to its 'think pieces'. Alan noted that several papers linked Peter's prospect of being freed with achievement of whatever was the principal IRA demand in their own commentary. His son appeared as a bit-player in a drama that had swelled again into a major news story.

Charles apologised for arriving twenty minutes late. Something had come up, he said. To everyone's surprise, his opening review didn't mention the newspapers. Instead he reported guardedly what he'd been told about the prospect of Peter's release, and said he'd authorised informal contacts with the IRA to facilitate this. He reviewed the security reports, and asked the chief constable and army general to fill them out.

At this point Dick murmured a silky intervention.

'Have you had an opportunity, Secretary of State, to glance at any of this morning's newspaper accounts of our affairs?'

Charles looked puzzled. Yes, he said, he'd flicked through them over breakfast, but since they seemed to contain the usual mixture of semi-literate fiction, he'd quickly turned to a turgid cabinet paper he had to get through. Was he missing something?

People began to mention whichever report, fact, or factoid had attracted their attention. Despite Charles's ostentatious boredom, the debate rumbled on for half an hour. The media are always more fun to discuss than terrorism. At last the secretary of state's patience ran out.

'Perhaps, in view of the clearly widespread interest in these press reports, I'd better make clear again what's happening. Our only objective – I repeat *only* objective – is to secure the release of Peter Houston. Our intermediaries will not be offering dates for withdrawal, or an independent Ulster, or a united Ireland. Nor even free trips to Florida so that Republican and Loyalist convicts can enjoy Disney-world together.'

Those who'd been taking the press reports seriously now giggled dutifully. Charles continued sternly.

'Our envoys are re-establishing contact with the IRA, with a view to going warily over the same ground we have been over so often before. But only when Peter Houston is free, and only when the IRA resume their informal truce will any serious politics be discussed. Perhaps not even then. Have I made that clear?'

Alan guessed that for the hour before the meeting Charles had been busy with media damage-limitation, for he had his own long-standing friends in senior Fleet Street jobs. He didn't want anybody outside his inner circle to know how serious the effect of reports about dates for withdrawal could be. What if the Unionists went crazy, or the IRA decided to hold on to Peter, to see if there was any truth in these press rumours?

Having laid down the law, Charles relaxed, and began to indulge his propensity to philosophise.

'I don't think editors of our great national organs ever notice how much of the material they give their readers comes from un-named sources. Not just in our affairs over here. People called "insiders" are always revealing City scandals to their reporters – though surprisingly few of these ever come to court. "Friends" disclose the sexual indiscretions of the entertainment industry, usually just before a new record or show is launched. Different "friends" defend various Royals over their peccadilloes. I would advise colleagues that it is inadvisable to become excited over such reports. They are suitable wrappings for our fish and chips.'

Several in his audience had difficulty in imagining their fastidious Secretary of State eating fish and chips from a newspaper. But Charles pressed on, saying the poor readers couldn't know whether such stories were pure imagination, or whether somebody was flying a kite, riding a hobby-horse, paddling their own canoe – 'or any of a large array of sporting and nursery metaphors'.

Alan caught the eye of Diana, who smiled at him. The reports about a date for withdrawal fitted in with what the Prime Minister had said to Charles and Dick many months before. Was she right that Number Ten was behind these two reports? Diana's smile said this smoke was not without a fire.

Alan thought it might all come from Rupert, with or without Downing Street nods and winks to encourage him. It might be James Butler of MI5, revealing his personal negotiating stance. Or Howard Considine, who believed the future lay in Irish unity. Even Dick perhaps . . .?

Alan's mind, as always, wandered off into speculation about what might be happening to Peter. Was he, at that moment, in some safe house near the border, about to be driven blindfold to Belfast and dropped off? Or would his jailers read the newspapers, and decide they might extract more advantage before they released him?

A colder thought could not be avoided. Was Peter still alive? As the meeting drew towards its close, he noticed the deputy chief constable, Patrick Kelly, being called out to take a phone call. After a few minutes he returned, went over to Diana, and whispered in her ear. Instinctively she looked straight at Alan. Then she went out with Kelly.

Alan's imagination raced ahead. Peter was dead! The hopeful reports were all wrong. The whispered conversation, that look of Diana's could mean only bad news. It was not likely to be about anything other than Peter. But why hadn't they called him out straight away?

He was about to leave his seat when the door opened and Diana beckoned to him. With his heart racing, he went out.

She kissed him.

'Great news! Peter's free. Paddy here's just had word from his headquarters that he was found alone, looking dazed, at the bottom of Castle Street.'

'Where is he now? When can I see him? Has Mary been told yet?'

Kelly replied that Peter was at RUC headquarters, and they'd already sent a car to bring Mary there. Alan turned to Diana.

'God, when I saw you look at me like that I was convinced he was dead.'

'Paddy thought if he announced it to the meeting, you would . . . well, just break down. That's why we got you out here. Sorry we alarmed you.'

It was then that Alan did break down, wept quietly, blew his nose, and apologised to Kelly. The policeman grabbed his hand, pumped it up and down vigorously.

'I can't tell you how glad we all are you've got him back. Many coppers have youngsters of their own, and we can never get the thought of such horrors out of our minds. Peter was a first. Let's hope he'll be the last.'

[45]

Alan found Mary in the duty room at police headquarters. She hesitated as he moved to embrace her, then slid into his arms, and gave him a tentative hug. Peter's release had left the Houstons confused about their relationship. For the moment none of this mattered, compared with their relief that Peter was free. That at least they could share.

The duty inspector told Alan his son had been distressed when the police found him on the street. The doctor had prescribed a pill to calm him, and said Peter ought to be allowed to sleep for an hour or so before they took him home. Mary said she had already seen him through the sick room window, and he looked all right. Alan had a look himself, and thought Peter's face seemed thinner.

A tall man in plain clothes introduced himself to the Houstons. He was Chief Superintendent Alec Wilson, and said he'd be in charge of the investigation into the kidnapping.

'Of course, we won't attempt to question Peter until he's had a full night's sleep at home, but I'd like you to keep your conversation away from the kidnap. It's always better if detectives can speak to a witness, especially a youngster, before he's been over his story with somebody else.'

Mary said huffily: 'We *are* his parents, you know. Surely we should let him get it off his chest as quickly as possible?'

Alan glanced at Wilson, and said they wouldn't do anything which might confuse Peter before Wilson talked to him. The policeman seemed satisfied, and spoke more kindly to Mary.

'I'm sure when you see how dog-tired he'll be, Mrs Houston, you'll just want to get some decent food into him, and give him an early night. I suspect he's not had enough to eat, and certainly not much affection since you last saw him.'

After an hour Alan's driver took the three Houstons home. How different, Mary thought, from her despair on the same journey with Alan and Brian on the day Peter was kidnapped! When they reached their house, she noticed that two policemen with automatic weapons were patrolling outside.

They had their meal in the kitchen. It was an anti-climax. Alan explained to Peter that they didn't want to ask him about his experiences until he'd talked to the police the next day. So they talked trivialities. Peter was still showing the effects of his pill. Once he emitted a vast yawn, without covering his mouth. When Mary exclaimed, 'Peter, really!' he relaxed for the first time.

'Well, you two seem boring compared with the company I've been keeping.'

Ludicrous as it seemed, his joke was the happiest moment either Alan or Mary had experienced in many weeks. Their son had come through his ordeal. Peter went to bed soon afterwards.

An hour later Brian arrived in a taxi. After Alan had telephoned him with the news at lunchtime, he'd caught an afternoon plane to Belfast. As he entered, he was smoking a cigarette.

'How did you come here?' Mary asked anxiously. 'I don't relish the thought of you on public transport with no security.'

Alan pursued a different strain of parental anxiety. He asked when Brian had taken up smoking.

'Since his lordship upstairs went off on his holidays – the ciggies kept me calm. Well, calmer. I'll go and have a word with him, if he's not asleep.'

Peter was asleep, and Brian didn't waken him.

His younger brother rose the next morning in good spirits. As Mary and Brian stood at the toaster, she murmured that it was as if Peter had never been away. Soon the two boys were scoring points off each other. Alan saw that Brian was engaged in his own form of therapy. It was always sobering when your offspring seemed more mature than yourself.

By ten o'clock, family life was back to near-normal. They still couldn't stop themselves fussing over Peter, but Mary thought it would be better for him to return to routine as quickly as possible. She threw the drying cloth in his direction, and said: 'Come on, dishes to be done!' Peter had always been a reluctant dish-dryer. Now he opened his eyes wide.

'Oh, really! What is this, the return of the long-lost son, or an army boot camp?'

'Boot camp, as usual – get on with it!'

Alec Wilson telephoned, and soon he and his Number Two, Detective Sergeant June Fisher, were interviewing Peter. Wilson again said firmly that he wanted them to see the boy on their own. When Mary protested about this, Alan told her not to make a fuss. The atmosphere between the Houstons grew chillier than at any time since Peter was released.

The two detectives were with him for more than an hour. They found he was a feisty boy, who answered their questions easily, and could remember a surprising amount about his captivity. The only time he came close to tears was in describing the encounter near the border.

When he'd heard the RUC car following the one he was in he began to hope he'd soon be free. He'd felt even more confident when they were held up at the border. He was sure the other policemen, the ones with different uniforms, would help the men in the patrol car to get him away from the IRA.

'Peter, I want you to listen carefully. Describe exactly what happened then, everything you can remember. It's important.'

Peter said that suddenly an older policeman had come out of the hut to speak to the driver of his car. He couldn't make out what he'd said, but he remembered that his own driver had got very excited.

'What did your driver say?'

Peter blushed, and looked at the woman detective before answering.

'He shouted "For fuck's sake let us through, and hold the Prod peelers back." Then the Sergeant – I *think* he was wearing stripes – he shouted "Away ye go, lads, and good luck to yez." That was the way he talked, a bit different from most people I've met over here. The tyres squealed as we started off again. I tried to look out to see if the patrol car got through, but the man beside me in the back seat yanked my head round to the front. That hurt.'

This account of events at the border would come in useful for the chief constable's discussions with the Gardai. What really interested Alec Wilson for his own investigation was any information about the places where Peter had been held prisoner, and about his captors.

It was June Fisher who asked about the house he was taken to immediately after his seizure. How long did the journey last?

Peter thought.

'Maybe about twenty minutes?'

Had he seen what the men looked like?

'They blindfolded me right at the start. When we arrived and the scarf was taken off, the men guarding me were wearing balaclavas.'

Could Peter remember anything more about them, anything at all, June Fisher asked, smiling at him.

'One of them had a dog,' Peter said, managing to smile back. 'Cathal, he called it. He was the same breed as two I saw on the Cave Hill, with men my Dad thought were in the IRA.'

When she asked if there was anything else he could remember, he thought for a long time.

'The room that first night was terribly dirty, with only a few chairs. The door squeaked a lot.'

Peter didn't tell Detective Sergeant Fisher one fact about his first prison. It was that the room smelled as if somebody had peed in it. He didn't think you should mention a thing like that to a woman.

She took down such details as he could remember about the other places he'd been held in, three in all. Peter's recollection had become blurred as his imprisonment dragged on. The police suspected he had slipped into despair, believing he would never be released. They asked how he had been treated. The boy gulped, but could say nothing. Wilson told him he'd done very well. June Fisher closed her notebook.

After they left, Brian suggested that Peter and he should kick a football around. Mary and Alan looked out of the window, and saw they were stringing a rope between two trees to form goal-posts. When Brian agreed to go into goal first, his parents both smiled. Despite the difference in their sons' ages, this issue had not always been resolved so amicably in the past.

Alan stayed at home just long enough to assure himself that Peter was not upset by the questioning. Then he spoke to Mary.

'I ought to go to the office. I want to know what Charles did to stamp on those scare stories in the papers. They might have delayed Peter's release.'

Mary shrugged her shoulders. On this of all days, for God's sake, Alan should be thinking about nothing except his family, and staying at home.

But ten minutes later, she was relieved he had gone to Stormont. The telephone rang, and it was Colin Newhouse, who said how glad he was Peter was free. It must be a great relief to Mary. And to her husband, of course.

It was an uneasy conversation. Phone calls with Colin had been a great comfort during the kidnap, but today Mary was nervous that Peter and Brian would come into the kitchen. Once Colin had talked about Peter, the other purpose of his call became clear. He had accepted a fellowship at Oxford, and would be going there in October.

'I hope you'll come with me, Mary.'

[46]

The atmosphere in the Stormont corridors was euphoric. People Alan scarcely knew clapped him on the back. But at Charles's meeting his cheerfulness was soon diluted. His delight at Peter's release was more important than anything else, of course, but Alan soon concluded that the British negotiating position he and Charles had been hoping to reconstruct was again disintegrating. His career in Ulster was ending in failure.

Dick Heston embarked on an agenda item he had sententiously called 'The Future'. He said because of their proper preoccupation with Peter's safety, there had not been time to review a great deal of activity between Government envoys and the Republican leadership. Charles grunted.

'I hope this "activity" wasn't responsible for the horse manure those two newspapers served up yesterday – time-tables for withdrawal and all that. I was afraid those fictional essays would delay Peter's release, so I personally jumped on them, with hob-nailed boots.'

His permanent secretary judged this a time for pomposity.

'It is not within my knowledge, secretary of state, that dates for British withdrawal have been discussed with Republicans. Though, as you know, some colleagues in Whitehall think that possibility ought to be investigated.'

Charles was irritated. Which colleagues, he thought uneasily – his or Dick's, or some of both? He remembered two oblique conversations with the Prime Minister, and almost spat out his response.

'That's cloud cuckoo land, Dick. First, it's subversive of democracy, takes no notice of what people have voted for. Second, remembering all the promises we've given, it's also a surrender to terrorism.'

Dick shrugged his shoulders with as much truculence as a civil servant ever allows himself.

As the meeting rumbled on, Rupert Rigby-Smith let slip that three more IRA prisoners serving long sentences in England for offences on the mainland were to be sent to the Maze.

The assistant secretary responsible for the prison service frowned. Heavens! This new PR genius had a lot to learn about the mystic skills of public administration. Any displeasing piece of information ought to be slipped into a minister's red box when he was overwhelmed with an entirely different problem. Several officials knew Charles Corbett would be writing an important cabinet paper this weekend. Nothing to do with Ulster – he was advocating a radical shift in government macro-economic policy, because of high unemployment. The man dealing with the prison service had agreed with Dick that Saturday would be a good day to inform the secretary of state of these additional prison transfers. He might overlook the prison report, of course. What a pity!

When Rigby-Smith made his gaffe, Charles raised his eyebrows.

'I'm surprised by this transfer of prisoners, considering how reluctant the home secretary was to move Tommy Hughes.'

Diana mouthed across to Alan: 'Times change.'

Alan looked at her. She was dressed in a lightweight grey suit, her long hair piled up on top in a style he hadn't seen her use before. Diana exuded detached amusement, though her face was too intense to seem kindly. Yet political disagreements with Diana didn't blind him to his own feelings. She now excited him more than Mary had done for several years. While Peter was still in peril he wouldn't admit this, even to himself. But now he knew it to be true.

Towards the end of the meeting, Charles said, 'I wasn't overly happy about that editorial in the *Chronicle* last night. Any comments?'

The assistant secretary responsible for the prison service winced. This was the second blow of a bad morning. The *Chronicle* had raised a much more embarrassing blot on his department's record than what, after all, was primarily a Home Office decision to transfer more prisoners.

The editorial began by endorsing the government's decision to bring

Tommy Hughes back from Wormwood Scrubs, to save Peter Houston's life. But then it went on to comment on what anonymous prison officers at the Maze had told the *Chronicle*'s crime correspondent. These officers claimed that the Maze Prison was out of control, and that the governor was now running it through Republican and Loyalist paramilitary commanders.

Dick, smiling, said he knew what lay behind this editorial.

'My university contemporary, Fred Hargreaves, confided this week that he's leaving Belfast soon for London, to be editorial director of his group. Sam McCluskey won't get the chair at the *Chronicle* this time either, so presumably this editorial was just a flexing of his political muscles.'

Charles grunted. 'All the same, I wish I didn't suspect he has justification for what he wrote. We've heard these rumours before, have we not?'

He turned to the official responsible for the prison service: 'I want on my desk tomorrow morning a paper on both these issues: why I wasn't consulted before we agreed to these Home Office transfers; and what is the truth behind the allegations that the governor is losing control.'

A telephone call later enabled Charles to piece together what lay behind the further transfer of prisoners. In the few days since the Prime Minister overruled Home Office reluctance to move Tommy Hughes, general steadfastness in that department had eroded rapidly. The permanent secretary, who had lost the battle over the transfer, was heard to mutter: 'What the hell! If that's what they want . . .' As soon as pressure came for others prisoners to be transferred, he was ready to agree.

Sinn Fein had already begun to demand the return of named prisoners in English gaols. The *Irish Times* carried a major article on humanitarian aspects of long sentences served far away from home and family. The *New York Times* picked this up, and fervently endorsed it in an editorial which made other disobliging remarks about British policy in Northern Ireland.

When Charles saw the New York paper he exploded in rage.

'"The good grey *Times*", as it so self-lovingly calls itself, is often stuffed with sanctimonious humbug.'

He noted that a careless American copy-editor had allowed this syndicated 'lift' from the *Irish Times* to appear on the same page as an American court report. This revealed that the civilised United States was imposing sentences of death and long imprisonment – improbable periods like 244 years – on people whose crimes seemed less heinous than those of Irish terrorists.

'American attitudes on crime and punishment seem to vary in direct proportion to the distance between Times Square and the scene of the offence.'

When Alan and Diana were alone, she asked whether he imagined the prison transfers were all that was going on? His response sounded weary.

'Do tell me more, if you must.'

'Well, you'd better know that talks with the Provisionals are far more ... well, comprehensive than even I expected. My old chum Howard Considine is busily spinning his webs, with the implicit support of the cabinet secretary.'

Alan's short fuse ignited.

'Surely even bloody Sir Philip wouldn't go freelancing again, after his rebuke from the Prime Minister last month?'

Diana smiled complacently.

'Want to bet, Alan? As I've told you more than once, politicians don't really control policy, for all Charles's play-acting this morning. Senior officials have a continuity that you priests of Demos can never match.'

'But what about the Prime Minister himself? Surely he's worked his way back to the plodding caution that's always been his political strength?'

Diana laughed at his innocence of the ways of her world.

'An old Whitehall rule is operating, my dear. No progress, no Prime Ministerial time. Tom Sanderson's interest span has never been long, and that's especially true when international financiers are breathing down his neck, just a few weeks before his party conference. You've surely read why Harold Macmillan deserted Eden over Suez?'

She said there had been earlier signs that the Prime Minister was getting bored with Ireland again.

'Why do you think he backed the transfer of Tommy Hughes? That scarcely presented a stern face to terrorism.'

'I had naively assumed it was to save my son's life.'

As Diana tried to apologise, Alan wondered at her brash insensitivity. She had been close to him during his weeks of anguish. Wasn't it rather soon for her to jeer at all he'd struggled for politically?

Alan had noticed before that a streak of condescension ran through his bantering friendship with Diana. She would have done well in the old Colonial Service, as a District Officer who'd stand no nonsense from the natives. He'd experienced her intellectual arrogance before, but never this ineffable air of a woman speaking to an ignorant underling.

It was at this moment that Alan Houston, puritan by temperament, but developing belated libertine tendencies, changed course again. Was it just a little while ago he had decided political disagreements were nothing compared with his desire for Diana? Now, because of this row, his feelings about her had altered.

For Alan was a political animal, more even than he was husband, father, or potential lover. Mary could have told him this long ago. Even now he was not introspective enough to realise that his convictions ruled not only his heart but his genitals. As he looked at Diana, he found he was not aroused, not at all.

Alan was angry, and that made him determined. The comradely hugs of yesterday meant nothing. Now, for reasons he did not understand, she was giving him a hard time. This startling glimpse of the vindictive side of her nature rang alarm bells in his head. He shoved a pile of papers into his briefcase.

'I'd better go home and hear the full story of Peter's talk with the police.'

'Feel like going out for a steak first?'

'No thanks, not tonight.'

[47]

Peter had spent an hour that afternoon telling Mary and Brian about his interview with the police. He was reluctant to begin again for his father's benefit.

'I haven't seen *Coronation Street* for years.'

'Years?' Brian said, with an elder brother's superior smile.

'Well, it seemed like that. Remember mate, while you were drinking port in your Junior Common Room I was a prisoner of terrorism.' He crouched, and pointed an imaginary gun at Brian.

Mary said he could watch *Coronation Street*, and talk to Alan later.

Brian lit a cigarette, and went off to telephone his new girlfriend in Cambridge. Alan said now the strain was off he ought to give up smoking. Brian exited with a murmured 'Yeah, yeah.'

As soon as they were alone, Mary said, 'Get me a drink, please, dear. It's been an exciting day, but a long one.'

As he poured the whiskeys, Alan thought how long it was since she'd called him 'dear'. His own feelings were a bewilderment of conflicting eddies, most of them provoked by his conversation with Diana. Perhaps Mary's feelings were confused too.

'Cheers,' she said. Then, after a long pause, 'Alan, I'm afraid this is going to sound like what my father's young soldiers during the war called a "Dear John" letter.'

Alan sat bolt upright.

Mary told him she'd been seeing Colin Newhouse for some months now. She explained what a horror his wife was, that they were about to be divorced, and that he'd asked Mary to go with him to Oxford, where he had a new job. Then she burst into tears, and said she didn't know what to do.

Alan was so stunned as to feel almost frivolous. He offered Mary a potato crisp, though his magpie mind told him you should feed a cold and starve a fever. He had no doubt this was a fever that Mary had caught. For Alan Houston thought affairs were things men had and women suffered.

Neither of them would remember later precisely what came next. Alan reverted to his most po-faced Ulster manner, and said something like while he quite understood Mary's need to weep – and would she like his handkerchief? – his limited knowledge of such affairs suggested it was not usual to consult your husband about your lover just when you were announcing to him that he was being cuckolded.

Mary said indignantly, 'That hasn't happened, Alan. Certainly not yet.'

'Thanks a million,' he said bitterly.

They discussed their marriage. Both agreed it had run out of steam, but they disagreed about the reasons.

'We've only made love once this year. That hasn't helped,' said Alan.

Mary puckered her brow.

'Symptom, not cause. I didn't want sex because what you call "making love" had become a formality, almost a contest. I felt you'd soon want a rosette as Green Star and Best of Breed.'

Alan looked shattered, but Mary was well launched into her grievances. If he wanted to hold an inquest, which was really a waste of effort, he ought to ask himself why she had fallen out of love with him. But did he really want to know that?

'If you wish to tell me, doubtless you will. But I warn you that I'll want you to listen to my side of the story.'

'You've lost interest in everything except politics, Alan. You're obsessed with peace talks that aren't really about peace. You didn't even notice how isolated and miserable I've been in Ulster, even before Peter was kidnapped. How could a man who's supposed to love me, who brought me out here against my will and the interests of my career ... how could you ignore that misery, rarely even notice it?'

'You would never say straight that you didn't want to come here. All I got was that old Home Counties, military family, stiff-upper-lip nonsense your mother taught you: "Always go with your man, dear, it's your duty." Where's all this duty now, then?'

Alan had a penchant for rhetorical self-inebriation. His own words and arguments fired his mind. He told Mary she was an upper-middle-class bigot, who'd made his job even more difficult because she'd never given life in Ulster a chance.

This was not a course of action a marriage guidance counsellor would have commended to Alan. But neither he nor Mary was thinking about reconciliation. More harsh words flew back and forward, until Mary suddenly said; 'Give me another drink, Alan. We'd better not be in the middle of this row when the boys come back in here.'

As he handed her the refilled glass, Mary showed a flash of fair-mindedness that surprised him.

'I must admit you *have* been more considerate during the nightmare we've just been through. But that was too late.'

It had come into Mary's mind that there was more than one comparison to be made between the two men in her life. She'd reflected all day on Colin's phone call that morning. He'd moved on quickly from congratulating her on Peter's freedom to what really interested him, his job in Oxford, and his hope that she'd join him there. Had he forgotten about her own offer of a plum job at the Tate in London? When speaking to a mother who had nearly lost her child for ever, hadn't he seemed a bit . . . well, a bit self-obsessed? Perhaps all men were like that.

There was one subject that symmetry prompted Mary to mention.

'This is a matter of purely historical interest now, Alan, but when I first got involved with Colin I suspected you were about to begin an affair with Diana. Would you like to tell me what you two were up to when the policeman arrived with the news about Peter? At Stormont you looked as guilty as I felt.'

Mary paused, and bit her lip. 'I may as well tell you now that the reason I was late in picking up Peter was because Colin and I spent too long over lunch in a pub. I've suffered the pains of hell about that while Peter was held by the IRA.'

Then she cried again, and this time Alan put his arms around her.

He didn't know how to answer her question about Diana. 'Just talking' would be less than the truth.

Fortunately for Alan, he didn't have time to reply. Peter burst in, humming the *Coronation Street* signature tune, and asked: 'Well, who wants to attend the second showing of "Tales of My Captivity, written and directed by Peter Houston, with additional dialogue by Seamus O'Hooligan of the Provisional IRA"?'

They both thought his captivity had at least left him seeming more mature, though his father worried that he might suffer a bad reaction in a few days' time. They must get medical advice. Mary hastily dried her eyes, then Alan began to ask Peter questions.

'Dad, go easy on the cross-examination, will you? You're a far more aggressive detective than the RUC people, and they get paid for asking questions.'

But the jaunty way he told his story for this second time did not deceive his parents. He'd had a miserable couple of weeks – short of food, locked up, often alone, and afraid he might be killed. The only awkward moment in his narrative came when Mary asked if any of his captors had seemed to feel sorry for him.

'Not a hint of that, Mum. I think they'd have shot me without a second thought.'

Mary shuddered. When Peter looked as if he had recovered from the memory, Alan asked casually. 'Were you able to tell the police about the places where they kept you?'

Peter said he remembered the first house, though the IRA had kept him there for only one night. He was certain it was in Belfast, because it had taken only twenty minutes to get there, and he'd heard a lot of traffic noise outside.

'What kind of a place was it?'

'Miserable room, really bleak, with a table and five or six mouldy old chairs. They threw a dirty sleeping-bag down for me before they banged the door. The whole place smelt as if somebody had peed there. I wondered if it was the dog.'

'The dog?' Mary asked. Peter hadn't mentioned a dog to her earlier.

'A big Alsatian, kept jumping up on me and growling. A bit like those ones we saw on the Cave Hill, Dad. One of the guys in the balaclavas seemed to own him. He kept saying "Down, Cathal!" but the dog didn't take much notice.'

Alan said quietly, 'Did you hear the men speak at all, Peter?'

'Well, none of them talked much, I suppose they didn't want me to remember them. But I noticed the one with the dog had an accent like Mrs Douglas's.'

Mrs Douglas was the woman who cleaned for Mary once a week. Alan was so little at home that he'd never met her. He asked where Mrs Douglas came from. Mary said her parents lived in Tyrone.

'She's quite a bore, is Mrs Douglas, when she starts talking about "Tyrone among the bushes", and how beautiful it is down there.'

Peter resumed his account of the room at the safe house.

'What I can remember most clearly is the door. Every time they opened or closed it, there was a terrible squeak. The IRA mustn't know about lubricating oil.'

Brian, who had just come in, said, 'I don't suppose they're much into DIY apart from Black and Deckers; but they're for knee-capping.'

Mary told him to be quiet. She looked at her husband, who seemed to be a hundred miles away.

[48]

'I've got a job for you, Alan. The Prods are on the rampage now!'

The next morning Alan's mind was still reeling from the double shock of Mary's affair and Peter's revelations. These two thunderbolts in his personal life were more important to him now than any political news Charles might have.

It turned out that Stormont had just learned of a general strike – at least, as 'general' as intimidation by the UDA could make it. Paramilitary leaders felt Whitehall had to be reminded who were the majority in Northern Ireland. Most Protestants might dislike these bully-boys, but this didn't trouble their commanders. Like the IRA they had their own ways of dealing with open defiance in their own areas – arson, the baseball bat and, if need be, the bullet.

Alan responded wearily.

'Of course I'll investigate the strike, Charles. But I've a huge weight on my mind this morning.'

'What's that? Is Peter all right?'

Alan told only half of what was troubling him. No mention of his shattering marriage, just the squeaking door and smell of urine in both the safe house where his last meeting with the IRA had been held, and in the house Peter's kidnappers used. Should he tell the police? Charles looked anxious.

'It's a terrible dilemma. If your evidence – Peter's too, come to think of it – if that convicted Sean, the IRA wouldn't forgive you. My own first reaction is that your family's safety must come first, even before our need to convict the kidnappers. You and Mary have suffered enough already. So has Peter. But whatever we do, it's not a decision that should be taken in a hurry.'

Then Charles's face lightened.

'Meanwhile, how about a fascinating piece of research on Prod attitudes to this strike?'

First he called in Dick and Diana. Dick said support for the strike was overwhelming.

'It demonstrates yet again that the so-called Loyalist community has no loyalty to Her Majesty's Government.'

Charles raised a hand.

'Hold your horses, Dick, we mustn't jump to conclusions. What's the evidence that this strike enjoys voluntary support? We all know what I mean by "voluntary" – unaided by kneecapping and other delights.'

Dick said the security services *knew* that the Protestant areas were solidly behind the strike and against HMG. He could not say more than that. Alan grunted that he didn't have much faith in the ability of either MI5 or MI6 to penetrate the Protestant ghettoes. 'They'd have more chance of infiltrating the Kremlin or the TUC's headquarters in Bloomsbury – assuming those obsessive McCarthyites can distinguish between the two organisations.'

Charles saw that Dick and Alan were, as usual, squaring up to each other, so he closed the discussion.

As Alan embarked on his enquiry, his most enlightening conversation that morning was not in the ghettoes, but with an old schoolmate, Martin Jacobs, who owned a clothing firm near Portadown. As a Jew from a Yorkshire family who'd been brought up in Belfast, he took a cool view of events. When Alan telephoned, Jacobs was blunt.

'I bet your colleagues in their Stormont ivory tower think everybody's supporting this strike. Right?'

Alan grimaced at the accuracy of this guess, and murmured assent.

'Thought so. Police and army bosses, shielding their backsides, have told them that. Well, it's not true.'

He then told Alan what had happened at his factory, where he employed eighty workers, evenly divided between the two religions.

'As soon as the strike was threatened, the two shop stewards – inevitably one of each "persuasion", as they say in these parts – came to see me. They said this wasn't an industrial dispute, their union was dead against it, and they all wanted to work on.'

So production had been going fine when, in mid-morning, three thugs with Glasgow Rangers scarves and baseball bats appeared outside the gates. Martin Jacobs laughed.

'Incidentally, Alan, the only bit of amusement I've been able to extract from this dreary affair is that if I allowed anybody in the factory to wear a football scarf like that, I'd be breaking the law. The Fair Employment Commission say they're provocative. Where were *they* this morning when I needed them?'

He said reports that the thugs were writing down car numbers spread through the factory. Workers asked what the management was doing to protect them.

'So I phoned the local police, who said they were overwhelmed: there were incidents of intimidation everywhere. At their suggestion I tried an army unit stationed nearby. One of its officers, a chap from Leeds, had a meal at our house last month. He said his soldiers were working their butts off to maintain petrol supplies to doctors and hospitals.

'I tried to argue to the shop stewards that there was no sign of active thuggery, just intimidation. The stewards wanted to be helpful, but I wasn't surprised when they came back and said the workers had decided to go home early, and wouldn't be back until the atmosphere cooled down.'

Alan had a lunchtime sandwich with a neighbour. This commuter said when his car reached the roundabout leading towards Belfast, four youngsters with staves were turning back the traffic. They wore Union Jack T-shirts, and couldn't have been more than fifteen. Three policemen and five soldiers were watching them, but from 100 yards away. When motorists complained to the police, they shrugged their shoulders sheepishly. Many people concluded the authorities had given up, so they turned their cars and took a day off work.

'That's a helluva contrast with the rough way English police often treat union pickets. I hear the thugs were out on the Belfast bridges too. This place won't be right until ordinary people like me combine to chuck a few of them into the Lagan.'

Alan smiled sympathetically. He could understand the temptation this man felt for righteous direct action. But he remembered that this was how the Ulster Defence Association had begun, a response to direct action by another set of hard men who thought of themselves as 'defenders' – the Provisional IRA.

Now these two sets of defenders were competitors in sectarian murder.

[49]

Alan spent a sleepless night. He thought less about the Protestant strike than about Mary's affair. He didn't even consider telling his wife the damning evidence he had against Sean. They had not spoken since she'd told him about Colin Newhouse two days ago. Towards dawn, Alan thought his head would burst. He rose, made a mug of tea, and set off for the shipyard, which had joined the strike the previous night.

Harland and Wolff's was part of Alan's family history. Not only had his father been a militant shop steward there after the Second World War; his mother's father had played an involuntary role in an incident that produced grievances lasting right up to the present.

Just before the Great War, at the height of the Home Rule controversy, this ageing man had been a Sunday school superintendent in a village near Belfast. He had taken the children on a Saturday picnic to a County Derry village. As they walked back to their train in the evening, men from the Ancient Order of Hibernians, the Nationalist equivalent of the Orange Order, led a crowd in stoning the children and their teachers. Alan's grandfather was cut on the head. The children fled in terror and wept through most of the journey home.

Belfast newspapers carried extensive reports of the attack. Many Catholics worked at the Belfast shipyard then; but the age-old curse of tit-for-tat took over that weekend and when these Catholics arrived for work on the Monday, Protestant workers threw several of them off the slipways into the River Lagan. Some were pelted with rivet ends. After this incident, few Catholic workers returned to the shipyard. It soon became almost exclusively Protestant and remained so.

Alan parked his car outside the shipyard gates. Nine or ten parallel streets of small terraced houses run from the yard perimeter to the main Newtownards Road. In earlier decades this was where the workers lived. There had once been 40,000 of them, the men who launched the Titanic and a dozen more fortunate liners, who built and repaired naval ships in both world wars. The workforce was now savagely reduced in numbers, and with narrower skills. The few thousand who remained thought themselves lucky to be churning out oil-tankers – when there were any on the order book.

Once he left the police grouped near the gates, Alan found himself in a No-Man's-Land, eerily empty of people. But on the main road, although pickets had stopped buses and other traffic, there was a buzz of activity. On every street corner stood groups of men armed with sticks or baseball bats. Many wore balaclavas to conceal their identities, though there wasn't a policeman close enough to identify anybody.

When Alan talked to them, he heard familiar grievances against Stormont, London, Dublin, an ineffectual feeling that Nationalism was in the driving seat, and that political control in Ulster was slipping away from the Unionist majority. The phrase 'they're gittin' in everywhere' might have mystified a stranger. Alan knew that 'they' were Catholics, and that 'they' were 'taking Protestant jobs', invading Protestant housing estates. This grievance was a mirror-image of Catholic grievances, and as lovingly nurtured.

A thick-looking man, who thought Alan was a reporter, spoke angrily to him.

'D'ya see me? If I could get m'hands on that skitter Corbett, I'd clack him one. He's in cahoots w' them scuts in Sinn Fein, and nivver bathers wi' us.'

One of his companions eyed Alan.

'Knackitaff, Jimmy. Yer man here's not from the papers at all. He works for Corbett. Give him a wide berth.'

One by one the pickets moved away from Alan. But soon a man wearing a cloth cap – 'a duncher', uniform dress of the shipyard worker and football supporter – approached him.

'You just come up from Harland's, mister? These glipes have Dee Street and most of the bigger streets covered. But d'ye think there's any way I could get down to the yard without gettin' me head bate in?'

Alan asked if he was opposed to the strike. The man rolled his eyes.

'It'd scunner you the way this lot's gettin' on. I just want to go to work. I've never scabbed in a proper dispute, over wages or a sackin'. But I was at work yesterday, and I'm buggered if I'm losin' today's pay over these gaunches.'

'Are there many feel like you?'

'Aye, most of them. But they're scared of the bully boys, so they are. Listen, I didn't come in m'car today, because they write down car numbers, and maybe set ye on fire later – the car or yer house. It'd sicken ye. We're livin' under lynch law, just like the Mickies are, only it's the UDA tellin' us what we can do. This place is gettin' like the Falls, or the bloody Wild West.'

Alan suggested a route that would lead him to the main gate without the risk of meeting anybody. Down the Newtownards Road towards the city, he could see army and police armoured cars parked about a quarter of a mile away. They were – as intelligence reports on Dick Heston's desk were doubtless informing him – 'avoiding any exacerbation of an already inflamed situation'. In other words, they were leaving the streets and the strike to the bully boys.

At Stormont that evening, Alan told Charles what he'd seen. The image of soldiers and police declining to control the streets was giving a dangerous message. Charles's predecessor had allowed the UDA to bring down a power-sharing government, the best hope of peace there had ever been. Now this passive attitude of police and army signalled that the government was accepting a second defeat at the hands of Loyalist paramilitaries. Alan spoke bitterly.

'God alone knows what the UDA hope to bring down this time. Maybe the United Nations?'

Charles looked horrified.

'Tomorrow the army and police will have orders to clear the roads. After that, the shipyardmen will have to decide whether they've the guts to go to work. Of course, if you're not right about their real feelings I'll have egg on my face.'

The next morning Alan arrived on the Newtownards Road just before eight o'clock. Many balaclavas were still on parade. Little knots of workers again stood wondering whether to risk the passage to the shipyard. Promptly at eight, there was a revving of engines further down the main road, and three armoured carriers, side by side, rolled up to the corner of Dee Street. A police inspector and half-a-dozen constables walked beside them.

The inspector told the pickets he had orders to clear the road. They replied that they weren't acting unlawfully. The policeman grimaced.

'And do you usually carry baseball bats when you go for a morning stroll?'

A picket uttered a foul mouthful of abuse. His face contorted with hatred, only a foot from the inspector's. Supporters raised an uncertain shout of encouragement. The inspector turned to his men.

'Draw batons,' he barked out. Black batons appeared in the RUC men's hands.

The inspector spoke icily. 'Are you going to do what I ask, and clear the road?'

A confused murmur greeted this. But the picket who'd already challenged him growled his considered response.

'I'm fucked if Ah'll clear this road till ye've cleared them Provo vermin aff uv the Falls.'

The inspector was not in a mood for dialectic. He struck the picket's shoulder sharply with his baton. The man uttered a shout of rage and pain. The constables, moving in behind him, raised their batons. But before a dozen blows had been struck, the pickets began to disperse, some running. At that moment, the Loyalist strike was lost, and not just at the shipyard.

Men who had been hanging around on street corners started to walk down the side streets that led to the main gate. Alan mingled with them as he returned to his car. Most were discussing how much they might find deducted from their wages. But he heard with satisfaction a couple of men express the opinion that the strike organisers had turned out to be a bunch of cream-puffs.

'The polis tuk them on, and they battled out,' said one man with a grin.

Alan smiled back. This sentence might sound ambiguous to a stranger, but the political adviser knew Belfast's 'o's' from its 'a's'. At least some things were going right.

[50]

No political victory could divert Alan Houston's mind for long from his personal dilemmas. He had no doubt that Sean had been involved in Peter's kidnapping but if he told the police and gave evidence against Sean, how would Mary react? She was now in a state of permanent anxiety about her family and herself. Surely she would think he ought to close the chapter on the kidnapping, for fear of provoking further reprisals?

These questions niggled away as he returned to Stormont. But soon they raised other questions. After what Mary had told him, why was he even considering the effect on their marriage? Surely he should just decide what was the right action to take. He wanted whoever had kidnapped Peter, and put Mary and Brian and himself through hell, to go to prison for a long time. If terrorists began to think kidnapping children was risk-free, that it carried no price, where would it end?

As Alan entered Stormont Castle he ignored the habitual antipathy of the guard dogs, howling from their kennels. By now he was wrestling with a question he had tried to avoid. It was what he should do about Mary and himself. That was if he wanted to do anything, other than walk away from a marriage she seemed to regard as over.

When Alan came into Charles's room, he received a congratulatory pat on the back for judging right about the Protestant strike. But that was no longer at the front of his mind.

He smiled wanly. 'Thanks, Charles. But have you had a chance to think about whether I should go to the police with this evidence against Sean?'

The secretary of state could be decisive about political matters, as he'd shown when dealing with the strike and disorder on the streets.

That was the kind of decision he believed ministers were employed to take. Solving personal dilemmas was not what he was best at, especially in the new mood of deep disillusion with all things Irish which was now upon him.

He heard himself mouthing platitudes, rehearsing possible courses of action, just as his civil servants mouthed platitudes in their option papers for him. All the time he was thinking how he could get Alan's dilemma off his own plate.

Charles Corbett was a kindly man. He had suffered more genuine anguish over the Houstons' loss of their son than anybody else at Stormont. But now that Peter was free, the single-mindedness that made him a successful politician engaged top gear again. Alan's was a political problem too, of course, but Charles closed his eyes to its uncomfortable implications for law enforcement in Ulster. For what Diana had said about the Prime Minister's recent shift in priorities also applied to his secretary of state for Northern Ireland.

With the collapse of Charles's efforts to broker a just peace – rather than just perpetuate the mixture of bully-and-surrender favoured in Whitehall – a chapter had ended for him. He concluded sadly that he could achieve little more here. Slowly, subconsciously, he was closing the file in his mind marked 'Ulster'. He was not yet sure when he should try to escape from the Stormont job, but that was now just a tactical choice.

Faced with Alan's hard question about going to the police with his evidence, Charles Corbett, philosopher as well as political operator, fell into a reverie. His Stormont interlude had at least taught him something. Most leading practitioners in the Westminster village, steeped in the life-stories of statesmen like Gladstone, Lloyd George and Churchill, secretly think of themselves as tragic heroes. Charles himself wanted to play a great role in affairs, though he knew that political careers usually ended in disappointment, even tragedy.

Now he wondered whether most politicians, including himself, might finish up not as tragic heroes, but as comic ones, playthings of events, even buffoons. But he thought: 'Well, that's the human condition, and there's precious little any of us can do about it, except hope to survive.' Charles Corbett, though by nature an idealist, was accepting his leader's Damon Runyon approach to politics, 'doing the best you can'.

He jerked himself back to Alan's problem, and reached a practical conclusion. Getting his political adviser to seek advice from others would allow him to concentrate on refuting the poisonous Cabinet paper he'd just received from his old adversary, the Chancellor of the Exchequer. He told himself this was what his fellow-citizens paid him for. It was certainly what the Left in the party wanted him to do.

'Why don't you talk it over with Diana, Alan? Come and see me again when you've done that. But talk to Dick first too.'

Diana listened to Alan's story with the same know-it-all air that had irritated him a few nights before. Then they had been talking politics, which was bad enough. Now it was the safety of his family, for heaven's sake!

'This,' she told him, with a smug smile, 'is a decision to separate the men from the boys all right.'

Alan was already painfully aware – but Diana reminded him – of what he had long argued: that the government and police must find ways of persuading ordinary people to give evidence against terrorists. Because several witnesses in serious cases had been murdered – one in front of his wife and children, on the eve of the court hearing – most civilians were intimidated from giving evidence.

'Look, Alan, we'll never get convictions while the courts hear evidence only from "Police Officer A" or "Soldier B". Even when the police secure a confession, the defence always say it's been extracted by ill-treatment.'

Alan nodded miserably. He could see where her argument led.

'So what do you think I should do, Diana?'

'You've no real choice – go to the police.'

'What worries me is that Mary and the boys could be IRA targets for ever. I knew one minister's wife who had Protection Squad police in her kitchen for years, all day and every day. It's no life.'

Diana gave him a cold, hard look.

'I hadn't thought you'd worry over-much about the convenience of the erring Mary.'

When he thought about it afterwards, Alan concluded that she might as well have kicked him in the scrotum.

'What do you mean by "erring", Diana?'

She showed a first, slight sign of embarrassment.

'I realise these matters can easily be exaggerated in this gossip-ridden province, but I assumed it was general knowledge that Mary has been seeing a man at Queen's. Colin Newhouse, isn't it? I take it you've known about this much longer than I have?'

'Mary told me a couple of days ago. I'm still trying to take it in.'

When she began to apologise, he looked into her eyes without speaking. He still found her achingly attractive. As he'd come into her room today – despite his worries, despite their recent row, despite the awesome decision he was asking her to help him take – he'd felt his flesh rise to her.

As he walked out through the door again, he concluded that while he'd like to have Diana in his bed, he wouldn't be able to stand her for long in the living-room. He still lusted after her – no doubt about that. Her body excited him, she had a sparkling personality, and in the right mood was wonderful company. But he couldn't imagine himself actually living with such a moody woman – a bully and an upper-class cynic who didn't seem to believe in anything worthwhile, whether in politics or human relations.

Strange how class and politics came into Alan Houston's mind, at the most unlikely moments.

[51]

Before Alan could arrange to see Dick, his telephone rang. It was Fred Hargreaves, the editor of the *Chronicle*, who had called to say goodbye. He was off to London sooner than expected.

'I've got some gossip I want to tell you before I leave. It must have been dreadful for you to watch that *Late Night Special* fantasy about the London Underground while you were still worried sick about your boy's safety. I told the BBC Controller here I thought it a disgrace.'

He chuckled, and said an old chum at the Television Centre had told him about a sequel in London that Alan might enjoy.

'Apparently Roger Corfield's programme has turned into one of those *causes célèbres* that the Beeb's so good at. The mother and father of all inquests is going on.'

'Oh, they've concluded the threat to the London Underground system was not altogether serious, have they?'

'Not as clear-cut a conclusion as that, I gather.'

Alan's opinionated interest in his old employer forced him to interrupt.

'No, the Corporation never is clear-cut. The *aficionados* down there will be waiting to see the Yellow Page minutes next week. If anybody can interpret those, hacking his way through the compulsory verbiage, he may discover what the truth has been *held* to be. It's a process of semi-divine revelation. D'ye know the favourite sayings at the Corporation when the ordure hits the air-extractor? "The buck never stops here" and "Deputy heads must roll".'

Alan had decided his own painful talk with Dick about his evidence could wait while he enjoyed Hargreaves's gossip. He was not disappointed by the malicious pleasure the story gave him. The editor knew a lot of details.

'Once doubts about the authenticity of Roger's programme reached the higher echelons, the inquests began, and they're still dragging on. Poor Roger!'

'Typical! One last interruption, Fred. Did you hear about the Mad Hatter's lunch party Diana and I had with the BBC team? Roger was quite keen then to claim it as all his own work, but Hugh Seabrooke was equally determined to establish that he was the big shot. So how's Hugh doing before the grand inquisitors?'

'My contact was funny about Hugh. Says he's been assiduously distancing himself from the programme ever since. Never did a presenter's smirk more eloquently signal: "Nuffin' to do wi' me, Guv."'

According to his deep throat at Shepherd's Bush, the story behind the inquest was one of BBC plotting worthy of *All the President's Men*. A year or so ago, when Corfield had been appointed to the plum job in Belfast, the London crime correspondent was an unsuccessful candidate. That made them rivals. So the crime man was delighted when a chum in the Metropolitan Police told him the truth behind the bomb threat.

'My contact says he's boasting that he saw a unique opportunity to "decelerate young Roger's upward mobility", as he put it.'

Alan said that from his own experience at the BBC, natural rivalries established themselves in every broadcasting generation, without the participants doing much about it. The BBC gossip machine – more formidable than any transmitter, more subtle than the most sophisticated technology – established the pecking order for them.

Hargreaves chuckled. 'That sounds like precisely what happened here. The crime correspondent concluded this might be an occasion when the list of runners-and-riders for the next-Head-of-News-but-two could be given a shake-up, to his own possible advantage. So he judiciously told all and sundry that the whole of Scotland Yard was rocking with laughter over *The Disaster Scenario*.'

Hargreaves said the Director-General had established a high-level enquiry.

'By the way, Alan, have you ever wondered why such enquiries are always "high level"?'

'Probably for the same reason that models are always "top". C'mon, Fred, your reporters couldn't really write about "a bottom model", could they? Anyhow, who would want to serve on a low-level enquiry? Certainly not the manoeuvrers and shakers who make up the administrative hierarchy at my late, beloved BBC.'

[52]

As Alan laid the phone down, Dick Heston came into his room.

'Charles says you want to discuss something personal with me?'

'It's about a difficult decision I've got to take. I've chanced on evidence that implicates one of the IRA men I've been talking to in Peter's kidnapping.'

The permanent secretary emitted a low whistle.

'Are you sure? It's not Liam, is it?'

Alan shook his head.

'No, Sean O'Brien, a much nastier man than Liam.'

He told about Peter's memories of Sean's Tyrone accent, his dog Cathal, sordid details of the room he'd been held in. Dick laughed nervously and said Alan mustn't expect terrorist premises to conform to the Shops and Offices Act. Then he turned to his real concern.

'Look, Alan, we rightly gave your son's release priority over negotiations for a ceasefire. But now my intelligence sources are reporting that the IRA has got the capability for a new bombing campaign, in Britain as well as out here. We need criminal charges against Sean like a hole in the head.'

Alan was disturbed. 'But surely I've got a duty to help the police find the kidnappers? We've spent enough energy and public money trying to get ordinary citizens to use the confidential telephone. Public servants like me aren't any different.'

Dick then argued that Alan had a right not to put his family in any further danger. This was precisely opposite to the position Diana had taken. The conversation ended inconclusively, and Alan was left with his dilemma.

When Charles heard about this conflicting advice, he wrinkled his brow. His mind was full of his row with the Chancellor. Charles was ignoring the old political maxim: 'If you can't ride two horses at once you'd better get out of the circus.' The economic direction of the government was now the only politics he cared about. He wondered whose side the Prime Minister would take. He also wondered ever more anxiously when he could decently get out of Northern Ireland and resume the hour-by-hour networking around Whitehall, which he had decided was the only way to achieve anything useful in government.

Reluctantly he switched his thinking back to Alan's dilemma. It was a rambling conversation that both found uncomfortable. Charles's only significant contribution came at the end.

'You must talk to Mary about your family's safety and convenience. You've put them through a helluva lot, Alan. Talk to your wife, and give her views just as much weight as what Diana's said. Above all, take your time.'

Alan had another sleepless night. He still couldn't bring himself to talk to Mary, because he knew she'd tell him not to go to the police. But Alan's stubborn nature said that Sean shouldn't get off with his part in kidnapping a little boy, possibly scarring his mind for life.

He spent more than a week dithering but he never spoke to Mary about it. Instead he telephoned Alec Wilson, the chief superintendent in charge of the investigation. They met later in the day. After Alan had told his story, Wilson looked over to his sergeant, who'd been taking notes.

'What d'ye think, June?'

The sergeant looked excited, and said she thought they had the makings of a case against Sean, though not against Liam.

Alan was startled.

'No, no, certainly not against Liam.'

He couldn't imagine giving evidence against Liam.

June Fisher said what they would need was some forensic.

'How'd it be, sir, if we give Mr Houston a ride in the streets near the **Irish Volunteer**? With luck he'll recognise the building they took him to. The fingerprint boys could dust it, and we might find O'Brien's

230

dabs there. Or even Peter Houston's. If so, we could take him round to identify the place.'

Alan blanched at mention of Peter. But when the chief superintendent put the crucial question – knowing the risks involved, was Alan still willing to help? – he received a firm nod of the head. Alan Houston had crossed a Rubicon.

That afternoon he identified the safe house without difficulty. The driver, who'd been selected because he knew the district well, affirmed that it was a building police had often seen IRA suspects entering or leaving. No surprise they used it as a safe house, he said. Just surprising they'd risked taking Mr Houston there without a blindfold.

'I guess they thought they could trust you,' he said blithely. Alec Wilson frowned, and looked uneasily at Alan. Then he said brusquely: 'Thank you for that, constable. Let's get out of here.'

The long-delayed conversation with Mary took place that evening. She thought the story emerged with tortuous slowness, but when she'd heard it all she could see why. She asked, with studied calm, whether he'd sought anybody's advice before taking this step?

He mentioned Charles, then Dick, then Diana. These names, too, came out like treacle. Mary supposed all of them thought he had a public duty to go to the police?

Alan said no, Dick had not wanted anything to upset new negotiations with the IRA. Charles had been ambiguous, said it was ultimately up to Alan himself.

'And Diana?'

'Diana thinks I have a duty to take the evidence to the police.'

Mary exploded in anger. She supposed it had not occurred to him that his wife had more interest in this matter than Diana?

'For heaven's sake, you've told me yourself that you think her political judgement is shaky. Yet you take her advice on your family's safety, against Dick's and Charles's, and without even asking me.'

She looked icily at him, and asked again if he was having an affair with Diana. Alan denied it and said what the hell had that to do with the decision he had taken? By now he was as angry as she was.

'If you want to know why I asked the three people at Stormont rather than you, it's because they're capable of rational thought. As your outburst has just illustrated, you think in emotional spasms.'

'But your supposedly rational thought has omitted the small fact that it's me, not Diana, who's in danger. It's your sons and me who'll suffer the wrath of the IRA if one of their thugs is gaoled.'

As her temper slowly cooled, Mary asked the questions Alan had dreaded. Wasn't his evidence circumstantial? How could the police be sure the house where he'd met Sean and Liam was the same one that Peter had been taken to immediately after he was kidnapped? Alan said they hoped they would find Peter's fingerprints there, as well as Sean's.

Mary asked, 'And if they do?'

'They'd probably take him there to identify the place.'

Mary closed her eyes. 'And then he'd have to give evidence in court, I suppose?'

Alan shifted uneasily, and said he wasn't sure about that.

Mary took a long time before she continued the conversation.

'By the time of any trial Peter and I will be well away from Ulster. If the RUC want him to give evidence, I'll make them get a court order to bring us back here. We'll have to endure protection for the rest of our lives.'

As the implication of her own words sank in, Mary began to cry. Alan moved to comfort her, but she pushed him away.

'I don't think you've taken in the reality, Alan. We've passed the point of no return. I'm leaving you. I'm going to live in England. After that, you can do whatever the hell you like, with Diana or otherwise.'

Alan asked if she planned to live with Colin Newhouse in Oxford.

'None of your business! This is just about you and me, nobody else. This time you've gone too far. We're finished. Our marriage is over. With you, bloody politics and even bloodier Ireland come first every time.'

Mary was not being completely frank. She did not tell Alan about her latest telephone conversation with the director of the Tate Gallery. He had called during the week when Alan was deciding whether to go to the police with his evidence. Her old chief in Impressionists was taking early retirement. How was Mary placed now that her son was free?

She said she'd like to be considered for the vacancy. The director laughed, and said she could forget about being 'considered'. If she wanted the job, it was hers.

The other incident she did not mention to Alan involved Colin. A few days after he'd asked her to live with him in Oxford they'd arranged to meet in the flat of a friend of his who was on holiday. There Colin had tried, clumsily and ineffectually, to make love to her. She had broken down, and told him to stop.

Later Mary asked herself why she was surprised? What had she thought Colin borrowed his friend's flat for? Why had she gone there, if not to make love? It was the most cliché-ridden plot, pure Mills and Boon.

Mary answered her own questions easily: a more sensitive man would have given her the time and space she needed. Mary always looked critically at other people's behaviour, rarely at her own. And never for a single moment did she admit that, once she knew she was going back to the Tate, Oxford seemed a less convenient place for her and Peter to live.

She was a woman who took care never to remain perplexed for long. Perplexity was an obstacle to action. By contrast with her husband she sometimes made her mind up with a speed that frightened even herself.

She concluded after the débâcle in the flat that Colin had been an oasis in the desert. (How quickly Mr Newhouse had moved into the pluperfect!) Their tentative affair, if that's what it was, had been merely a reaction against what Alan's dreadful job had done to his personality, against her whole experience in Ulster, the people she met, the attitudes she loathed. Her suspicion that Alan was involved with Diana had made her susceptible. That was all.

Mary told Alan none of this. Even in this last encounter with him, her reticence prevailed. She was very angry but she just said that she was finished with him. That was all he needed to know.

[53]

'This Court of Oyer, Terminer and General Gaol Delivery for the County of the City of Belfast is now in Session. God save the Queen!'

Alan sat through the legal archaisms of opening ceremonies in the Victorian courthouse. As a young reporter he'd spent many hours here. He'd once seen a man sentenced to death for killing an old woman to get money for his shotgun wedding. The Appeal Court freed him on a technicality – the jury had been taken on an evening coach trip, instead of being locked up – but the acquitted man kept getting beaten up in dockside pubs, so he emigrated to Canada.

In terrorist cases they now had judges sitting alone. The IRA had discovered ways to intimidate jurors, thus offering a valuable lesson to the criminal community in England. The poor old English cons had an uneven record of success. When the IRA fixed a jury it stayed fixed.

Alan was aroused from his reverie when the clerk called: 'Put up Sean O'Brien.'

The prison officers then went through their own ancient ritual. Long before the court sat Sean had been led through the tunnel which runs from Crumlin Road prison beneath the main road, and was now lodged in a cell just below the dock. But everyone in court could hear the echoing sound of warders' voices down below, shouting Sean's name to one another, as if they might have mislaid him.

At last he appeared in the dock, blinking in the bright sunlight. First his gaze took in the judge, then the clerk, who was asking him to confirm his name. But soon Sean's eye lighted on Alan. It was a long, steady gaze.

He pleaded Not Guilty to kidnapping Peter Houston, seizing him unlawfully in Holywood, County Down, on a date in June last passed, and thereafter unlawfully detaining the said Peter Houston against his will. And conspiracy to kidnap, seize and detain the said Peter Houston. Not Guilty to all of these. Sean's austere glance seemed to enquire of the clerk whether there was anything else he'd care to mention?

Detective Sergeant June Fisher gave evidence of arrest. The accused had declined to make any answer to the charge. A man from the police forensic department said Sean's fingerprints were in all parts of the safe house. There were also smudged prints on the arms of a chair in the main downstairs room. These appeared to match Peter Houston's.

Defence counsel rose, swished his gown up on to his shoulders, adjusted his wig, and said, 'Appeared?' Here was something he must get his teeth into right away, for it was crucial to the Crown case.

The police expert explained that the smudging affected three fingers of the right-hand print they had found. But the index finger and the thumb were, in his opinion, a match for those of the boy.

'They were the only prints from a child among the many on the furniture in that room.'

'Let me be sure', said defence counsel with ostentatious patience, 'that I understand what you are saying. It is because my client's fingerprints are among those of many other adults in this room, while the room is *not* smothered in the fingerprints of other children, but contains only a doubtful impress of Peter Houston's thumb and forefinger . . . that's why my client is accused of kidnapping? Isn't that all the prosecution case amounts to?'

Crown counsel jumped to his feet to protest that this was taking an expert witness far beyond his competence. The judge said the witness must answer only what he knew about.

The forensic expert took the cue. It wasn't for him to say what the strengths and weaknesses of the case were. But he believed these were definitely prints of Peter Houston's index finger and thumb.

Defence counsel prefaced his next question by saying that the forensic evidence seemed extremely tenuous. Why did the witness have such faith in his judgement of what he acknowledged were smudged prints? Wasn't the only reason that police had told him the boy Peter Houston had been held in this room? Was Peter Houston to be called to the witness box to identify the room?

The fingerprint man said that this, too, was beyond his personal knowledge. Defence counsel looked towards his colleague for the Crown. The prosecutor made no response until the judge spoke.

'Are you calling the boy, Mr Arkwright?'

The lawyer rose to his feet slowly. His words came out slowly too, for this was the flaw in his case that had worried him for days.

'My Lord, it was judged that this boy, who is only twelve years old, had already suffered enough potential psychological damage from his incarceration in appalling circumstances. The Crown did not feel he should be subjected to an ordeal in court, facing a public gallery occupied by many members or supporters of the organisation which kidnapped him.'

Defence counsel jumped to his feet.

'M'learned friend has made an outrageous suggestion, M'Lord. It's a slur on the reputation of every single person in the gallery who has come to observe this important case.'

His intervention was a signal for the public gallery to erupt in angry shouting, and it took the judge and the court usher several minutes to command silence.

Crown counsel said he would now call Alan Houston, the kidnapped boy's father, who would be able to identify the room and witness to the accused man's apparent familiarity with it.

As Alan walked to the witness box, there was a stirring in the gallery, and a woman's voice screamed 'Quisling! Brit-loving bastard!' Two policewomen pulled at the arms of a pretty, dark-haired girl in a black dress. As they led her out of the court, one of them emitted a sharp cry of pain. The policewoman's ankle hurt, so she carelessly stood on the dark-haired girl's foot. The judge said if there were any more disturbances he would order the public gallery to be cleared.

Alan's evidence-in-chief was brief. Afterwards he reflected that the Crown silk had not made much of his assertion that Sean had shown intimate knowledge of the safe house where they met. Alan mentioned the squeaking door and the smell of urine, and said he knew Sean had a dog called Cathal and spoke with a Tyrone accent.

But when he said this was the accent and the dog's name Peter recalled, defence counsel challenged again. The judge agreed this was hearsay evidence and Crown counsel was left even more uneasy.

Alan's cross-examination was also brief, and defence counsel concluded it with a sneer.

'A squeaking door, Mr Houston. That's what this whole case, which you have concocted almost single-handed, that's what it really comes down to, isn't it? Your son, who's not to give evidence today, told you he heard a door squeaking. That's hearsay evidence in itself, but we'll let that pass for the moment. Then you think *you* heard a squeaking door, on an occasion when you had a quite amiable conversation with my client and a friend of his in this room. Not very substantial, is it? It's almost as squeaky as the door, don't you think?'

The public gallery erupted in giggles. Alan was irrationally angered by the suggestion that his conversation with Liam and Sean was amiable. He could recall that evening vividly, how his stomach churned as he worried about whether Peter would ever be freed, while all Liam and Sean wanted to talk about was fresh negotiations with the IRA. He spluttered out most of this, knowing the impression he was making on the judge could not be good.

Alan suspected the case against Sean was collapsing. His own evidence was not strong enough to make up for Peter's absence. That was his fault too. When Mary had heard that the prosecution proposed to call Peter, she'd telephoned Alan from England. Her conversation was of undiluted fury and hatred.

The next morning he had told Alec Wilson that if Peter was brought to court under subpoena, he would withdraw his own evidence. Alan knew his son's absence might undermine the case against Sean, but he feared what Mary shouted down the phone was true: if Peter was responsible for Sean going to prison nobody would be able to protect him. At best his entire youth would be spent looking over his shoulder. At worst he would be killed. Peter had suffered enough. If any more risks had to be taken, Alan would take them alone.

But in court today it seemed to him that he'd taken the risk without achieving justice against the man he believed was a key figure in Peter's kidnapping.

Defence counsel rose to ask the judge to dismiss the charges.

'The Crown case is so insubstantial, M'Lord, that I feel no need to call my client to rebut this concatenation of rumour and hearsay.'

He began to enjoy himself as he ridiculed the Crown's effort to link the two recollections of a squeaking door. One of them came from the mouth of the father. The other might have been put in the son's mouth by him. This, he argued, was a man so obsessed – understandably obsessed, he added, with a show of sympathy – by what had happened to his son, that he didn't care who got hurt. Anybody with Republican connections, however tenuous, was fair game to Alan Houston. Justice was far back in his thoughts.

Crown counsel tried to argue that Peter Houston had first spoken of the squeaking door to two RUC detectives, one of whom had given evidence that day. He would recall her if necessary.

The judge shook his head, and murmured: 'Hearsay again, as you very well know, Mr Arkwright.'

Counsel said the story could not be a concoction of Alan Houston's. He maintained that the fingerprint evidence established that the kidnapped boy had been held in that room, despite bungled efforts to erase his prints.

Alan could see that his heart was no longer in the case. He knew he'd lost, on the oldest legal trap, hearsay evidence. It was Peter's absence which was responsible.

The judge was brief. There were deeply suspicious circumstances in this case. Defence counsel had stretched credulity to its limits by implying that the accused man's Republican connections were tenuous. He had, after all, been sentenced for firearms offences only four years ago, and he made no secret of his continuing admiration for the IRA.

But that had limited relevance to the present charges, and the evidence to convict him of these was simply not available. The judge could understand, even sympathise with the reason it had been decided not to call Peter Houston, but without him the Crown never had a real hope of proving the connection between the two events which allegedly took place in this room. He cleared his throat, looked wearily towards the dock, and said: 'You may go now, Mr O'Brien.'

In the Bar mess later, he murmured to Crown counsel: 'I was tempted to add that chestnut from the old Munster Circuit: "You have been acquitted by a Limerick jury, and leave this court with no other stain on your reputation."'

[54]

Sean was carried away on the shoulders of cheering supporters. The railings of both courthouse and prison were lined with banners: 'What price British justice?' 'Free the political prisoners *now*!' As Alan was driven away in a police car, the jeering crowd saw him almost too late. He watched a sprinting youth fail to catch up. Then he spied a single banner that puzzled him.

'Free Sean O'Brien – he's suffered more than any father should.'

Alan missed another slogan which was causing problems for the reporter from BBC Television. The tough-minded Angela Hayter had taken over in Belfast from Roger Corfield, who was still enduring the interminable BBC inquiry into his programme about the London Underground. Angela had recorded her interviews with Sean and with the chairman of the 'Free the Political Prisoners' committee. These were on their way to Broadcasting House, in the centre of Belfast, to be sent to London for the lunchtime News.

Now she was preparing her piece to camera. She wanted to have a backdrop of the portico of the prison, across the street from the courthouse. But directly behind where she needed to stand was another banner. This said: 'Fuck the Brit-loving basterd Houston'. Alan's name had joined a distinguished Belfast gallery, which included the Pope and the Queen, though in different districts.

Angela spoke to her producer, Nigel Grant, a recent recruit to the news department.

'What can we do about that bloody thing, Nige? If we try to move it, this bunch of thugs will do their nuts.'

He had no suggestions. She adopted a tone of frigid politeness.

'Do you think it would be possible for you to organise a table? If I stand on that, and the cameraman crouches really low, we'll get the prison gates in, and avoid that "fuck". Otherwise, assuming somebody in the gallery notices it before we go on air, they'll drop my p to c until after the nine o'clock watershed.'

A substantial 'bung' to a nearby householder secured the kitchen table. The £20 was to appear on the producer's expenses as: 'To hire of table, needed to avoid misspelt basterd (sic).' This greatly enhanced Nigel's reputation for wit among his colleagues, who saw the ludicrous side of their work more readily than the focused Angela.

The table came quickly enough, but the lunchtime News took longer to reach the Belfast item.

'I thought we were top of the bulletin?' Angela said testily, as she balanced on her shaky perch.

Nigel had phoned London from a nearby kiosk.

'No, once O'Brien was acquitted, they decided we weren't worth it. They'll reach us about 1.15, I'd guess. But you'll have to stay on your perch longer than that, Angela. They want to finish off the programme with a two-way interview between you and the presenter. "What more can you tell us?" kind of thing.'

Angela emitted a low oath, and said it was so windy on her table that by the time they got her on air she'd be lucky to remember the IRA man's name. Everything she had to say was in the package, or in the piece to camera. The two-way was just a sop to the presenter's over-developed ego.

As Angela glared down from her table Nigel smiled to himself. This was a perennial argument to which there was no conclusion. Nigel felt happy in the belief he shared with editors, producers, directors – almost everybody in broadcasting who worked behind the cameras. Anyone who appeared in front of those cameras, whether reporter or presenter, must be assumed *prima facie* to be a self-regarding, self-obsessed fool. Overpaid, too, in many cases.

[55]

Alan's office telephone rang late that afternoon. It was Liam, who said they needed to meet. Alan said he couldn't see much point – their time of usefulness to each other had passed.

'I haven't made myself clear, Alan. This is not so much an invitation as a summons. You've got some form with us now, and we need to sort it out. Don't worry, we'll meet in the bar of the Europa. Even I couldn't kidnap you from there.'

Looking back to their first encounter in the tawdry atmosphere of Joe's Café, Alan found in these more luxurious surroundings an incongruous contrast. This most frequently bombed hotel in Europe had become the favourite watering-hole for the Belfast political classes, of every hue.

Liam was grimmer than Alan had seen him before. He said quietly that giving evidence against Sean was 'misguided'.

Alan repeated the word 'misguided'. Was Liam telling him Sean hadn't been involved in the kidnap? It turned out that this was not the issue Liam was addressing. But before he had time to explain, Sean O'Brien himself appeared at their side, a pint of Guinness in his hand, and sank into the third chair at the table. Alan was staggered. The man he'd confronted in the dock that morning was sitting beside him. He wondered if this was a trap, and wished he'd told somebody where he was going tonight.

Liam said he thought Sean ought to be present because of what they had to tell Alan. First of all, Alan needed to understand the reasons he had his son safe and well at home – 'or rather, in England with his mother, I believe.' Ice gripped Alan's heart. The IRA knew all their movements.

Liam said the story about a plan to bomb the London Underground system had been 'a freelance fantasy'. Sean cut in to say that after the police had carted the fantasist back to Ireland, he'd been seriously considered for 'a head job' (a bag over his head, and a bullet in the back of it). But the powers-that-be had relented, and let him off with a good beating.

'He won't enter the Belfast Marathon for a year or two. The reason nothing worse happened to him was that, by mistake, he served our purpose.'

Alan looked puzzled. Liam laughed.

'The crazy thing is that our intelligence people are convinced what made the Brits bend and move my cousin to the Maze was not the use of your son as a hostage, but the supposed threat to the London tube. Maybe we should *really* be making this eejit our Chief of Staff.'

Sean laughed malevolently.

'You see, friend, your British chums were quite prepared to sacrifice your wee boy, but the mere possibility – spurious as it happened – that some of the *real* Brits, the Londoners, would be killed on the Underground – that's what changed their minds about Tommy Hughes.'

Alan couldn't resist his sarcastic reply.

'Well, I happen to know what went on inside Whitehall, and you've been misinformed. I can say no more than that.'

Sean shook his head in disbelief.

Liam said, almost apologetically, that Peter's kidnapping had been 'a painful necessity'. He described the boy's release as 'a piece of disinterested kindness'.

'You've a nice turn of phrase, Liam.'

'Ach, well, a poor, under-educated Falls Road Mickey does the best he can with the limited amount he learnt from being regularly hammered by the Christian Brothers. Anyway, the point I'm making, Alan, is that you might have been less keen to put Sean behind the wire if you'd just had the humility to remember that you owe us one.'

Alan breathed deeply, and his hands gripped the table. He looked sadly into Liam's face.

'The only thing I owe you and your friends, Liam, is a final loss of innocence. I know now that each of us, ultimately, is on his own, completely, utterly. Humanity, human decency, the fact that we're all Irishmen – these things only stretch down so deep. Below that, there's a dark place, where you can trust nobody. You're on your own.'

Sean wondered what he was talking about. Liam looked thoughtful. Alan talked on.

'I'll be withdrawing, not only from this job, but from politics. I'll stop seeking solutions for other people's problems. I'll concentrate on my own affairs, and find what happiness I can in whatever's left of my family life, which is not much.'

Sean spoke softly.

'At least you have them alive, Alan. My wife and our only wee girl were killed early on in these Troubles.'

Alan looked embarrassed. So that was what the banner saying Sean O'Brien had suffered enough was about!

'By Loyalist paramilitaries?'

Sean couldn't get any more words out. Tears came into his eyes, and he took a long pull at his Guinness.

Liam said, 'No, it was an IRA getaway car.'

Alan murmured that he was sorry. At last Sean spoke again.

'Unlike you, my fellow Irishman, I don't have any religion any more. No faith. No family. Just Fatherland, some would say. I would say "just the Republic".'

Then Liam got to what Alan had been waiting for, what the IRA were threatening to do to him. He said they could not tolerate the presence in Ireland of a man who'd given evidence against one of their members. (Alan noticed that there was no talk of 'tenuous' connections with the IRA now.)

'I intend to go back to London anyhow,' he said.

Liam shook his head.

'That's not going to be enough. We don't want you anywhere in these islands, Britain as well as Ireland. We're already pursuing our political agenda with the Brits, and your presence, even in London, might put your Whitehall masters off some necessary concessions.'

'So you're saying I have to go into exile from my own country, whether you define that country as Britain or Ireland?'

Sean glared at him. 'Aye, that's right. Our leadership think your life should be buggered up, the way ye tried to bugger up mine. Though, looking on the bright side, the Costa Brava'll be nicer for you than Long Kesh would have been for me.'

Alan took a long pull at his Guinness.

'What if I don't agree?'

Liam said it was not only Alan's life which would be at risk. If he refused the IRA's order to live abroad the lives of his wife and two sons might be forfeit. They also knew he had a sister and family in Belfast, and they'd regard these as legitimate targets also.

They parted soon afterwards, and Alan thought they would never meet again. He and the other two had been born in the same province. They shared political problems that went back centuries. As human beings they could touch each other.

Sometimes, as when he heard about what Sean had been through, he felt emotionally closer to him, at least in suffering, than to his colleagues at Stormont or Westminster. But for all the chance he and these fellow Ulsterman had of bridging the deadly divide between them, they might as well have come from different planets.

[56]

Alan's postscript: Paris, Christmas 2000

It's almost a quarter of a century since these events ruined my life. Perhaps if I'd told Mary then about the IRA sentence of exile it would have worked out differently. But I didn't want her living in daily fear that she or one of the boys would be murdered. I didn't tell Charles about the threats, or Dick or Diana, or the police. Nothing any of them could do to help, so least said soonest mended, or so I thought at the time.

When I settled in Paris I fully expected that the next communication I would receive from Mary would be divorce papers. Instead she sent me Christmas and birthday cards, that year and every year since. 'With love', they always said. The ones I bought here to send to her said 'Salutations!' The French express everything with nuances, but I wonder whether the word struck the right note back in London.

I had assumed Mary would marry or at least live with Colin Newhouse. When Brian stayed with me on his way to ski in the Alps a year later, the affair had petered out. I suspect what happened in 1977 was that Mary fell out of love with me, rather than into love with Professor Newhouse.

My silence about the IRA threat that forced me to live outside Britain left Mary and the boys thinking I had simply deserted them, through those self-obsessed, maverick faults of character that Mary has always seen in me, and doubtless told Brian and Peter all about. I could find nothing to say that would correct that impression.

I would like to have been closer to my sons as they grew up, but my secret kept the barriers up between us. I could see that Brian and Peter were offended when I didn't come to London for their weddings. They thought it was my antagonism to Mary that kept me away. On the phone Brian murmured something like 'nobody should stay that bitter'. I had to let that pass. It's not me that's bitter, it's the Provos.

The IRA have not forgotten me. I've earned a reasonable living here, first teaching English to French people, then lecturing at the Sorbonne in English literature. I've augmented this by journalism, mostly travel articles for French papers and for a magazine in New York. Strictly no political journalism, until some more than usually bizarre development in Ireland tempted me to write a letter to the *New Statesman.*

And that was when I learned that the Provos remember me. I had a phone call, Belfast accent, said he was speaking for the IRA. He explained, with almost bureaucratic politeness, that their sentence of exile also extended to publications in the UK. If I wanted my wife and family to be safe, he said, less politely, I'd better 'jack it in'.

Charles and I kept in touch for a while, mostly through gossipy letters. When he came here as Foreign Secretary he invited me to dinner at the embassy. After leaving Stormont Charles swiftly inoculated himself against Irish politics. 'Graveyard of ambitions' and all that. When I reminded him of our efforts to defeat terrorism, from both Republicans and Loyalists, he said sadly that the caravan had rolled on.

It's rolled even further since Labour were chucked out in 1979. Endless constitutional conferences under Thatcher, culminating in a Mandarin's dream, the Anglo-Irish Agreement, which Lady T. decided – soon after leaving office, naturally – had been a mistake. She told one of her cronies that the Americans – her chum Ronald Reagan? – had turned the heat on her.

Family regrets aside, am I enjoying myself here? Marvellous city, nice people, and I'm happy most of the time. I revel in the look of Paris. I travel round on the buses, because you have more human contact there. The modern Metro's quick and clean compared with the London Underground, though I've never quite forgiven them for abandoning the defining scent of my student days – Gauloises and garlic.

How else do I spend my time? I go often to the opera. When I came here first my aural French wasn't good enough for ordinary theatre, so I got hooked on opera. I meet friends mostly in the restaurants and cafés of the Left Bank, and round the Bastille, where the newer Opera is better for hearing and seeing than the Second Empire glories of the Garnier, though with less atmosphere, and no memories of my honeymoon visits with Mary.

Seven or eight years ago I had a long letter from Dick Heston. It was so remarkable I've kept it. Began as a sort of *apologia pro vita sua*: sorry he'd been such a pain in the backside when we were working together, had seen the error of his ways, about Ireland and much else. I wouldn't have recognised the arrogant Sir Richard if it hadn't been for the handwriting.

It turned out he's had a religious conversion. Perhaps I should say 'reconversion', since Dick was a candidate for the priesthood in his youth. After Stormont he became permanent secretary at Defence. When he saw the scale of Britain's nuclear weapons he began to have qualms, especially with a more aggressive international stance under the Tories. That's when he started to talk with a bishop who'd been in the seminary with him all those years before.

There was a touch of the old Dick in the part of the letter where he told me what had turned him back to the Church.

I don't suppose your Prod education embraced a fine Catholic poet, Francis Thomson? A piece of his, 'The Hound of Heaven', seemed to describe my years in the civil service, especially the period supervising the means of blowing all mankind to oblivion.

I fled Him down the nights and down the days;
I fled Him, down the arches of the years;
I fled Him, down the labyrinthine ways
Of my own mind; and in the mist of tears
I hid from Him, and under running laughter.

So in the end, I stopped running, maybe stopped laughing so cynically at the woes of humanity. That last bit, at least, I hope you'd approve of.

I was moved by the letter, moved that Dick felt our relationship had been close enough, even if combative, for him to tell me about the conclusion of his intellectual journey.

What mildly irritated me was his doubt whether I'd welcome his embrace of Catholicism, what my harsher Anglican friends used playfully to call 'Poping'. Ulster's 'Them and Us' mentality has left its scars on Dick.

I wrote back saying how pleased I was, and that I couldn't see as much difference between the Pope and Luther as he did. I kept to myself what really struck me – that a church which could turn such a harsh, egotistical, unyielding man as Dick into a decent and kind human being had a lot going for it.

He has got a new woman in his life, someone he met through the church. He's researching a book on the history of English Catholicism, and seems to be settling into a scholarly old age, with unexpected composure. 'Nowt as odd as folk,' as Dick himself would say.

My closest French friend is Pierre Lefevre, features editor at one of the papers I write for and the only man I know here who wants to discuss Ireland, though he's quite innocent about its politics. Like him, I'm glad they've stopped shooting each other, more or less, but I'm unsure about the politics. The 'modalities' – as the civil service loved to call them – have changed since my day.

The Government have been talking to terrorists for years now, with or without ceasefires, and making concessions galore. Shades of Howard Considine! Remember the fuss there was about transferring Tommy Hughes from an English prison? Now they're letting them out altogether, Loyalists and Republicans. So murderers laugh in the dock when the judge says they're going to gaol for life, because they know he's wrong. No talk of demanding a quid pro quo, like a straight surrender of Semtex or guns. Just waffling on about institutions of government, as if it matters who supervises the painting of the park benches.

Meanwhile, no doubt what 'community policing' means to the Provos and the Loyalist paramilitaries. Within their own ghettoes both behave like Hitler's Brownshirts. Lynch law – beatings, knee-cappings and 'head jobs' – still go on. And I'm not the only exile from Ulster, not by a long chalk. All sorts of people, for all sorts of reasons, are advised that if they don't get out and stay out they'll be killed.

This is how the bully-boys maintain the discipline that allows their collar-and-tie terrorism to go on – rackets in protection payments, drugs and money-laundering that make the black taxi scams of the seventies look childish. It seems that what Dubliners used to call 'the men in the mohair suits' – in London and Belfast now, as well as Dublin – reckon the poor old working-class are expendable in their Brave New World.

Pierre's the only person I've told why I'm living in Paris. Safe enough, for he shows no great wish ever to go to London, much less Belfast. A very French Frenchman, my friend Pierre – he takes his holidays in Aquitaine. He's happy enough to argue gently with me about what he calls 'a peaceful outcome', which I suspect he thinks French logic could deliver in a week.

He mentions how de Gaulle got out of Algeria. When I point out that it makes a difference who's in the majority, who in the minority, Pierre gives a Gallic shrug.

I had one such conversation with him last week. I'd just heard on the World Service that the Colombian rebels have held 1,400 people hostage in the past month or two. Fourteen hundred! Including a school bus-load of children, and the entire congregation of a church. What for? To raise funds to fight their government. I told Pierre about this.

'How bad is the Government in Bogotá, Alan?'

'You and I don't know, *mon vieux*. Anyhow, I've long since stopped adjudicating such grievances. None of the Irish grievances, whether against London, Dublin or Stormont, would detain millions of starving Africans for a nano-second.'

He raised a sceptical eyebrow. He had to be convinced.

'Look, all I'm saying is that one of the first places where democracy lost its innocence is in my own benighted homeland, because it's gone on for so long that nobody can distinguish right from wrong. What's annoying me is that the world, including the peacemakers, are still missing the wider message of Ireland's thirty bloody years. Violence has a veto on democracy.'

Pierre just laughed at my vehemence. For him Ireland is a diversion.

My life was chugging along gently when one day recently Diana came into it again. That set off old memories, old yearnings, but Diana had a story to tell that was even more astonishing to me than her many past bombshells.

[57]

Diana has left the Foreign Office and is teaching at St Andrews. She was in Paris for a conference of foreign affairs academics. As beautiful as ever, more mature, but with that smouldering sexuality undimmed by the passing years.

The story she had to tell came out over a long lunch on the Boul' Mich'. Diana has developed a more laconic way of speaking than the machine-gun rhetoric I remember. She got to the point with tantalising slowness. Once I'd tucked napkin into collar and savoured the first spoonful of my favourite onion soup, the first question I asked was why she'd left the Foreign Office.

'It left me, more or less.'

Surely they hadn't sacked her? No, not quite. But when Charles was foreign secretary he'd wanted to send her to Dublin as ambassador, which made sense after her long experience in the North. But he encountered a high blank wall in Whitehall.

'They made it clear that I did not have a dazzling future in the diplomatic service. Didn't you ever wonder, Alan, why I was sent to such a no-hoper's corner as Stormont?'

I ignored her tactlessness about what had been my own brief arena of public service. She took a long sip at her wine, and then told me a fuller version of the Czech story I had heard from Charles all those years before. Again, as on the cliffs above the Giant's Causeway, I didn't reveal to her that I already knew.

'Our people said my Czech friend was an intelligence agent, though I was never sure. Anyhow, even in our most torrid moments together I'd never told him anything remotely secret, or even sensitive. But when I was summoned back to London and underwent a tough debriefing, I apparently wasn't able to convince my interrogators. How do you prove a negative? A shadow came over my career, over my life too. Stefan was the only man I've ever been certain I loved.'

Diana gulped, then smiled sadly at me, and said there had been others she might have loved if they'd given her a chance. I admit my heart-beat seemed to falter at this, but I said nothing. Just as well, as it turned out.

How her Czech affair ended came out like glue from a narrow-necked bottle. One evening her lover told her he was going to remain with his wife. This had been a terrible blow, even before she was recalled to London in disgrace. I could see she had a sneaking suspicion that Stefan had betrayed her to the British authorities for his own marital convenience. It was the kind of doubt I knew she'd never get out of her mind.

But Diana had another story to unveil that was a much greater surprise to me. After Labour's 1979 election defeat, when internal strife doomed them to long years in opposition, Charles had abandoned front-line politics and taken the peerage that came with his cabinet rank. He and I completely lost touch after that, though I had read that he had a fellowship in Cambridge and spent most of his time there. I asked Diana whether she ever saw him. She came as close to blushing as such a self-confident woman could.

'Were it not for our peculiar geographical arrangements, Alan, you might say that Charles and I are living together. We've been what they call "an item" for some years, though we've never got our working and residential acts together.'

She laughed, in an embarrassed way that surprised me, and looked to judge my reaction. I smiled, encouraging her to go on, though I couldn't keep the phrase 'chalk-and-cheese' from bubbling into my mind.

'We never discuss Ireland, in case you wondered. It might make us quarrel.'

Charles had suggested they should be married, but she valued her independence too much. She liked living in Scotland, and they were together either there or in London or Cambridge when their commitments allowed.

'I sometimes think the Hebdomadar – that's the academic at St Andrews who's responsible for discipline – takes a sniffy view of my domestic arrangements, but he hasn't dared to say so. After all, it's something for the University to have a former Foreign Secretary visiting a lot, even if our liaison is irregular. He gives an occasional seminar to my classes.'

[58]

A few years ago I had an even warmer encounter with my past. In 1986 the French Government put right a mistake the Compagnie des Chemins de Fers d'Orléans made in 1900. The railway had then bought a prime Parisian site, just down the embankment from the Foreign Office, for their terminal. But by the thirties railway mechanisation had made the Gare d'Orsay unsuitable. In 1945 they used it as a clearing-house for prisoners-of-war, and in the sixties as a set for an Orson Welles film. There was even talk of tearing it down and building a hotel.

In 1900 a painter called Detaille had said that the original plans for the railway station looked more like a museum. Eighty-six years later France, after years of discussion, finally decided he was right. With the successive encouragement of Presidents Pompidou, Giscard d'Estaing and Mitterrand, they turned the Gare d'Orsay into the Musée d'Orsay, and moved in from the Jeu de Paume all those paintings Mary had so envied.

The happy result of this was that I now had one of the most enchanting galleries in the world just round the corner from my flat. Each time I went there seemed to produce a new experience, so monthly visits to the d'Orsay became a habit.

There I was, wandering through the Impressionists, when the figure of a woman struck me as familiar. She was studying a picture by Berthe Morisot – Manet's sister-in-law – of a mother looking at a baby through the draperies of an old-fashioned cradle. I came up behind her, and said quietly: 'Feeling broody?'

Mary swung round, all the emotions imaginable spreading across her face.

'Alan!' she said, and seemed speechless. Then, searching for something to say that would bridge the decades since we'd last seen each other, she picked up my remark about the picture.

'I was babysitting for Brian and Heather last week. Morisot's caught precisely what young babies do to women, even women of my age.'

We talked about the gallery. When I asked why she hadn't let me know she was coming, Mary reached in her pocket to show me a piece of paper with my address and phone number on it. She'd been going to call later in the day.

I said there was no time like the present. We should have lunch. First we spent another hour wandering round the pictures. I must have gained something in tact in the years since Mary and I broke up. As she was trilling away about how imaginative it was of the French to turn a railway station into a gallery, I forbore to remind her of a conversation many years before. Then, when the transfer of her beloved Impressionists was first being mooted, she had jeered at the idea. A railway station indeed!

It was only when we'd relaxed over a couple of glasses that I risked my little joke. She used to enjoy my Franglais, so I said: 'Dare I mention, Mary, that there was a time when you thought the d'Orsay was having *des idées au dessus de sa gare*?'

She blushed, and said we all made mistakes. Remarkably, this broke the ice. For me the lunch was magical, and I think it was for her too. We talked about everything, our lives and work, the boys, Brian's wife and two little girls, Peter's wife and new baby son. I hadn't seen my grandchildren, and as I thought back to our encounter earlier at Morisot's 'Le Berceau', I knew how much I'd missed.

I said this, and Mary posed the question left unspoken until then. Why had I chosen to live in Paris? In 1977, even though she and I were breaking up, it had seemed daft for me to break with England. A corner of the old, aggressive Mary peeped out from the calmer woman I'd seen that day. I was stumped for a reply.

'Let's just say there are reasons why I can't sensibly live in England. I can't tell you what they are. That wouldn't do either of us any good. I know this has curdled the boys' attitudes to me, yours too, Mary. Sadly I'll just have to live with that. Indefinitely, I suppose.'

As you can guess this produced a hiatus in our conversation. Up till then the warmth we still felt for each other was flowing across that table like electricity. But the secret I was keeping from her was bound to come between us. The atmosphere, previously so hopeful, was curdled.

We were rescued by a bizarre little scenario, the kind of incident that reminds you Parisians are not cool Anglo-Saxons. Three middle-aged men, wearing business suits and clutching brief-cases, were lunching at the next table in this tightly packed room. (It had the best cuisine in the 16th, after all.) As they rose to go, one of their coat-tails touched Mary's glass, and tipped out what was left of her claret.

What a scene! Mary said later she wished Renoir had been around to record it. The man pronounced himself 'désolé', and fussily ordered the proprietor to bring salt cellars, cloths, and another whole bottle of the best claret in the house to make up to us for the very small quantity we'd lost. Mary kept assuring him that it had mostly fallen on the tablecloth, only the tiniest specks on her skirt, but he still left the restaurant proclaiming his undying shame.

Mary visited Paris several times over the next dozen years. She stayed with me and we went round all the museums together. I introduced her to a little private gallery in the suburbs, the Marmottan, where there were good Impressionists she didn't seem to know about. Or perhaps she was just being tactful. That's the change: Mary has become more tactful. So have I.

We also went to the opera together. Mary dressed up for it, and I made what effort I could with my limited wardrobe. She still looked ravishing. I saw a number of women in the smart bunch who patronise the Garnier eyeing her surreptitiously, and felt proud.

The relationship continued in this on-off way, not satisfactory to me – to either of us, I suspect – but certainly better than nothing. During her stays we usually made love, not the raging, hilarious passion of our younger days, but maybe more loving. She said I'd become 'more considerate'. That made me wonder what kind of boor I must have been before.

[59]

27 January 2001

My chance encounter with Liam and his granddaughter happened last summer. We didn't discuss my exile in front of her, of course, but just this week I had a telephone call from Liam. He made it sound quite casual, said he'd bumped into a few Republican friends now influential in the IRA.

'The younger generation, Alan! Myself, I'm spending more time with my family, just like those Tory toffs used to say when they passed their sell-by dates.'

I couldn't bite back my instinctive response.

'I wish I could have spent more time with mine these past couple of decades.'

'That's what I'm phoning about, Alan. It may seem a bit late in the day, but now you can. Sorry for the delay, but my friends had to talk to the IRA Army Council. Turns out they've no objection to you living in London now, if that'd suit you better. This latest Peace Process is very shaky, but all their Brit contacts seem to think you're irrelevant to that. Funny how time heals old wounds!'

I've written to Mary. After all these years, I was able to reveal why I hadn't told her or the boys about the threat to their lives and mine. I said we should talk as soon as possible about our futures, told her my heart is almost bursting with anticipation, but left the rest till we meet.

So I'm sitting here now, happy as Larry, finishing off a bottle of Burgundy, and thinking. About Mary and me, about Peter's kidnapping, Sean's trial, and all that followed. About Ulster itself, the bloody past and apparently endless, hating future of my native land.

These Troubles remind me of that phrase from the 1966 World Cup. When spectators ran on to the field after the third England goal the commentator said: 'They think it's all over . . .' And then, as Geoff Hurst thumped in a fourth: 'It is now.'

I still have my doubts about this latest of the many ceasefires since the one I nearly brought about a quarter of a century ago. What I wonder is whether the killing is all over this time. I pray it is.

Nothing much has come of all the mandarins' plotting since then. It never does, but it's a dreadful distraction from serious politics. Sir Philip Radley has long since gone, first to the House of Lords, then to be with his ancestors. The constitutional status of both parts of Ireland remains roughly where our sagacious cabinet secretary found it.

However, since Liam announced to me the IRA's gracious reprieve I'm thinking not so much about politics, but about my own future, our future. I'd like us to live in London again. At last I'd be able to spend time with my sons and my grandchildren. I wish I didn't feel quite so old and tired.

[60]

Mary's Postscript: London, 1 January 2001

I spent this second edition of the Millennium alone last night. Plenty
of invitations, but I preferred a glass or two of wine while I listened to
music and read a book. It was a nostalgic evening, naturally. What else
is on December 31st menus except nostalgia? So I thought about what
happened to Peter in 1977, and what's happened to Alan and me since
then.

I've had a satisfying career, many happy times with the boys and
their wives, now with my grandchildren. I've plenty of friends, enough
money, far too many interests and activities for my own good. I don't
think I've just 'kept myself busy', as widows are always being advised
to do.

Widows – there's the rub! Apart from that foolish flirtation with
Colin Newhouse I've never looked seriously at a man since Alan and I
broke up. For a dozen years or so he and I have been seeing each other
again. Warm and friendly most of the time, even a bit more than that.

But always we've met in Paris, and therefore fleetingly. His
inexplicable decision to move there in 1977 has always rankled with
me. I wasn't planning a reconciliation, certainly not in the early years,
though I never considered divorce. But it would have been convenient,
when Brian and Peter were young, to have had my husband – late
husband; no, former husband; whatever the hell he is! – to have had
Alan available to share the strain. Newspaper columns by divorcees
kept informing me about those laddish Saturdays fathers and sons
spend at football matches, allowing the mother time to see her friends.

Instead, Alan was mooning away his life in Paris. Hard up at first, I
would judge, though he always sent me some money to help with
Peter. Anyway, with my more senior job at the Tate, I was well enough

off as a single mother. But Alan's freelance travel writing began to hit jackpots, and then he lavished gifts on us all – holidays for the boys, jewellery, perfume and clothes for me. Quite an imaginative shopper, my Alan has turned out to be, since he learned his way round the Grands Boulevards.

My Alan! How did that slip out? For years after the events of 1977 we just exchanged Christmas and birthday cards. His were rather formal – 'Salutations' kind of thing, not much warmth there, I thought. Then came our magical encounter at the Musée d'Orsay. As we looked at that cradle picture of Berthe Morisot's and I said it reminded me of Brian's younger girl, the hurt in Alan's face almost made me cry. He came up with one of his eternal quotations, about 'the years that the locusts have eaten'. For once I thought it appropriate, for both of us.

Not that I've been pining for Alan, or any nonsense like that. I've had far too fulfilled a life, with my work and my family. But isn't it incomprehensible that a man who's so clearly still in love with me should absent himself for more than twenty years from the city where anything that was going to happen between us again would happen?

Unreasonable though he's been, both over that dreadful trial and in this mad Paris enterprise, I can't get Alan out of my system. When we had our first lunch near the d'Orsay I found him as funny as ever. We had an odd encounter in that restaurant, when a businessman spilled a drop or two of wine on my skirt and appeared to be on the verge of suicide. Later Alan invented an entire fiction of 'the life of Alphonse': his wife, mistress, office colleagues, drinking chums in his village, aspirations to win the mayoralty of his commune away from the Left. By the time we parted at the airport Alan had turned 'Alphonse' into Monsieur Hulot.

I'd be happy to restore to him 'the years the locusts have eaten', or as many of them as are left. He hasn't been looking after himself – growing paunchy, eating too much, and with rather more red wine than is strictly necessary to decoke his coronary arteries, I'd say. But I want to continue at the Tate for as long as they'll have me. This new gallery in the old Bankside Power Station – shades of the Gare d'Orsay! – has given me more scope in the original Tate. Sojourns in a new marital home in Paris are simply not compatible with my career.